Tastes So Sweet

"There is nothing better than a
friend, unless it is a friend
with chocolate." —Linda Grayson

Happy reading,

Tastes So Sweet

An Everheart Brothers of Texas Romance

Kelly Cain

TULE
PUBLISHING

Tastes So Sweet

Dedication

This one's for my dad, Van Cain, and my lovely memories of his garden of greens and other deliciousness that inspired this book and Ryan's grandfather.

And to my daughters, Diamond and Kamryn, because they're the loves of my life.

CHAPTER ONE

Flynn definitely hasn't changed. Smh.

THESE DANG EVERHEARTS will be the death of me. I swear.

I rush down the hall from my office, passing the large storage room filled with kitchen equipment on one side and the employee break room opposite it. I catch the weeping employee heading toward the back door of the restaurant before he can open the exit. "What happened? Where are you going?"

He takes in a deep breath, makes a valiant effort at quelling his emotions, then releases another sob before pulling off his chef's hat and hiding his face behind it. "Mrs. Landry…"

"Ms. And please, call me Ryan."

"Ryan, I don't think this is going to work out."

I don't need to ask why because this is the third chef who's departed through this same back door in the month since the second of Flynn's three sons unceremoniously quit. I'm all for Knox and Declan venturing out on their own paths, but it would have been helpful if they could've spread their departures over some time, like two or three years instead of weeks. Heck, even months would have been helpful.

I offer the man a small smile. "I'm sorry to hear that, Chef. I'd hoped with your Michelin experience, you would understand our special circumstances."

He lifts his hazel gaze to mine, bright with tears, and hiccups, then places a hand on my shoulder.

I resist the urge to pull away from both his touch and his intense, unwavering stare, understanding this is more a comfort for him than me.

"I've worked with Michelin chefs who overstrained and corrected me to no end. Their training made me a better chef. This is something different." He squeezes my shoulder and glances up at the ceiling, sucking in a raggedy breath. "Chef Everheart's goal is total denigration, and I value my health—both physical and emotional—too much to be subjected to his unearned punishment. I see why his sons left." With one more squeeze of my shoulder, he storms out the door without a backward glance.

I take a deep breath to steel myself, then trudge to the kitchen. Before picking up the abandoned knife, I wash my hands and don the white jacket I pull from the dish-washing area. There's a chef's jacket in closer reach, but I don't dare. This one is close enough.

Flynn marches my way, his fair white skin turning almost purple, chef's hat askew.

After putting the knife down, I place a hand on my generous hip and narrow my eyes. "You can't keep running off the chefs I hire. Pretty soon, we'll need to start looking outside Austin. Maybe even the state at this rate."

He scrunches his thin lips together and takes a moment to calm before speaking. "If you'd hire someone worthwhile, they wouldn't run as soon as I explain how I want something done. I'm a Michelin-star chef. Surely you can attract better quality personnel to work under my wing."

"You're a Michelin-star chef who won't give anyone a chance. You're lucky we've been able to retain the ones we already had. They've been here long enough to know you're not normally this over-the-top, but if you continue, we may be in a bigger hole than either of us will be able to dig out of." I pick up the knife again and wave it at the seating area of the restaurant. "You forget you're on display. At some point, our customers will tire of the show."

He opens his mouth, then shuts it and glances at the nearby chef's table that separates the kitchen from the front of house. When Flynn designed his restaurant, he wanted to show off, calling attention to himself and his ridiculously handsome chef sons. Now that he is down to one offspring, the one he often forgets about, he's probably rethinking his life choices. Flynn's parting rebuff from under his breath floats back my way. "We'll discuss this later."

I go back to chopping because while I need to contact the next person up, there is an immediate need for a pile of sliced onions and as short-staffed as we suddenly find ourselves, there's nobody else to do it.

When the restaurant closes and the staff initiates the nightly ritual, I finally trudge back to my office and turn my monitor back on so I can print out the list of chefs we've already interviewed. I only had time to press the button underneath the screen before rushing to head off our wayward now ex-employee. Leaving my laptop on and accessible is a huge faux pas, but it couldn't be helped.

I'm just about to kick off my shoes and massage my aching insoles when Flynn barrels into my office, still spry considering the long night. "You need to get me someone competent."

"Working on it, Chef. Next time, try to give the new person at least a couple days before you jump down their throat. Maybe we can retain someone."

He shoves a hand into his pocket and jangles the coins within. Who actually carries real money around anymore, less known change? Old-school Michelin-star Chef Flynn Everheart, that's who. "We wouldn't need to retain anyone if you'd done your job to begin with."

Here we go again. "Your sons leaving the fold is not my fault." I raise my eyebrows, daring him to counter.

"Perhaps if you'd given me notice when you found out, I could have stopped it."

I'm not usually a rolling-my-eyes kinda gal, but if this conversation continues down this path, I may have to change my policy. "Perhaps if you hadn't tried to strong-arm your sons into working for you, they'd still be here."

And now we're heading back to purple skin. "That is none of your business. But keeping me in the loop on kitchen personnel changes are in your wheelhouse, isn't that true?"

I throw my hands up in surrender because he's right. I should have told him. I never thought his sons would abandon him without a heads-up. "You don't pay me enough to jump in the middle of you Everhearts. I have enough to do without navigating your family drama, Chef."

And therein lies the problem. He pays me nearly thirty

percent lower than my counterparts because I didn't have the same level of experience coming into this job. It doesn't matter that I've proven myself over and over again the past four years I've had this job. It's why we have this contentious relationship, though, and why he allows me to speak my mind. Sure, he could fire me, but he'd be hard-pressed to replace me. He earned that Michelin star during my tenure here. Not that I don't believe he wouldn't dismiss me if I went too far or broke one of his golden rules. But now I do have the experience. I only stay because my salary puts me in a good position when it's time to fill out the financial aid forms for my twin sisters. And I only have one more year before they go off to college. I just need to hang on until then.

"Back to your compensation, I see. Do you really want to go there? Especially now?"

May as well. In for a penny, in for a pound, right? After all, it's the principle of the thing. "My assistant general manager earns nearly as much as I—"

"That's your issue, not mine. You have free reign to pay your staff as you see fit."

"Right. And I compensate them at the market rate so we retain our high level of excellence. Just like you pay your chefs. I'm the only one getting the short end of the stick here."

"Your compensation package is in line with the market for your experience, Ryan. I've explained that to you before." He sighs and pulls his hand out of his pocket, readying his stance for his exit. "Just ensure that we are properly staffed. Night."

I watch his retreating back, completely dumbfounded. Not that I thought he'd magically give in all of a sudden, but because of how cavalier he is about it, then ordering me to dig even deeper.

That's all I do these days. Dig deeper here and at home. The time to pay the piper is coming up soon, and I need to solidify my plans.

I SMELL WESTON before I see him. A slightly sweet and yeasty scent meets me at my open door. Soon his big body shadows across the hood of my car, his smiling face leaning down to catch my eye. "Do you need some help, Ryan?"

Giving up on the heavy crate I'm attempting to pull out of the back seat of my SUV, I pass it to him instead. "How'd you know?"

He shrugs and easily balances the box under one strong arm.

I smile and shake my head. I'm certainly no small person, but the box is not only heavy, it's bulky. Where I struggle to wrangle it with two hands, Weston makes it seem like a small box of packing peanuts. "Thank you, Chef." I can't help the title when he's decked out in his gear for work. We established long ago that it is a visceral reaction rather than a conscious decision. He finally relented and just goes with it.

"Anything for you?"

Most of the time I can tell when he's really asking a question rather than ending his sentence with a curious-sounding lilt, but only because we've been such close friends for so long. Without Weston, I'm not sure I would have been strong enough to persevere those first few months of managing the restaurant. Knox was nice enough but busy, and Declan was...decent most of the time, but Weston really went out of his way to help.

"Thanks, Chef."

We walk to the door in the rear of the building, the same one Weston just came through. The more potent Weston-smell catches me right in the nose and jets down to my stomach. "What in the world are you making?"

"*Zwetschgendatschi*."

I frown and glance in the direction of the kitchen. The restaurant won't open for another couple hours, but the crew is already well into prep work for lunch. Thankfully we are fully staffed for the next two days, giving me a little time to find another chef. "Switch-Dutch-who now?"

Weston laughs, a bright twinkle in his gleaming blue eyes. "It's a German cake made with Italian plums. I thought it would be a nice addition to the dessert menu."

I walk down the hall to my office with Weston trailing behind, carrying my burden. "You can just put it over there on Nancy's desk, please. She won't be in today." I place my purse in the bottom drawer and turn back to Weston. "The cake sounds delightful, but did you run it by your father? You know how he is when any of you try to slip in anything Italian around here."

His shoulders slump and he bows his head, having the nerve to look ashamed when we both know he isn't. "Why bother, Ryan? It's not like he'll notice anyway."

"Oh, he notices everything that goes on in his restaurant, trust me. You can't keep changing the dessert menu."

He bends forward, balancing his forearms on the chair facing my desk. "When I added the chocolate brioche, he didn't even mention it."

"He most certainly did. Why do you think I had you switch it to the triple-chocolate mousse cake?"

His mouth drops open in disbelief. "Ryan, how could you? You said it was your favorite?"

I shrug and switch on the monitor topping my desk and connect my laptop. "Two things can be true. Flynn nixed the brioche."

"As if you don't have enough to do. I don't understand why Dad can't just tell me himself. Does he have you making any other menu decisions?"

"I'm sorry. It wasn't my decision. I was just the messenger." We both know why Flynn doesn't tell his only remaining son about the dessert menu. He'd have to remember Weston existed first.

Good-naturedly as usual, Weston straightens up and grins. "It doesn't matter anyway. The fruit is only in season this month." He gives me an eyebrow wiggle. "Speaking of which, isn't your birthday coming up?"

My heart beats a little faster. "You know it is."

"Calm down—you're turning blue."

I do a quick check on my phone camera and examine my skin color. Still medium brown, but I can agree it has paled some. I smooth my closely cropped curls over my ear. "I am calm. You know I don't want to talk about my birthday."

"Come on, Ryan. Can't this be the year we celebrate

your special day? You never do?"

"That's a firm no."

"But why? At least let me make you something special."

"You're already making my favorite, remember? And the way you make it with a hint of raspberry really sets it apart. I'll just grab a slice of that."

His friendly smile doesn't falter, but he does run long fingers through his wavy black hair. His fair olive skin reddens ever so slightly, and his usually bright eyes dim. "We'll table this until later. I haven't given up."

"I won't change my mind."

He tilts his head to the side and purses his lips, then snaps his fingers. "I almost forgot. I heard what happened last night. Sorry I missed it?"

"Be glad you did. Your dad is not making my job any easier. Pretty soon word will get out and I won't be able to pay someone to interview."

"I wish I could help, but all my friends from culinary school have great jobs. Nobody wants to come here."

"It's okay. I plan to ask your brother for help. I already texted him this morning."

Weston's eyes widen considerably. "Uh, Ryan. Not the brother I think you're talking about."

I suck in a deep breath. "I already know, but I'm desperate. Your dad will just have to deal with it. At least we'll have someone worthy of Knox's replacement."

"I'm not sure anyone will ever be able to replace Knox. Especially in Dad's eyes." His expression doesn't change, which is even more heartbreaking because he's so used to his father's snubs.

I soften my expression, giving Weston a small smile. "Your father thinks the world of all of you. He misses Declan, too, and if something were to happen and you left, that would create a big hole. You're the best pastry chef around."

He smiles brighter, but his eyes stay the same. Clearly placating me.

Although Knox was the star chef in the family, I really do believe Flynn misses Declan being here to bounce investment ideas off and would truly feel Weston's loss if he were to leave. He just has a terrible way of showing his love for his sons. But that's not my business.

"Are we all still heading over to Lady Bird Lake tomorrow?"

"As far as I know. Restaurant's closed, so I'll be there for sure. The twins may come after school if we stay long enough and the others said they would meet us there, but I'll check with them later to verify. I already told you Lisa can't make it. That's it for the cousins."

Weston claps his hands and releases a high-pitched sound. "I'm so excited. We haven't all been together in ages."

I could catch up on my rest, do some cleaning, and maybe even read a book tomorrow, but it's totally worth going to witness Weston's glee. "Me, too."

"Okay, I better get back to the kitchen. I also want to get a little writing in before the rush starts. See you later, Ryan?"

"See you later, Chef." I watch him stroll through the open door and smile how lucky I am to have such a great friend like Weston.

CHAPTER TWO

Only a small problem. Not.

S WEAT ROLLS DOWN my back, but I try my best to ignore the stickiness in the air and not be a spoilsport per usual. Weston hurries ahead when he spots Jerome. Often, Weston calls me his best friend, but we both know that's not exactly the truth. I circle back and fall into step with Diedra, Naomi, and Darryl. "Why is it so humid?"

"You act like you just moved to Austin a minute ago." Naomi frowns at me.

I snicker because my Austin cousins always think it's humid. "Yeah, but I spent my formative years in Houston and what y'all call humidity is not normally what I consider wet. Today is muggy."

"I guess. Hey, Ryan, can you bake some of your delicious brownies for Kieran's bake sale next week?"

"Sure." I choke down a sigh since I have zero time to bake brownies and Diedra should maybe learn to cook since she's been responsible for a whole human the past six years, but hey, I'll just add it to my ever-growing to-do list. "What day do you need them?"

"Thanks, luv. The bake sale is Tuesday, so could you bring them by Monday night?"

Naomi gives me a look behind her sister's back.

I ignore her because obviously I should say no sometimes, but I never can. Naomi doesn't have that problem, which is why Diedra would never ask her even though she's a much better baker than me. And I've forbidden any of my cousins to ask baking favors from Weston. We had a huge falling out over it.

"Um, I guess. You can't pick them up?"

"She has cheer practice way in Round Rock on Mondays, so she'll be too wiped out to go by your place, too. I can hear the whining now." Diedra shakes her head like she can't imagine doing more than one task a day.

Must be nice.

"Okay, I'll drop them off at seven."

She kisses me on the cheek and fast walks ahead to where Weston and his friends are renting paddleboards and kayaks. Weston owns both but rarely brings them unless we're going camping for an extended stay.

I direct my attention to Darryl. "Did you remember to send Fred a card? His birthday will be here before you know it." Fred is his only uncle on his mother's side. Darryl always says he wants to keep in touch but doesn't make the effort unless I remind him.

"Ugh, no, I forgot."

"I have a box of cards at home if you want to swing by after this and pick one up."

He gives me a one-arm hug as we approach Weston and crew. "You're a lifesaver."

I wave at the only one of Weston's friends who's looking my way. Jerome is picking up a kayak, so he gives me a head nod. His brothers are already in the water on paddleboards. Their friend is picking out a kayak. Weston is standing by the rental booth on his phone as usual, typing furiously, eyebrows drawn together, transforming his kind face into a scowl.

"What's wrong?"

"Sorry, just a second." He types even faster.

I roll my eyes even though he isn't paying attention to me. My pet peeve is people on their electronics nonstop, and Weston stays on his overtime. It's the only source of contention between us.

"Okay, done." He slips his phone into the pocket of his cargo shorts and grins at me. "Nothing's wrong? I was just capturing a particularly dark thought."

"You're writing dark fan fiction now?"

He fidgets with the bottom of his T-shirt and looks anywhere but at me. "Not really."

"What aren't you telling me?"

He shrugs. "Are you going on the lake? Or we could walk the trail?" His easy smile is back.

I narrow my eyes but don't press him. "The trail sounds good." Even in this oppressive air, I'll take a walk over getting out on the lake and messing around with our crew any day. They play too much. Plus the trail is shady, which will block out most of the sun, and being alone with Weston always recharges me.

Weston strolls over to Jerome at the edge of the lake and speaks to him. Presumably about our walk.

Although I can't hear them, Jerome looks at me, then back at Weston with a smirk on his handsome face. His dimples pop when he laughs at whatever Weston says in reply.

When we set out on the trail, Weston reaches for the phone in his pocket but stops when he witnesses the scowl I send his way. "Sorry."

"Is it that major?"

He shrugs. "So where's Lisa today?"

"Work." Most of our little pocket of family and friends have a flexible work schedule, which lends itself to days like today where we can hang out in the middle of the day. The restaurant is closed on Mondays, so that's the only off day I can count on. Weston has a little more flexibility since he has another pastry chef under him, but he works most days, too. His schedule is set a couple weeks ahead of time so he can plan.

Lisa is the only one of my cousins who has an even stricter schedule than mine. A law associate trying to make partner is never an easy climb. Diedra's days are free until she picks up her daughter from school. I still don't know what Darryl does. And then there's Naomi, an accomplished editor at a medium-sized publishing house. She works long hours but sets her own schedule. Sometimes I envy her life, but then realize I need more structure than her job affords.

"I don't even know why I asked. She's always at work."

I bump his shoulder. "Why're you asking about Lisa?"

He quirks a half smile my way. "Because Jerome asked?"

"Oh. I thought maybe you were asking for you." The energy I put into waggling my eyebrows is all bravado. I would die if Weston liked one of my cousins. Too weird. "So Jerome likes Lisa, huh?"

Weston grins. "He does." He bumps my arm. "Were you worried about me liking Lisa?"

"No, of course not." I bite my lip and look away. "They would make a cute couple if she had time to date. Everyone can't be a partner in an architecture firm and make their own hours." I whip my head around as thunderous laughter barrels over to us from the river. "Speak of the devils."

"Hey, guys! Come jump in," Jerome calls from the lake.

I shake my head, but Weston walks toward the water's edge, then hops back with a quickness belying his size. "Snake."

The architecture bros, as I like to call them, move away from the bank like it's on fire and continue down the river.

"Jeesh, what kind of snake?"

"Probably harmless, but could've been a cottonmouth. I didn't stick around long enough to find out."

I release a sound—half laugh, half groan. "This is why I don't mess around with this so-called lake. The Colorado River is not to be trifled with, but y'all stay in that water."

Weston kicks pebbles my way. "You love kayaking. What's with you and this particular lake?"

After dancing out of range of his teasing, I turn to face him, walking backward a safe distance away. "Too many things happening in here. You're not allowed to swim, but you can paddleboard. You can fish from a boat but not from the bank or bridge. I can't keep up with their arbitrary rules. Lake Conroe was so much easier to navigate." And therein lies the real reason, if I admit it to myself. I compare everything in Austin with growing up in the northern suburbs of Houston and find the city lacking, whether it's rational or not. "So anyway, what's up with you being so secretive about your fan fiction?"

He bites the corner of his lip, then looks to the bench I just passed. "Wanna sit?"

I double back and happily rest next to him, pulling a bottle of water out of my backpack purse. "Want some?"

"Thanks." Weston takes a couple sips, then hands it back to me. "So this morning I pulled the Ace of Cups." He looks at me expectantly.

"Okay." I only have a very cursory knowledge of tarot and only because Weston's so into it. Austin's Sixth Street is a little try-hard when it comes to keeping up with New Orleans, if you ask me. More of my Austin prejudice.

"Remember cups is emotion, right?"

"Okay, sure."

"And the ace…"

"Beginning. That I remember."

"Right. So when you put them together, it usually means being more receptive to love."

I open my mouth to object, but he looks away, and I feel bad because I know Weston wouldn't mind at least exploring something between the two of us.

"Or creative opportunities. I'm starting a book."

My eyes stretch so far, the breeze under these trees extends to parts of my eyeball it has no business reaching. "Really? A real book?"

"As opposed to all the fake books I've been writing until now?"

"No, I just mean, you know. The fan fiction."

He nods. "I haven't given that up. I used to think it was

the fandom that spurned me on? And I guess part of it is that, but I've finally figured out writing is my passion. That's all I thought about as a kid." He shrugs, then leans back against the bench, spreading his arms wide. "Not that I'll ever do anything with it, but it's fun. I've already written over four thousand words today. It just flows out of me and that's all I want to do."

I take a deep breath before addressing the proverbial elephant. "What about baking? I thought that was your passion."

A small, sad smile creases his lips. "I think you know better?"

I do, but I also need to know where he stands with the restaurant. Losing Weston right now would be a disaster. "You aren't thinking about quitting, are you?" I bump his shoulder.

"Not now."

He doesn't offer anything else and I don't really want to pressure him, but it's my job to know where his head is. "*Not now* as in you want to see if this writing thing sticks? Or *not now* as in maybe next week?"

He leans into me, inches away, and looks me straight in the eyes. "I would never put you in that position, Ryan. I care about you too much."

The air from his sweet words wisps across my face, he's that close, his breath smelling of cinnamon. A reminder of our closeness and his trustworthiness. "I know you wouldn't. Are you going to let me read it?"

"It depends. Two conditions."

I sit back and take a swig of my water. "Okay."

"One, you can't tell anyone. I'm not ready to share this with other people yet. Let me see how it feels first."

"Okay, easy enough. What's the other condition?"

"That you're brutally honest with me. No holding back, Ryan. Seriously."

Weston knows *brutally honest* isn't in my repertoire, but I'll try for him. "Okay."

"Okay."

WHEN WE'VE HAD enough lake, Weston takes off with the architect bros and, since I rode with him, I catch a ride back home with Naomi. I glance out the tinted window of her Audi sedan and watch the tall buildings of downtown Austin pass by.

"What has you so melancholy?"

"Me?" I snort because there's no one else in the car. Who else would she be talking to? "I'm fine. Just a little preoccupied. How's work?"

She flashes a wide smile. "I'm really excited about the manuscript we acquired. It's sci-fi about someone who falls in love with an AI. But the kicker is that the AI falls in love right back. It's really good."

I raise an eyebrow because although I like sci-fi fine, that sounds a bit more than I'm ready for. "Sounds, uh, interesting."

"I know the premise seems farfetched, but if you read it, you'd see what I mean." She glances my way quickly, then turns her attention back to the road. "What have you been reading lately?"

"Well, I'm listening to *The Innkeeper's Daughter* by, um…what was her name?"

"Oh, Bianca Schwarz, right? Historical thriller?"

"Yup, that's it." I pull a book from my purse backpack. "And I'm reading one from Reese Ryan. It's really good, where two best friends wake up married in Vegas. I'm almost done with that one."

She slows the car at the yellow traffic light, then stops altogether. "That's a great one. You can't go wrong with that author."

"I know, right? I can't believe it took me this long to discover her."

Naomi spares me another glance, then puts her foot on the gas when the light changes to green. "What else is happening? I know something's wrong."

This is what happens when you finish high school at your grandparents' and your cousins live right down the street. Everyone knows each other a little too well. "I, uh." I don't want to bother her with my financial problems. She already has enough on her plate. "It's nothing. Just planning for the future. With my sisters."

"The future? Could you be a little more specific? Like their weddings? Retirement? What?"

"Ha-ha-ha. Let's start with college. They both plan to go to UT, and although it's a state school, the tuition along with everything else is a hike. I'm just trying to figure out how I'll pay for it."

"Understandable. It's high enough for one person, let alone two. I'm surprised Uncle Robert didn't set up a college fund, though."

"No, they did. For all of us, but they had sixteen years to pay into mine and only a couple for the twins. Mimi put money in from the life insurance, but I still need to come up with at least a thousand a month to cover room and board for both, plus books. At least according to the calculator on the website."

"You know we'll help you, though, right?"

I sigh and slow blink my eyes. "Yeah, but I can't let you. As it is, you and Lisa are carrying all the extra medical bills for Mimi and Papa. I haven't even been able to do my part."

I don't look Naomi's way, but I can almost feel her rolling her eyes. "Neither Lisa nor I have two extra mouths to feed. We don't press Diedra with her single mouth that she actually birthed."

"I know, but—Hey, watch out."

Naomi swerves to miss someone riding an electric scooter who darted into traffic right in front of us, and I instinctively reach for the grip handle above the window and hang on, my heart pounding. I don't have time to register anything else because there's a loud crashing sound, and I'm jerked hard against the door, my head crashing against the window, then the airbag explodes into my face before everything goes black.

"Ms. Landry."

The sound of someone calling my name penetrates the ringing in my ears, but I have zero intention of opening my eyes. Instead, I reach up and press my wrist against my pounding forehead.

"Oh good, she's conscious."

Who is she talking about? Why is someone holding my other wrist?

"Ms. Landry, can you open your eyes, please?"

I croak, "What?" I still don't open my eyes because whoever's talking is not the boss of me.

"You were in a car accident. We need to check you out."

My eyelids pop open, but there's a bright light pointing right at me so I squeeze them closed again. Then panic rises in my chest. "Naomi?"

"She's fine. They're treating her at the scene."

"At the scene?" I reopen my eyes, and that's when I realize we're moving. I attempt to sit up but dizziness roils my stomach and I give up.

"Whoa there. We'll be at the hospital in just a moment."

"The hospital? Why am I going to the hospital?" I finally glance over at the person speaking to me. A woman with thick glasses and a dark blue uniform hovers over me with a pen light.

She turns the blasted thing on again and squints at my face, shining the light back and forth between each of my eyes, then nods and clicks it off. "Although there are no obvious injuries, you were unconscious for quite a bit of time. They'll need to run some tests to ensure you're okay."

I close my eyes again and take a deep breath, then wince at the pain in my head. "Are you sure my cousin is okay?"

"Yes, ma'am. Just some minor cuts on her face and neck from the airbag."

My mind moves on to the next people on my list, my sisters. They should be out of school by now and wondering where I am. "Do you have my phone?"

"I believe your belongings are in a plastic bag up front. We'll transfer them to the ER admitting nurse."

I squeeze my eyes shut and thank the universe the accident wasn't worse than it was. I shouldn't have distracted Naomi with all that financial talk. What if I left them, too?

"We're here."

The back door of the ambulance swings open, and I'm rolled into the hospital and into a curtained-off room. Someone lifts the sheet I'm on to transfer me to another bed, and my stomach flips, vomit rising up before I can stop it.

The ER nurse sticks a bed pan under my chin before I can make a mess.

I flop back onto the bed and fling my hand against my forehead, suddenly slick with sweat, and watch the nurse type on the bedside computer.

"Your full name?"

I inhale and hold my breath, battling the pain in my head. "Ryan Yvette Landry."

"Address?"

"I can answer. I have her wallet as well."

After blinking a couple of times, I swing my gaze to where the curtain has lifted and Weston is standing. He's holding my purse and steps through, letting the curtain fall. His expression is...I'm not sure. I've never seen his face contorted the way it is, with red streaks running the length of his cheeks. "West?"

"Will she be okay?"

The nurse looks my way, then back to Weston. "And you are?"

"Her brother?"

Great time to inflect your voice. "Yes, my brother."

My caretaker twists his face in confusion but shrugs and turns back to the screen. "We'll need to run some tests as a precaution."

Weston takes my hand and squeezes, forcing a smile into his worried face. "You okay?"

I nod slightly, not trusting my voice. All of a sudden I'm weepy, touched by Weston's unexpected appearance. I'm guessing Naomi called him and he rushed over. He's still wearing the board shorts and tank top he had on at the lake, so he must not have made it home yet to change.

He pulls up a chair and answers all of the nurse's questions, only confirming a couple of past history details with me. Everything else he knows.

When they wheel me away for the MRI, Weston gives me a bright smile and nod. "I'll be right here when you return."

Of that, I have no doubt.

WESTON EYES ME like a hawk watching a chicken. His blue gaze doesn't ever move from my face.

I adjust myself in my bed and reach over to the nightstand for the glass of water he placed there a little earlier. "I'm fine, West."

"The doctor said to take it easy at least forty-eight

hours." He glances at my laptop near his feet—the one he caught me on just a few minutes before—and shakes his head, shifting in the chair next to my bedroom window. "Clearly you can't be left to your own devices."

I hang my head but feel the need to defend myself. "Your father called and needed me to review the inventory for the bridal shower this weekend. I was only doing a quick survey."

"Isn't that what Kerry is for? And what about Ace? He's the assistant executive manager, but honestly..." He huffs and runs a hand over his stubbled jaw. "I hate to say this, but I don't really see him doing much assisting. He's a nice guy, but shouldn't he be able to cover for two days without you having to log in?"

I hide a small smile because that's about the harshest commentary I've ever heard Weston express about another person, especially someone employed by the restaurant. "I feel okay, I promise."

"Dad shouldn't have called you."

Shrugging, I lift the glass to my mouth and take a long sip, then put it back on the table next to my bed. "We both know Flynn would call even if I was in the hospital in traction. He wouldn't care as long as he gets his needs met."

He only nods.

"Plus, he's down a pastry chef. He's probably running around in a haze."

"Thankfully Francis was able to pick up my shift yesterday. I was already off today. I'm sure Dad didn't notice."

I avert my eyes because it's too painful to look at Weston when he talks about his relationship with his father. He does his best to hide behind his sunny smile and bright eyes, but the pain lurks just underneath and is easy to see, especially for me.

"Do you think you should take one more day off? Just in case?"

"I'm ready to get back to the restaurant. I'm doing great." Which is true, mostly. Weston may have caught me on my laptop reviewing the inventory for an upcoming event, but he missed all the calls I've fielded today along with countless emails and too many text messages from Flynn and others. Going back to the restaurant will ease the strain of working remotely.

After giving me a good, long stare, he finally flashes those perfect teeth and shrugs. "You know yourself better than I do. If you say you don't need one more day, I believe you." He stands and moves to the door. "Be back in a few minutes with dinner."

I slink down in the covers, guilt for my lie scratching at the back of my head. "Thanks."

CHAPTER THREE

Saron with the surprises. Ugh.

"WHAT TIME ARE the twins getting home?"

I glance at my phone and frown. "They should have been here by now." I hit the Send button after pulling up Meagan's contact entry. I know better than to call Saron because she doesn't do phone calls, only text. Or better yet, Snapchat if she had her way. Meagan doesn't answer so I call again, fingers shaking as I press the key. It's been a week after my accident and my anxiety has ratcheted up considerably. When my sisters are even a few minutes late, my thoughts go to a bad place.

"We're in the driveway, Ryan." Meagan disconnects before I can respond.

After taking a couple of deep breaths, I rotate to Weston, who's hanging out per usual when we're both off. "They're here."

The pitying look he gives me is so out of place on his face.

Before I can say anything in my defense, my sisters come through the garage door into the kitchen, chattering excitedly.

I tamp down the need to explain why I was worried.

They already know anyway. "What's good, y'all?"

Saron's usual subdued smile is wider than I've ever seen it. "You remember it's college day, right? That's why we're late."

I nod, though I didn't realize it would be after normal school hours.

"Well, I've made up my mind that I definitely want to go to Howard."

After blinking a couple times, I glance at Meagan.

She's smiling, but the tremor of sadness is lurking just beneath.

I turn back to Saron. "In DC?"

"Do you know of another one?"

"Snarkiness doesn't become you." I circle back to Meagan for support. "I thought you were both going to UT."

She shrugs. "I still am."

My stomach drops and I concentrate on the movement out of the corner of my eye.

Weston comes to stand so close to me, the heat from his body caresses my arm.

It takes a moment, but I finally regain my footing. "Why the change, Saron? You had your heart set on UT. Isn't that what all the hard work has been about? So you'd graduate in the top six percent and be automatically accepted? Both of you together?" I want to keep asking questions, but I've ventured into rambling territory.

There's a light brushing against my arm—Weston reminding me he's here for me. Like I could ever forget.

"I've been thinking about it for a while, but today really sealed it for me."

"Maybe visit, at least, before making any final decisions." Weston really is clutch.

"Yes, exactly. At least do a campus look-see. You don't want to commit and then not like the environment." My breathing hasn't settled yet, but at least I can string together a coherent sentence without giving away my heavy anxiety over this. I can't imagine anything worse than this news. How will I take care of her fifteen hundred miles away?

"Obviously I want to visit, but I've mostly made up my mind. It'll take a huge disappointment in DC to sway me." She smiles and shrugs, then lilts down the hall to her bedroom, not a care in the world.

Meagan squeezes my hand, then pushes her glasses up on her nose. "What's for dinner?"

My sisters never get rattled. I suppose when you lose your parents at such a young age and don't die from heartbreak, you can't imagine anything worse happening in your life. I was a high school sophomore and wouldn't have survived if it hadn't been for my sisters so much younger than me. Although we moved in with our grandparents, they needed me, and I had to be strong for them. Now the worst thing in the world I could ever fathom is being separated from them—not being there at a moment's notice when they need me.

"Lasagna today. I'm also making a meat loaf and enchiladas to last the remainder of the week."

"Okay, thanks. I've got some homework to do. Call me when it's ready." She walks toward the entrance of the hallway, then rotates back. "Weston, you wouldn't happen to be making any of your famous *cannelés*, would you?"

"Meagan, don't bother Weston on his day off."

Weston laughs and heads toward the kitchen. "I just happen to have been thinking the same thing, Meg."

I can only shake my head as I watch her bound off down the hallway. It's incredible that they're seniors in high school. Saron with her serious disposition more like seventy than seventeen. And Meagan more like seven. It's unbelievable that they're twins because they couldn't be more different.

The shuffling of pans in the kitchen brings me out of my thoughts. I follow the noise and find Weston on his knees, deep under one of the cabinets. His butt right in my face, clothed in cargo shorts. Uncovered long, muscular legs for days. "What in the world are you doing under there?"

Weston backs up slowly, carefully avoiding the low cabinet ceiling. He raises a stack of small cup-shaped pans. "Pay dirt. I knew I stashed these here the last time the girls asked for cannelés."

Of course I hadn't even noticed them under there. Daddy taught me to cook, and I fell in love at a young age but never had the desire to do it for a living. Nowadays I take all the shortcuts I can because I don't have a lot of extra time lying around. "You can't indulge their every whim."

"Why not? You do?"

"I…" I can't deny it because I do. "Well, they expect that from me. You're just spoiling them. And not for the first time."

"Even though I'm an average chef, you know I enjoy baking for the people I love." He plops the pans into the sink and turns on the hot water.

My heart sinks. "I know we've had this discussion a

thousand times and I'll never convince you otherwise, but you're an exceptional pastry chef. Your mom would have been proud." I truly believe that from everything Weston's told me about his mother. Not that I wish anything bad on Flynn's head, but if Lia Everheart were the parent here instead of Weston's father, he'd have more confidence and know his worth.

He shrugs and adds soap to the dishwater he's making in the sink. "Thanks." It's said with an upbeat tone, but the underlying mood is doubt. He washes and rinses the molds before swiftly changing the subject. "How do you feel about Saron's revelation?"

I hadn't forgotten about my sister's news exactly, but talking about the Everheart family dynamics gave me a reprieve. My chest tightens and I pull a glass out of the cabinet and fill it with water from the pitcher in our modest fridge. After taking a long drink, I face Weston. "I'm devastated. She's never mentioned going out of state for school. This is completely out of the blue."

"As is the Saron way."

"Yes, that's right, for sure."

There was the time she decided to run a marathon despite never having run a day in her life. She came home one afternoon during her freshman year and announced her training plan, including meals I needed to improve on. Six months later, she finished the Austin marathon. Now she has ten under her belt.

I drag a deep inhale of air into my lungs, then release. "Dang it if this one didn't catch me all the way off guard."

"Rum?"

"Hmmm? No thanks."

"Do you have any rum left?"

"Oh." I open the cabinet above the built-in microwave and pull out a pint-size bottle of the dark alcohol. "Here's what you left last time. Is it enough?"

He holds it up to the light. "Plenty. Thanks." He opens the pantry and retrieves flour, sugar, and salt. Then eggs, butter, and milk from the fridge. After rummaging through the spice cabinet, he turns my way, eyebrows raised. "I don't suppose you have any vanilla beans, huh?"

I snort and water dribbles down my chin from my up-turned glass. "Do you know how much one of those little vanilla beans costs from the grocery store?"

He smiles and shrugs. "No?"

"No, you don't because Kerry buys all your beans and everything else you need at the restaurant. Trust me, it's cost prohibitive on my salary." I move him aside and fish out a bottle, then hand it to him. "You can use the vanilla extract. At least it's pure and not imitation. The girls won't know the difference anyway."

"You need a raise."

"I deserve a raise."

"Have you asked Dad?"

I pull out a wooden chair at our four-person kitchen table and take a seat. Our home doesn't have a formal dining room, but we're fortunate that whatever furniture we have is good quality since we inherited it from our parents. There's more in my grandparents' shed I was saving for whenever we bought a bigger house, but that day never came and who knows what will happen now with Saron moving across country. It's been fine because when we are able to eat together, which is rare, there's only the three of us—or four when Weston joins us.

"I'm not pushing him on it because if I make too much more, the girls won't be able to get financial aid. But I have shown him the salary comps for similar restaurants because he needs to know my worth, but he refuses anyway." I rub my hands across my forehead and groan. "He has me over a barrel because he knows this job is all I've ever wanted. He also knows how much I need it while the twins still live here. He has one more year before I get serious with him. He either has to pay me my worth or I'll walk." The truth is I hope he pays me because I'm comfortable and don't want to start all over at another restaurant. Equitable positions for a woman—a Black one at that—aren't just hanging off trees for the taking.

Weston pours the batter in the molds while looking at me. It's really quite amazing how intuitive it is for him. "I'd offer to talk to him, but that would just make it worse."

He's right, but I won't hurt his feelings by agreeing. "I appreciate the offer but I'm going to figure this out. I have to. I already didn't know how I was going to close the gap on in-state expenses. I don't even want to think about out-of-state private school money." My chest tightens again, and I take another long pull of water, thinking back to my conversation with Naomi just before the accident last week. "But one thing I know for sure, those I love will never go without. I'll figure out a way."

"Well, you could always move in with me to save money. Sell your house?"

I take a deep breath, then stand and pull Weston into a tight hug. "If only it were that simple." It's not like this isn't the first time he's hinted at something similar. *Just room-mates,* he said. I'm not sure how long that would last if we were under the same roof.

He kisses me on the temple, lingering for a moment, and goes back to his task.

I sigh and gather the ingredients for the three meals to last us the week.

If only it were that simple.

THE SHED IN the back of Mimi and Papa's house covers half the backyard and is divided into three sections. Mama and Daddy's belongings take up two sections, and Papa has his hundreds of books, which is who I learned my love of reading from; the overflow of pots and pans from the kitchen; and other odds and ends in the last section. Years ago, he used the space as a workshop where he whittled miniatures of everything anyone could think of. He lost his passion for his hobby when his oldest son died and hasn't carved anything since. There are still carvings here and there throughout the house, but they, too, have lost their luster.

I dig around for a small box with wedding rings and fi-nally find it behind an old record player Daddy had held on to since he was a kid. He loved that thing. He and Mom would wait until I went to bed on Saturday nights and play records and dance until late into the night. There was a vent between the hallway and the family room, so I would sneak out of bed and listen through the shaft. They would laugh at Daddy's corny jokes and prance around the hardwood floors until the wee hours of the morning. That was before the twins came along, of course.

I wipe a tear and inhale slowly before walking through the shed door.

"Find what you were looking for?"

I show Papa the rings. "I did. The box was wedged behind a lot of stuff just where I left them." I've never forgotten them there but wanted them out of sight until I needed them. With Saron leaving, it feels like a good time to wear them close.

He wipes his hands on a rag sticking out of the back pocket of his coveralls, then stands. "Good deal."

"The garden's still looking very nice. I didn't think you'd have all those peppers this late in the season."

He nods, surveying the rows of vegetables. Most have gone to seed, but there's still quite a few bearing. "Pretty soon I'll dig up those tomato plants and get it ready for some greens."

Daddy said he could eat greens every day if possible. I've never been able to see the allure. "Collards?"

We walk to the back door. His steps are slower than when the twins and I first moved here a few years ago, but he's still spryer than any other eighty-year-old I know.

He opens the screen door for me to walk through. "Yeah, we'll do some collards and some mustards, too. Diedra wants some Swiss chard so I'll put a couple plants out there and see how they do."

I swallow the sigh creeping up my throat. Diedra strikes

again. You'd think she was the baby of the grandchildren instead of Saron and Meagan.

Mimi lumbers down the hallway, pushing her walker. "Y'all sure are up early."

The pang in my chest makes itself known as I walk over to my aging grandmother. I can't imagine our lives without her, but her health has been declining steadily since the twins and I moved out a couple years ago. I wanted my own space for so long but held off until my sisters were old enough to drive themselves around, considering my loaded schedule. It had been a blessing, too, because I was able to concentrate on my career and finally become an executive manager last year.

"I have to be in the restaurant in a few minutes but wanted to pick up my parents' wedding rings. I stored them in the shed." I kiss Mimi gently on her forehead. "How're you feeling this morning?"

"Not too bad. I'm ready for my coffee, though." She makes it over to her recliner and sits with a relieved sigh. Her full face of makeup belies her advanced years, and although she has traded in her signature pantsuits for decorative house dresses, she's no less fashionable than she always was.

Mimi often chastises me for my lack of care when it comes to my appearance, urging me to at least use a hair stylist, but my wash-and-go short style gives me the freedom to take care of my many responsibilities without spending unnecessary time or money in a salon. A biannual trip to the barber for a trim is all the time I can spare on trivial tasks.

A knock on the door pulls me out of my thoughts on self-care.

Papa opens the door to a smiling Weston. "I've come

bearing treats."

I can't help but smile back. "Hey, you. Whatcha got there?" I grasp for the pastry box, but he pulls it out of reach. "Hey."

"These are for Mimi and Papa." He sets the box on the end table residing between the matching recliners and leans over to kiss Mimi on the cheek. "I brought you some beignets and fruit kolaches."

Mimi leans over the box and inhales, closing her eyes. "These smell divine, and right on time. Papa was just getting my coffee." She rubs her hands together after opening the lid to the box.

Weston claps. "I thought so. I tried to time it just right."

"Well you sure did. Thank you so much, Weston."

"Anytime, Mimi."

He follows Papa into the kitchen.

I trail behind them. "I can make the coffee, Papa. I'll have a cup, too." I rotate to Weston. "How about you?"

"No, thanks. I'll just have some water." He reaches into the cabinet next to the refrigerator and pulls down a glass, then fills it from the dispenser in the fridge door.

Papa sits at the kitchen table, perches his glasses on his nose, then opens the newspaper. "There's some fruit in the ice box if you want some."

I'm not sure if he's speaking to me or Weston, but my friend opens the door and removes a container of loquats. "Yum. Where'd you get these?"

Papa doesn't look up before responding to Weston. "Naomi picked them up from the Whole Foods."

I look at the fruit before pulling out the French press

that's rarely used in favor of the Keurig. "Have you had those before?"

The wheels in Weston's brain are clearly churning. He's concentrating so hard on the basket in his hand that he doesn't acknowledge me.

"Weston." I nudge him out of the way so I can fill a pot with water from the dispenser.

He blinks down at me. "What? Oh, sorry?"

"I asked you if you've ever had loquats before. Are they good?"

"Really good. Aunt Kara has a tree in her backyard in Berkeley. Growing up, I would gorge myself on these. Declan preferred the persimmon tree, which wasn't my favorite by far, and Knox liked the pomegranates. They were so good but a lot of work. He didn't seem to mind, though." Weston's gaze is wistful, clearly thinking back to another time when the brothers were all together.

I take a moment to wonder if his memories are from before his mother died but don't ask. Weston never seems to mind talking about her, but there's definitely a difference between "before Lia" and "after Lia." Weston spent more time with his mother than the others, taking an immediate interest in the sweet confections his mother made as a pastry chef. After she died, poor Weston took up his assumed place as the typical middle child: ignored by his father, playing peacemaker between his brothers, and generally trying to please everyone. He finally embraced a "found family" with friends from school who are still part of a close-knit group today. Then finally me and my myriad of cousins and grandparents.

"I hope you aren't thinking what I believe you're thinking."

He grins, then removes a few pieces of the fruit and washes them under cool water in the sink. "If you believe I'm thinking about turning this wonderful fruit of my childhood into a fabulous dessert, then your hopes would be dashed?"

"Oh, goodness gracious, Weston." I dump way too much coffee into the press before Weston stills my hand.

"Not for the restaurant, sweetheart. I got the message loud and clear."

I inhale, drawing in most of the air in the kitchen. "Sorry." I know I'm only the messenger, but I hate being the tool used by his father to hurt him.

He kisses my cheek, then spoons the excess coffee back into the jar. "You're fine." He pops one of the loquats into his mouth and grins. "Almost as good as I remember. I gotta go, but I'll see you at the restaurant later?"

Even though it wasn't really a question, I nod anyway and watch him fist-bump Papa then stroll through the kitchen door. What did I do to get so lucky to have a friend like Weston?

CHAPTER FOUR

Cynthia has all the answers. Right?

THE RESTAURANT OPENS in less than an hour, but I've been fighting an unsettling feeling all day. I finally relent and pick up the phone to video chat with Cynthia. At least for a few minutes.

I watch the screen while it rings, thinking how fortunate I am to have Mom's best friend a phone call away. Days I'm missing my parents terribly, I can connect with Cynthia, who's like a balm to my grieving soul. I palm my parents' wedding rings hanging around my neck while I wait.

"Hi there, honey bun."

"I hope I didn't catch you at a bad time." She's dressed in a conservative navy blazer with a pearl blouse underneath. I figured she'd be at the hospital where she counsels in-patient clients, both individual and group therapy, but hoped I would catch her during administrative hours. If she were busy, more than likely she wouldn't answer.

"I have a little time. Everything okay?" She squints into the phone screen. "Why are you in the dark?"

"Just grabbing a few minutes to myself before we open. I'm hiding out in the storage room for privacy."

She nods and offers me a small smile. "You didn't answer

my question."

I sigh hard, choking down a shuddering breath that threatens to turn into a sob. "I'm failing the girls again, and I'm not sure how to fix it."

She rolls in her chair across to the open door to her office and swings it closed, then returns to her desk—and me. "There's so much to unpack in that sentence. We'll get to the fact that they're not your sole responsibility and what you're afraid of. But first, let's start with the obvious: You haven't failed your sisters in the past."

Tears prick the back of my eyes and I blink rapidly to control them. "If it weren't for me begging to go to that basketball game, my sisters would still have their parents."

"Oh, dear. I can't change your mind. Lord knows I've tried so many times over the past ten years, but your parents chose to make dinner plans that evening. Transporting you less than a mile to the high school isn't what killed them. A drunk driving on a foggy night did."

I shrug because she's right—I'll never believe I'm not responsible for what happened that night. I just had to make it to every event whenever the school doors opened. The fog didn't deter me in the least, as long as I got what I wanted. I wouldn't let Mama rest until she agreed to drop me off. They would have never thought about leaving the house that night if it weren't for me. I'm just grateful Cynthia babysat my sisters instead of my parents taking them along. It was fortunate Mama lived across the street from her best friend. And unfortunate Cynthia was usually unoccupied to babysit because of a failed relationship she never quite got over. "Mama and Daddy aren't here, but I am. I have to care for them to make up for their loss."

"Your grandparents have custody. They're ultimately responsible for Saron and Meagan. They never wavered."

The outer door opens and one of the waiters comes in, searching the shelves.

I sink back into the shadows and put a finger to my lips.

When the waiter finds a waist apron in his size, he finally leaves me in peace. He should have already had an apron in his locker in the employee break room.

"Sorry about that. I don't have much time before I need to be out front. I wanted to hear your voice." She can't help me, but when we speak, she reminds me of Mama. Not that they're alike in any way, but they were best friends, closer than sisters. She knew Mama better than anyone, except Daddy.

"What is it, Ryan?"

I take a couple of cleansing breaths. "Saron has decided on Howard for college. I feel so helpless. I can't lose her." This time a sob does break my voice.

"Oh, honey. You won't lose her. Your sisters are grown and ready to branch out and establish their own lives. We've discussed this before. You have to let them live."

"Well, of course, I know that. But why does she have to go so far away? What if something happens to her so far?"

"You just had a car accident a few miles from home. You better than anyone know anything can happen close by. It's not just far away."

I clasp the rings on the chain hanging around my neck. The medal warms my cold hands. "I know, but it's just so hard to let them go. I want to protect them."

When the outer door opens again, I resign myself to my plight for the remainder of the day. "Thanks for talking. I have to get back out there."

"Okay, but please promise to call me later when you're off."

I'm shaking my head before she finishes the sentence. "It'll be too late, but I'll call you Monday for sure."

She frowns but doesn't say anything.

I wave my goodbye and disconnect the line.

AFTER THE LAST customers depart, I go to the office I share with the three managers who report to me and fall into my executive leather chair.

"That bad, huh?" My assistant general manager places a tumbler of brown liquid in front of me along with a printed list of chefs we interviewed, lines crossed through the first three names. We've gone long enough without replacing the last chef.

"Thanks, Ace. I don't think this list will cut it, though. We started with the best candidate, and now we're working down the list. I don't see this process getting any better." Besides, Knox is working on this for me, but I can't tell Ace that.

He folds his tall frame into one of the comfortable chairs on the other side of my desk and crosses his legs. "That's a good point. What do you need me to do?"

"Flynn's been no help at all. He depended on Knox too heavily, and now we're all paying the price."

Ace huffs, then blows out a hard breath. "Chef Everheart probably wouldn't agree."

"Agree or not, we're in damage-control mode at this point." I sip the smooth whisky and raise a brow at Ace.

"I figured you'd be in need of the good stuff."

"You have excellent intuition, my friend."

He clears his throat and leans forward. "I know this is the worst timing, but we talked about a raise during my evaluation over a month ago. I realize it's been wild around here since, but when do you think that'll happen?"

I lean back in my chair and close my eyes. Yes, it has been frantic around here since his performance review and we've just been holding the ship together, but Ace deserves the raise, that's not a question. Despite what Weston believes, Ace is an integral part of our continued success. Even though Flynn leaves employee decisions to me, the problem is that if I bump Ace up the seven percent he wants, he'd be the highest paid non-chef. Including more than me.

After taking a long pull on my drink, I nod. "Would you settle for five percent?" At least we'd be making the same amount.

He bites the inside of his mouth, thinking. Or perhaps calculating. "For now, I suppose so. I can work with you on this, but we need to revisit soon."

"Appreciate it, Ace. You're an incredible asset to Everheart Bar and Fine Dining." I smile, hoping to convey my sincerity. "And to me."

He nods and walks back to his desk to pack up.

I check the time on my cell phone and groan. Another extremely late night. So late, it's blending into morning. One more night I won't see Meagan and Saron because they will have been in deep sleep for hours when I finally make it through the door, then up early for school while I get at least a few hours shut eye. Something has to give.

"DID YOU HEAR about Corey and Shay?"

I overhear the whispered question just as I turn the corner on my way to get some work done in my office.

Jenny straightens when she sees me, then averts her eyes and rotates toward the employee bathrooms.

Weston gazes at me with sad eyes. "Couldn't you have turned your head on this one?" He follows me through the door to my office and it clicks ever so silently behind him.

"I wouldn't have even known about it if it wasn't for your Chef Francis. And he told me right in front of your dad, so…" I shrug and plop into my chair, a heavy weight on my shoulders pushing me into its leathery depths. "Shay was our best waitstaff. The last thing I wanted to do was let her go. Your father and his stupid rules."

Weston's eyes darken for a moment before he scrubs a large hand over his face. This is as close to down as he gets. And as far as sucky situations go, this one sits pretty close to the top. "I'm going to talk with Dad."

My gaze pops up from the screen on my computer and lands on his worried face. "You're what?"

He closes his eyes for a moment. "I know. I'll only make it worse. He would probably put out the word to blackball both if I fought for them."

I frown, but what's the use of saying anything? Lord knows Flynn is just that petty. "What would have been nice is if your pastry chef told you instead of me in front of your dad. What business is it of his anyway? Why would he care?"

The door opens and Ace comes through, dinner plate in hand. "Hey, Chef."

"Hey." Weston turns back to me and says under his breath, "I'll tell you later."

I nod, then purse my lips. "You know, maybe I can have another word with him. I'm not sure if he even knew Shay by name. He certainly praised her skills and even had me assign her to the chef's table." I shrug, then click off my computer screen. "It's worth a try at least."

Weston stands after I get up and walks toward the door.

Before I can reach him, Ace clears his throat. "Hey, boss, did you see this?" He flips his screen my way, displaying an open email.

I bend to take in the headline with Weston leaning over my back, a hand casually resting on my shoulder, reading it for himself. *National Restaurant Executive of the Year.* "Oh, wow, Ryan, you should totally enter."

My mind churns with the possibilities. Recognition is welcome, for sure, but the prize money would go a long way in helping me send my sisters through school. I scan below and read the rules. "I can't just enter, Chef. Your dad would have to recommend me." My stomach drops after working itself into a joyful frenzy.

"Why wouldn't he? This place wouldn't be where it is without your management. Even Dad admits it, however begrudgingly."

Ace nods in agreement and flips the screen back his way. "Listen to the requirements: *Someone who has a high ability in restaurant management; establishes key achievements in their current job; demonstrates staff development and supervision, proven market trend insight and promotion, exceptional food and beverage planning, superior customer service, and inventory control and budgetary management.*" He blows out a hard breath. "Boss, you fit that bill if anyone ever has."

"That's very kind of you, but it's a team effort. I couldn't do this without you, Nancy, and Kerry. You know that, right?"

He smiles, then shrugs. "Thanks, boss."

Weston squeezes my shoulder and runs his hand down my arm. "Looks like you have another item to run by Dad."

"Indeed."

This time when I head through the door, Weston hangs back and starts up a conversation with Ace. It's just as well because sad as the thought may be, if Flynn sees Weston beside me, he'll be less likely to listen to reason.

After looking throughout the restaurant, even in the supply rooms, I find Chef in the last place he ever spends any time—his office with a golf club in hand, staring down an indoor putting green. I'm talking real grass taking up about half the floor, the other half covered in some sort of expensive tile. No fake turf for Michelin-star Chef Flynn Everheart. He's built a whole gym onto the restaurant for his sons, but the only one left to use it is Weston and he prefers outdoors activities. It's sort of sad if you think about it, but considering this is a situation of his own making, I don't linger on his feelings.

I knock on the open door. "Chef, I need to run a couple items by you."

His grip tightens on the putter, and his face reddens. "I'm busy."

"I see that." I walk farther into the room, then sit on the leather sofa. Chef spends a ridiculous amount of time in this restaurant, even more so since Knox's departure. As the cliché goes, he works hard and plays even harder, even in his advancing age. Not that he's old. From what I've heard from Weston, his parents started their family right out of culinary school. If I had to guess, I'd put him in his late fifties. He's still fit and quite handsome but doesn't hold a candle to his genetically gifted sons. "I'll wait."

He lines up his shot again and easily sinks the ball in the hole. "What is it, Ryan?"

"Well, Chef. First, I'd like to revisit the HR issue we had yesterday. I realize you have this rule, and I mostly understand why, but Shay is our best server. Her job hasn't suffered because of her romance with Corey."

He finally turns my way and stares me down, eyes narrowed and brows drawn together.

I don't flinch or cower because I've become accustomed to his intimidation tactics. They worked on me in the beginning, but after a while, it just makes him look silly. I love my job and certainly need it, but he and I both know I'd need to do something egregious for him to fire me.

He blinks, then walks over to his desk but doesn't sit. Instead, he balances his weight on the back of his chair, then looks at me again. His stare is back to normal but no less intense. "Do you know how many frivolous lawsuits I spent money on before I instituted this policy? No, you wouldn't because it was in place before the boys came of age." He rubs the smooth skin around his chin in thought. "There were several. And productivity usually takes a nosedive when employees are sneaking into the supply room or, even worse, they break up and can't stand to work together. You should be thanking me. That scheduling nightmare would fall onto your shoulders."

He's laid out a good case. "I'm not asking you to change the policy, but could we make an exception in Shay's case? I don't want to lose her."

"No. What's the other item?"

Since I've been customarily dismissed on that topic, I ease into the next. "We're doing well, would you agree?"

He leans against the wall and crosses his arms over his chest. "We've seen better days, but yes, I would agree that we are keeping up our usual excellence."

No way am I touching the *better days* statement. Clearly he's referencing the loss of two sons to the outside world, but since he only has himself to blame, there's no reason to go down that road. I make a note to myself to ask Weston if his father even speaks to his wayward brothers. Then again, Flynn would have to speak to Weston first. "I believe I'm a big part of maintaining our high quality and Michelin status."

His posture stiffens. "We discussed your compensation just last week, Ryan."

"I'm not asking you about a raise. You've already laid out your compensation plan for the chefs and me." I don't agree, but what can I do. It's his name on the building. "I'd like you to enter me into the National Restaurant Executive of the Year contest."

His eyebrows raise ever so slightly.

"Besides the hefty monetary prize, there's industry recognition and would be even more publicity for the restaurant."

That last part gets his attention. I can see when he realizes the benefit to himself. "I'll consider it. I need to see the materials before I decide."

I prepared for this moment by bringing my laptop with me. I only need to open it and show him the website already queued up.

He scans the entry instructions and rules with his normal scrutiny. "*Three examples of both key successes you've had in your management role and how you've ensured customer satisfaction. Two examples of food and beverage...* Listen, Ryan, if you can think of all of these various examples, fill it out and I'll submit it."

After checking in with my feelings, I simply say, "Thanks," and close my laptop. I should have tears in my eyes or maybe clench my jaw with anger, but I don't feel anything at all. Flynn is as selfish as they come and only recognizes his own achievements. If he doesn't give his sons credit, there's no hope he'll give me any recognition ever. I have to look elsewhere for that and perhaps this contest is the answer. I can think of a hundred examples for each question. I just need to get to work on it.

CHAPTER FIVE

Jerome doesn't know what he's talking about. Nope!

I CHECK MY phone and note that I'm a little early, but I didn't have much going on this morning at home, so decided I may as well head over to barbecue. It's great when both Weston's and my off days fall on a weekend. We can hang out and everyone's usually available, including my sisters.

Weston's house is simple but yet somehow chaotic. He has a ranch-style three-bedroom down the street from Knox and not too far from where Declan lived before he sold his house and decided to become a world traveler with his film-making love. None of the brothers live more than a stone's throw from Everheart Bar & Fine Dining. I should be so lucky but could never afford to live that close to the prime real estate where Everhearts call home.

I set my container of paper plates, eating utensils, and napkins on one of the tables in Weston's backyard because when there's a potluck at a professional chef's house, what else are you going to bring?

From the looks of everything else already here, I'm guessing the architect bros had the same idea, except with alcohol.

There's open coolers of craft beer as far as the eye can see and a couple filled with bottles of water.

Jerome comes from the direction of the garage, pushing a wheelbarrow full of bags of ice. "Hey, Ryan." He sets the cart down and kisses me on the cheek. "When'd you get here?"

"Hey. About five minutes ago. I came straight out here. Where is everyone?"

"Weston's in the kitchen getting the corn together to bring out. That fire is roaring."

Somehow I missed the huge barbecue pit blazing with sky-high flames. If you could call it a pit. It's more like the hearth at the restaurant. "Wow."

"Yeah. My brothers ran to the store for more beer. They didn't think we had enough." He chuckles and shakes his head. "Lisa's in the house." He looks longingly to the second-floor windows. "Darryl's up there, too, playing in the game room." He picks up the first of the ice bags in strong arms and unceremoniously dumps it into the nearest cooler.

"Let me text and see where the others are."

I send a message to the twins first, then fire off a message to Naomi.

"So what's been happening at the firm lately?"

He smiles wide enough for those gorgeous dimples of his to pop. "We just landed a huge project downtown. Fifteen stories, living space in the top stories with various entertainment businesses down below."

"Oh my goodness. I hadn't heard. Congratulations!"

"We just signed everything this morning, so now it's official. Looks like you'll have to keep Weston busy the next few months because this is our last hang for a while." He winks before dumping more ice.

I scrunch my face, trying to decide how he meant that wink. "You know Weston and I are only friends, right?"

He looks up from his task and chuckles. "I think I may have heard something like that."

"Okay, Jerome. What's the deal? What are you not saying?"

He wipes his hands on his khaki shorts. "Look, I get what you're saying. I hear you." He shrugs and grabs the back of his neck, looking around. "For those of us on the outside looking in, lately it seems like you and Weston are getting...closer. That's all."

I blink several times. "Did Weston say something?"

Jerome throws his hands up, waving me off. "Nah, not at all. Don't get me in trouble with my boy. I'm just making an observation."

"Yeah, an observation. You said 'those of us' so I'm assuming everyone's gossiping behind our backs, so you can go back and let everyone know that Weston and I are friends. I love him like a brother."

"Sure, sure. Whatever you say, Ryan." He picks up the wheelbarrow and heads back to the garage before I have a chance at a rebuttal.

I zip over to the back door and stumble through narrowly losing my balance completely. Jeesh, Jerome has me feeling some kind of way.

Weston rotates my way, then moves to come help me. He steadies me on my feet and kisses me on the temple.

The kiss feels more intimate for some reason. "I'm okay. Carry on."

He smiles. "What has you all flustered?"

The question of the day is do I answer this or not. If I do answer, the proverbial worms will spill all down the can. This is not where I want to go with Weston. He's my best friend and I'd never want to lose that. "I probably need some water. It's hot as Hades out there."

He laughs and turns to the cabinet to take down a glass.

"I can get it. You keep doing what you were doing." We both reach for the glass and our fingers brush like they have a thousand times, but this time something moves inside my chest. Maybe because what Jerome said is fresh on my mind, but I don't move my hand. Instead, I allow the heat from his finger to penetrate my skin. I slide my gaze to him, meeting his perplexed expression, eyebrows drawn together. "I—"

The twins burst through the back door—Meagan giggling and Saron rolling her eyes. "Hi, Ryan and Weston" reaches through the air in stereo.

"Hey, what do you two have—"

"Hey, everybody. What's happening?" Darryl comes into the kitchen and heads straight for my sisters, gaming instrument in hand. He's closer to their age than mine, and they usually gravitate to each other when we have these gatherings. During our extended family dinners, too.

The three of them ignore me completely and circle back toward the stairs.

"Wait a minute. Where are you going? You just got here."

Saron and Darryl bound up the stairs like I wasn't even speaking. Meagan stops midway and pushes her glasses up her nose, then shrugs. "Darryl challenged us to *Fortnite*.

We'll be back down when the food's ready." She follows her sister and cousin without another word.

"Hmmph."

"Kids today." Weston faces the sink, but his shoulders shake ever so slightly.

I haven't forgotten the unusual moment we just shared, but if he's willing to ignore it, that's probably the best route to take. "Hardy har har."

He barks a laugh before slapping a wet hand over his mouth.

"I hope you didn't have meat juice on your hands. Yuck."

"Just corn juice." He holds up a freshly shucked ear of corn with the husks wrapped back in place. There's a large bowl filled with more soaking corn. "These are ready to go outside. Get the door for me?"

"Sure." I move to open the door and bump into him as he rounds the counter. "Sorry. I don't know what's wrong with me today."

He cocks his head to the side and studies me. "Everything okay?" He smiles. "I mean, other than all the other things."

I snort. "Yes, I'm fine. Other than all the other things." I open the door and let him through, but before I can close it, Naomi places a hand on the knob.

"Whew, it is *hot* hot out there. Thank goodness for air-conditioning."

I stand back and let her through. "Isn't that the truth. Where are you coming from?" She's dressier than a backyard barbecue calls for. The deep purple dress has cap sleeves, and she's wearing heels.

"I had a meeting with marketing this morning. Matter of fact, I only have a couple hours before I need to head back. I'm on deadline with this manuscript."

My smile turns into a frown. "Ah man. I haven't seen you since the accident. I was hoping to catch up."

She puts her purse on the wide windowsill lining the breakfast area. "We can still catch up. Just a couple hours' worth." She flashes me a smile, then pulls out her phone.

"Ugh, you're always busy these days."

She finishes typing out a message, then sets the phone down on top of her purse. "You're one to talk."

"Yes, I know, but I've always been busy." I laugh at my own ridiculousness. "Sorry. What are you working on anyway?"

"That same AI manuscript I was telling you about. The contracts are dry, so we're in full swing." She plops into one of the kitchen table chairs and clasps her hands. "I'm so excited."

"Sci-fi seems to be all the rage these days. Even Weston's writing one." I suck in a startled breath as I realize what I just said.

"Excuse me?"

"I wasn't supposed to say that."

She crosses her arms over her chest. "Do tell."

"He's going to kill me, and you definitely can't tell him I spilled, but Weston's been working on a real novel. He's still doing the fan fiction, too, but he says writing the novel has been freeing and just pouring out of him."

"Wow."

"I know, right? He's been letting me read ten thousand words at a time, and it's really good."

She nods, quirking one side of her mouth up. "This is an interesting turn of events, but I have to say I'm not surprised you think it's good. I've read some of his fan fiction, and it's really great."

"Do you think... I mean...would you consider reading it? To acquire, I mean."

"Is that what Weston wants?"

I sit in the chair next to her and lean in just in case Weston comes back through the door. "I think he would love to be a published author, but after everything with Flynn, I'm not sure he has the confidence to do anything other than what he's doing. Even that doesn't feel comfortable for him. He thinks he's an average chef at best. Can you believe that?"

"Man, it's such a shame. His father is really an asshole."

"Tell me about it." I lean back in my chair and stare at the ceiling. "He's run the other two sons off, and if he ever remembered the one left, he'd probably do something to make him leave, too. As it is, Weston's just skating by, but I really don't think he's happy. There's also the thing with his mother's memory. That probably holds him to this job more than anything."

Naomi's phone buzzes and she shoots me an apologetic glance. "I have to get this." She takes her phone into the living room and her voice fades.

Left with my own thoughts, I move the curtain a little and look out the window. The other architect bros are back. Along with Weston, they're all standing around the hearth, beers in hand, laughing and talking. I could go out there with them. I've fit into their group comfortably for a while. But between Jerome's accusation and that lingering touch with Weston's finger, something feels a little off.

I continue watching, feeling a little dirty for the intrusion, but somehow I can't peel my gaze away from Weston. I sigh and shake my head. Weston is too important to me to let my thoughts wander this way. Time to stuff those wayward ideas back where they belong.

CHAPTER SIX

It's only a dance. Seriously.

I WANT TO run and jump into her arms, but that would surely be frowned upon. After witnessing Chef Sinclair put Flynn in his place, again, I can only saunter back to my office, sit in my chair, and slip off my heels, grabbing the thick carpet with my toes, the padded friction a welcome relief to my sore feet. Then I fire off a text message to Knox, one of many I've dispatched him over the past two weeks since he sent our way the new wonder-chef that is Charlotte Sinclair. *Chef Sinclair is working out just as you promised. I can't thank you enough, Chef!*

A response doesn't come immediately, but that's unsurprising considering he's knee-deep in renovations of the space Rowan finally decided on for her restaurant. Considering what an amazing chef Knox is, it's unbelievable he excels even more as a consultant. I have a perfect new chef to attest to that.

"What's that smile for, boss?"

I want to roll my eyes so hard, but again, that wouldn't be a great response to an employee—but goodness gracious almighty, I've asked Nancy and the rest of the staff not to call me boss at least fifty-leven times. "I'm just so relieved how well Chef Sinclair is working out. Looks like we've found the one."

Nancy perches her glasses into her bright red hair and sits back in her chair with a wide grin. "That's fabulous. I'm so sick of filling out new employee paperwork for the same position every week."

A snort escapes my nose before I can clamp it down. "Who are you telling? I can finally take a breath and resume running the rest of this restaurant without putting out the same fire over and over again." I squeeze my eyes closed and shimmy my shoulders, squelching a squeal. "I'm so relieved."

"Hard same." She checks her watch and stands. "I'm going to meet the tech guy down the hall. There's still a glitch in the voice assistant technology."

"Let me know if you need anything."

With a wave, she leaves through the office door, closing it behind her.

I turn back to my laptop and review the schedule for next month. Now that we have what looks like a permanent addition, scheduling should be a breeze. I'm sidetracked by Nancy's task, though. Flynn has allowed us to incorporate every tech possible no matter how expensive as long as it makes his restaurant run smoother and keeps up with the latest trends. Yet he won't pay me my worth.

Before I can fall too far down that rabbit hole of defeatist thought, there's a heavy knock on the door.

"Come."

Weston eases the door open, tablet in hand and tense lines around his eyes even though he's smiling. "Hey?"

"Hey. What's up?"

He shrugs and falls into the chair across from my desk, whooshing the scent of caramel my way, extending his long legs underneath, then taps my foot with his. "Just taking a break. I'm a little stuck on my story and not sure where to go next."

"I can't imagine just writing hundreds of words in one sitting. That's why I went the MBA route. English essays were never my favorite."

He shakes his head and laughs. "Not mine, either, believe me. This is different. I don't know how to explain it. I just start typing and all of a sudden, I'm telling a story to myself without much conscious thought. It usually just flows."

"What's the problem now? Everything I've read has been amazing." We've been here before with his doubts. There's nothing I can really offer, but it seems to help him when he can just talk it out a little.

"I don't know exactly. I'm having trouble capturing the lead alien's voice. The one from the intergalactic court."

I nod, recalling some of the story I've read. His fan fiction always crossed many genres including fantasy and sci-fi, so I wasn't surprised by his choice of story to tell. "Are you not able to identify with them?"

"Hmmm, that may be the problem. They're too close to me, and writing them seems personal. Almost invasive?"

"Oh, interesting. How so?"

"Well, they're a middle child, making their way through life in a profession that was more expected of them than something they wanted. But they don't believe they're capable of anything else, barely getting by in what they're doing." He looks over at Ace's empty desk and shrugs.

"Oh, Chef, really?" I reach across my desk and tap the edge, reaching for his hand.

He eases his hand into mine but doesn't face me. "It's all fine."

It's so not fine, but I can't instill the confidence in my friend his father has taken years to strip away. *Unfair* is an understatement, especially when Weston is so talented and intelligent but doesn't recognize his strengths. I stroke his palm and nearly pull away from the spark that flies up my arm. The same feeling I've been fighting ever since I first felt it at the barbecue. He needs me, though, so I continue the movement. "Dearest, I wish you could see yourself through my eyes."

Now he does rotate my way and glances down at our joined hands before looking up at me with warmth in his eyes. "It really is fine, Ryan. I'm just grateful I have you and you're always in my corner. It means a lot." He bites the side of his lip before releasing a deep sigh. "I better get back."

I pull my hand back, but the tingles still course through my skin where we touched. I barely whisper, "Okay."

THE RESTAURANT IS finally closed, and I can get off my feet for a few minutes at least. There's plenty left to do but traveling from one customer to another, querying their dining experience isn't one of them. Or running interference between Flynn and Chef Sinclair. She's got his number, all right, but I can't rest on my laurels. Losing her would be a disaster and going back to Knox again wouldn't be an option. He gave me a freebie, but the man has a lot on his own plate right now.

I relax in my chair and kick off my low-heel pumps and just breathe with my eyes closed. It's so late and my team has been gone for hours, so I have peace in the office. For a few minutes at least. My body may be relaxed, but my brain is going a mile a minute so I sit up and turn on my computer screen. I gave Flynn the prefilled application for my entry to the National Restaurant Executive of the Year contest last week, but as of yesterday, he hasn't actually submitted the entry. I double-check my email, and as suspected, there's no welcome message from the contest organizers.

Before I can fire off yet another reminder, my phone rings, breaking the silence of my office. I frown and look down at the screen, then panic and answer with fumbling fingers. "Meagan, what's wrong?"

Background music blares through the phone, and Meagan giggles before speaking. "Heyyyyyyy, Ry."

I take a couple of deep breaths before responding. "Hi. What's going on?"

"Need a hiccup. I mean pickup?" More giggling.

"Where are you?"

I write down the name of the Sixth Street bar even though it's right around the corner. Just to be sure. "I'll be right there."

My restaurant duties have to wait. The waitstaff is still bustling when I walk down the hallway and the chefs are breaking down their stations as well.

I spot Weston and race over to him. "If anyone asks, I'll

be right back. I have to go get the twins." I take a deep breath and close my eyes. "They're drunk and need a ride."

Weston's smile drops and his eyes widen. "That's new. Do you want me to go?"

I'm shaking my head before he finishes the question. "No, I want to lay eyes on them. Like you said, this never happens, and I would rather interrogate them while they're liquored up and have looser tongues."

"Good plan. At least I'm happy they called you instead of trying to drive."

"I've always let them know they could. And they would never put their lives or anyone else's in danger like that after what happened to Mama and Daddy."

He rubs my arm in comfort. "That makes sense. You go ahead, and I'll cover if anyone asks."

"Thanks, Chef."

I sit behind the wheel of my car, hands shaking. Ever since the accident, I've had to think twice about taking off into the night. And a time like this, I just want to tear my way there to get my sisters. But that thought scares me because this time of night, there are always drunk drivers around. Just like the one who killed our parents.

By the time I get to the bar a few minutes later, both sisters are sitting on the curb of the wide sidewalk. Plenty of people are still milling about in drunken hazes, but bars and restaurants are closing up for the evening. Sixth Street has many different businesses, all related to tourism or the local college crowd, but is especially known for its bars. Usually it's closed off to traffic, but luckily that won't start until tomorrow night heading into the weekend. I'm not sure how

I would have handled parking and hustling my sisters back to the car.

As it is, they're sloppy drunk, leaning on each other to keep themselves up. A tear pricks my eyes with the thought of them not having each other always. Saron's decision to go to school a thousand miles away still has me perplexed and more than a little in my feelings. I wipe at my eyes and exit the car because they aren't even trying to look for me.

"Hey—ready?"

Saron raises her head ever so slowly, eyes unfocused. "Ryan?"

I want to be mad because they are extra toasted, but I promised to always be their ride in times like these and this is the first time they've tested my pledge. "Yeah, it's me. You ready to go?"

I help them up and into the car. There's no more giggling, only tired and droopy eyes.

As I turn off Sixth Street, I clear my throat. "So what happened?"

Saron's head lolls my way. "You're mad."

"No, honey, just concerned." I look in the rearview mirror, but Meagan's sleeping, soft snores escaping her mouth.

"Why?"

"Well, because you've never been out drinking before. As far as I know at least. Did something happen today?"

"Do you really not know what today is?"

I blink. I've been so busy and preoccupied with the living, I hadn't given a thought to the dead. "The anniversary of Mama and Daddy's deaths."

"Bingo." She slumps down in her seat and tries—and

fails—to rest her head in her hand.

"You've never taken to alcohol on this day before."

"We never had fake IDs before."

My breath catches and anger rolls down my spine. Tonight isn't the time to hash this out, but I'll have to let them know how dangerous it is to play with something like that. So many bad things could happen—like being arrested and then being ineligible for financial aid. That's just the least that could happen. "Let's talk about that tomorrow."

When there's no response I spare a glance. She's joined her twin in sleepland.

We make it home, and I wake the girls, load them into the house, and give them plenty of water and an aspirin with promises from them to hydrate.

I have my purse in my lap, but the tiredness and emotion of the day have me locked on the sofa. Maybe just two more minutes and I can will my body to move and get back to the restaurant.

There's a soft knock on the front door before the lock unhitches and the door swings open.

I barely see Weston through the blurriness of my eyes, but the closer he gets, the sharper he comes into focus. He's changed from his chef's jacket and black pants into board shorts, a loud orange tank, and flip-flops. He joins his thigh to mine and places an arm around my shoulder.

"Hey."

"Hey. Everything okay?"

"Yeah. Just willing myself up and back to the restaurant."

"Dad left not too long after you. Everything's been reset for tomorrow, and I locked up. Whatever's left you planned to do can wait until the morning if you want."

Happy tears well in my eyes. "Really?"

"Yes, really." His voice contains the tiniest bit of scorn. It stands out from his usual ultra-pleasant tone.

"Are you mad?"

He kisses my temple, then leans his head against mine. "No, of course not. Just a little frustrated. You never ask for help when there are those in your life who are willing."

Clearly he's referring to himself because I can't think of a single other person who doesn't take more from me than they give. Even my family. Especially my family. "I'm fine doing it myself."

"Okay."

He doesn't argue with me because that isn't his way. He'd rather barrel through and ask forgiveness later, but he doesn't usually do that with me. Maybe because I get everything done on my terms first. I shrug, then burrow into the crook of his arm, laying my head on his firm chest.

I love you. I'm not sure if he said it or if I did. Sleep pulls me under before I can decide.

"UGH, CAN YOU guys finally just get a room already?"

I pop my eyes open and push off Weston's lap, then wipe the drool from my chin. You'd think I was the one up drinking last night by how foggy my head is. "Jeesh, what time is it?" I already know the answer because Meagan's fully dressed with her backpack slung over her shoulder.

Weston shifts beside me, then stretches his long arms

over his head, groaning. He slept sitting up. I'm stiff, so he must be doubly so.

"It's time for you two—"

"Okay, that's enough of that. Where's Saron?"

Meagan pushes her glasses up on her nose and shrugs. "Still in the bathroom. Tell her I'm in the car waiting." She strolls out the front door like she wasn't up until zero dark thirty drinking last night.

Saron doesn't fair as well as her twin. She plods down the hallway, dragging an overstuffed backpack behind her. Her natural curls stick out in several directions and her elbows are ashy.

I stand up and head to the kitchen. "Go get some lotion for your arms before you walk out."

She grumbles but rotates back toward the bathroom.

There's a bowl with milk in the sink, so Meagan must have at least had some cereal. I fill up with water two of the Yetis Weston gave the girls for their birthdays one year and grab an energy bar, then meet Saron at the front door before she goes through. "Meagan already ate, so this is for you. Make sure you both hydrate plenty today."

"Thanks."

I turn back to a grinning Weston. "What?"

"I don't know…" He shrugs. "Watching you and your sisters is so different than how my brothers and I grew up. I was constantly playing peacemaker between them, and of course they never listened to me. Declan was oldest and we didn't really listen to him, either."

I walk back into the kitchen and pull down a couple glasses and fill them with water, then join Weston back on the couch and hand one to him. "If we were closer in age, they probably wouldn't listen to me, either. Or maybe if I wasn't a surrogate parent…"

He places his glass on the table and rubs my back. "You want to talk about it?"

Do I? We've talked about it before plenty of times, but after last night's events, I definitely wished for my parents to be here to handle the teenage drinking part of the program. Really to handle it all. "I guess it's just hard sometimes. I love my sisters to death, but I'm a little resentful sometimes, too. Not because I'm taking care of them, but because all those years went by and I'd gotten used to being an only child, I guess." I take a long pull of my water. "Then my parents did in vitro because they wanted another child and hadn't been successful, and voilà…twins. I resent the universe because they died and didn't get to raise them. But in truth, it's all my fault so I'm more mad at myself than anyone else."

Weston twines his fingers with mine and squeezes ever so gently. He doesn't speak because we've hashed this out before. Just like with Cynthia, no matter what he says or how hard he attempts to reason with me, I'll always blame myself for being so selfish that I just had to go to that basketball game and wouldn't take no for an answer.

"You always say I'm a great listener, but it's really you."

"You absolutely are." He sighs and kisses the back of my hand. "And I'm only quiet because I'm powerless to take away all your pain."

"Well, I appreciate you all the same. They say time heals all wounds, and I suppose that's true to some extent.

Wounds heal, but do they ever disappear completely?" I shrug because I already know the answer to that question. If I live to be a hundred, I'll never forget how guilty and helpless I felt the night my parents died.

He rubs fingers over his chest, the tattoo almost completely exposed under his twisted tank. "Maybe not."

I grab my phone for the time because I probably should go in a little earlier today since I didn't close last night. I notice a new playlist created by my music app in my notifications and click on it because…why not?

Beyoncé plays first, and I smile, imagining the video complete with top hats and tails. I love that video.

The music sinks into my soul, the rhythm moving my shoulders. Soon my head bounces from side to side, and when Beyoncé hits that chorus, I jump up and move. Arms join shoulders and head, then hips sway, and I can't help but pop my fingers.

Weston watches me with a wide smile on his face.

I reach for him. "Dance with me?"

His response is to get up and do a little shimmy of his own. He moves in time with the beat, keeping his eyes on me as he dances my way.

I giggle to myself because the brothers would always tease Weston about his dancing, but in reality, neither Declan nor Knox could hold a beat to save their lives and I truly believe they were jealous of Weston's moves.

He grabs my hand and twirls me, then we dance around the room, moving and swaying with each other in perfect sync, laughing and being silly.

With Weston, I'm floating without a care in the world.

CHAPTER SEVEN

Oh, you thought Flynn was playing. Never.

I HANG UP the phone on my desk and spare a moment for a smile, then clasp my hands together.

Nancy walks into the office and glances at me, then does a double take. "You're smiling. You were just out there defending the new waiter from Chef's onslaught, and now you're smiling. What gives?"

That recent memory brings the corner of my lips down. These days, just the mere mention of Flynn's contemptuous behavior sets my teeth on edge. But I won't let him steal this bit of joy. "I just hung up with Shay, giving her the great news that I found her a new job."

"Oh, that is great. I'm not surprised, though. She was a really good employee." Nancy sits in the chair behind her desk and pops the top on her can of soda. "I am a little surprised Chef didn't try to blackball her."

Flynn's reputation really isn't great, but even he doesn't go out of his way to hurt someone unless they've committed a grave offense against him. Or shares his last name. "I doubt he even remembers Shay's name. He's feeling her loss, though." Promoting Henry to chef's table and hiring a new waiter hasn't gone over well with Flynn. There's been too much change in such a small amount of time.

"Well, I'm really happy for her. She deserves to land on her feet. What about Corey?"

"He went back to working at his mother's dry-cleaning business. This was just something to do. A change of pace for him."

"That's a shame considering what it cost Shay."

I shrug because while I agree getting fired over someone who doesn't care about the consequences of losing his job is a shame, Shay wasn't forced to start up something with him. She knew how strict Flynn is about his *no fraternization* policy. "I'm going back out there. See you later?" Nancy works a nine-to-five job here as the administrative manager, and it's almost quitting time.

"Maybe." She looks at her cell phone for the time. "Probably not."

"Well, if not, you have a great evening."

"You, too, boss."

At some point, I'm going to believe my employees are just messing with me with the whole "boss" thing. I close the door behind me and tread down the hallway, preparing myself to do a last round of checking on the waitstaff and greet the early-bird-dinner diners.

Weston and Jerome enter through the front door and wave. Weston laughs because he must register the surprise on my face. If he isn't working, he isn't here as a rule.

Before I can make my way over to them, I stop at a table with an older white couple I haven't seen here before. "Good evening. I'm the manager, Ryan Landry. How is everything?"

The man raises his eyebrows, but the woman responds

before he can open his mouth. "The service was excellent and the food even better. Thank you so much for asking." She's strikingly beautiful for any age, with midnight-black hair and sharp blue eyes. Maybe they have been here before because she does look familiar now that I'm engaged with her. Then again, even sitting down, she's quite tall, so maybe she was a famous model or something. Who knows.

"You're very welcome. I'm happy you enjoyed your meal. Have a great evening."

"Thank you." She tuts, frowning at her dining partner as I walk away.

I don't take offense, even though it's offensive. A lot of our elderly patrons are confused when I introduce myself. Or sometimes outright rude in their disbelief. One thing Flynn can be given credit for is hiring me. Most executive managers of these types of restaurants don't look anything like me.

"Hey, you." Weston pulls me in for a quick hug, brushing his lips across my ear, leaving a trail of heat behind.

"Hi. Are you two here for dinner?" I try to breathe through the sensation throbbing at my earlobes, but Weston's proximity makes it difficult to concentrate.

Jerome pops those dimples my way. "It took a lot of harassing, but I guilted Weston into bringing me here. No more fancy dinners for a while after tonight."

I frown, then remember. "Oh right, because of your new project. It's starting already?"

"Yes, already in prep mode. We put our collective heads down starting in the morning. It'll be a while before you see us anywhere again."

"That's a shame. We'll miss all of you, but happy for this

incredible opportunity." I turn toward an unusually subdued Weston. "What are you going to do without the fellas?"

Before Weston can open his mouth to respond, Jerome puts his two cents in. "I'm sure you can occupy his time. Right, Ryan?" He's doing his best to hide a smile behind a big hand.

Either Weston is oblivious or choosing to ignore his friend's teasing because he makes puppy-dog eyes. "She's always working. I'll have to fill my off days with writing, I suppose."

"I'm not always working. We have Sound and Cinema with Naomi and them later this week, and don't forget Lisa's birthday bash coming up."

"Yeah, yeah, yeah. Okay, that'll have to do."

"I better get back to work. It was good seeing you, Jerome." I lean in so nobody else can hear. "Don't order dessert because our best pastry chef is off tonight."

Weston and Jerome's chuckles follow me as I make my way to the next occupied table.

FLYNN DOESN'T STROLL in until five minutes before the restaurant opens for lunch so I don't have an opportunity to talk with him about why my application hasn't been submitted. The deadline is still two weeks away, but I would rather not cut it close. Plus, worrying about the submission is taking up too much space in my head.

I catch him before he slinks out the back door, an hour before we actually close. I've noticed more and more that he's only here when the doors are open, and sometimes, like tonight, not even then. That's his prerogative, of course—he owns the place—but many customers patronize this establishment specifically because of the Michelin-star chef.

"Chef, do you have a minute?"

He visibly stiffens before rotating my way. His eyes are guarded, but he pastes on a smile.

It's the least he can do considering I'm running his restaurant with minimal hiccups.

"What can I do for you, Ryan?" He looks at the expensive watch wrapped around his wrist with a matte black stainless steel oyster strap. Yes, I've looked it up, and it's nearly a year of my salary. "I'm late for an, uh, engagement."

That doesn't sound shifty at all. "The contest deadline is a little over two weeks away. It doesn't look like you've submitted my entry."

"That's correct."

"May I ask why?"

"I'm still reviewing. I have a few concerns about the contest."

My stomach flips. "Concerns? Such as?"

He crosses his arms. "For instance, all of the past winners have been men. Seems as though this contest may be sexist."

I swallow the snort rushing over my tongue. As if Flynn would care whether or not the contest or anything else is sexist. Clearly this is an excuse for something. What, I don't know yet. "I think that's more of a reflection of the industry in general. Most restaurant executives are men on this level."

"Did you see that Buccola is judging?"

Well, that didn't take long. Herein lies the problem and

why I need to prepare myself for disappointment. Chef Buccola has committed many sins in Flynn's eyes. The least being part of the judging team that awarded Rowan and her family the grand prize over the Everheart team. The biggest transgression, of course, is hiring away Flynn's number one son, Knox. "I didn't see, but why should that matter?"

"I don't believe he will be fair and impartial. The last thing Everheart Bar and Fine Dining needs is to have its reputation varnished by a judge who's out to get us." He glances at his watch. "I don't think it would be wise to enter this year."

"I need this contest prize money. This year. If you don't want to enter me, we need to revisit the raise. I realize that my personal circumstances shouldn't be the driving force around asking for a raise, but I've been patient considering I make significantly less than most of my male counterparts."

His eyes narrow and the wheels spin behind his eyes. Flynn is smart enough to recognize a threat when he hears one. "I will consider the entry over the next two weeks and let you know what I decide." He spins and marches over to his car, which is parked a short five steps from the door.

I fume and watch him drive away. When he's out of sight, I reach for the door, but my hands shake too much to grip the knob.

Ace walks past, then doubles back peering through the glass from inside the restaurant and opens the door. "Oh, there you—What's wrong?"

"I just need a minute. I'll be in shortly."

He looks at me a long moment, but whatever he sees convinces him that now may not be the time to pile something else on my shoulders.

I lean on the wall next to the door and close my eyes, replaying the conversation I just had with Flynn. I've never exactly been appreciated by Flynn—that would be too much to ask because of his self-centeredness—but I at least thought he valued me enough to understand I work hard and long hours, keep on top of the staff and the inventory, put out any fires that try to pop up, and do everything within my power to ensure he maintains that Michelin star. I didn't even take a real break after the car accident. Is it really too much to ask to submit my name for an award? One that will not only bring me needed money but him more exposure?

A tear slips down my face and I quickly wipe it away before a customer or, worse, an employee happens by. As it is, I just complete the move before the door opens again.

Weston leans against the wall next to me, crossing his legs at the ankles, staring out into the employee parking lot. Or maybe the buildings beyond.

After a few minutes of neither of us saying anything, I finally take a deep breath. "We should probably go back inside."

"It's covered. We can stay out here as long as you want."

"I don't actually want to be out here." Smells from the restaurant waft out to us, which isn't terrible, but the sticky heat has me wishing for the air-conditioned comfort of my office. "I just can't force myself off this wall."

"Is there anything I can do?"

If only he were Knox. Or even Declan. "No, it's just your father being an ass again." Unfortunately, Weston can't help in that area.

"Must be a day ending in a *y*, I guess." He shrugs.

I laugh a little because it's so true. Flynn normally doesn't affect me this much, though. "He's thinking about not submitting me for the award. Because Chef Buccola is a judge."

"Ouch. I can only imagine how that went over."

"I didn't even look to see who the judges are. I'm a strong candidate whoever they are. Had I known, I wouldn't have even suggested Flynn enter me. But now I've lost precious weeks to figure out something else for Saron's tuition."

"You could let me—"

I put up a hand and finally push off the wall. "Please don't. We've already discussed this. I can't allow you to pay huge sums of money for my sisters. It would ruin our relationship."

"Well, there's the other thing where you sell your house and move in with me."

"How's that any better?" I rub my hands across my face.

Weston turns to face me. "We could make it work, Ryan." His features are so serious, I hardly recognize him.

"We could. Or maybe we could destroy everything. And you'd never ask me to leave, but I'd be in a worse situation than now. At least I'm not homeless because I would never let your kindness make you miserable."

"You're right. I'd never ask you to leave because I'd never want you to leave. At least consider it as only friends."

I snort because although Weston may believe we could live together as best friends, I know better. If the past couple of weeks have taught me anything, Weston and I have some unexplored feelings for each other that need to remain unexplored. Cynthia's situation is never far from my thoughts when I even think about Weston in a romantic light. Losing her best friend after going against her better judgment is a constant reminder for me that I would never want that to happen. Cynthia has never married, and I truly believe it's because of the intense loss. "Let's table that discussion for now. Flynn hasn't said no for sure. He'll let me know in two weeks before the deadline."

"Whatever you want."

He follows me through the door back into the restaurant, and we split off. He turns right to go back to the kitchen, and I turn left back to my office, the string that connects us suddenly feeling a little loose.

CHAPTER EIGHT
Sound and Cinema. Mood.

T HE HUMID AIR hangs on until the last minute as the sun finally makes its slow decent. I adjust on the blanket, unsticking my thighs and hiking up the skirt on my sundress to catch some sort of breeze. Then I lift my lobster roll and inhale the buttery goodness. "I love this event."

Weston nudges my arm, then stretches his long legs across the blanket before taking a bite out of the *bánh mì* taco he grabbed off the Peached Tortilla food truck. "The food is incredible. What's the movie tonight?"

I snort and nearly lose the bite I just took of my roll. "You're kidding, right?"

He shrugs, smiles, then takes another bite.

"You seriously don't know what's playing tonight?"

"It's always something good. Besides, I'm here for the food and the company." He sends a sizzling lopsided grin my way.

My face heats.

Diedra takes that moment to plop down onto the blanket with her daughter, Kieran, both carrying several big cupfuls of Amy's Ice Creams but somehow avoiding any spillage on their matching capris and yellow halter tops.

Weston grins around his mouthful of food. "See?" He passes my little cousin the quesadilla he bought when he got his tacos.

I hand over Diedra's lobster roll. "Where's your sister and Lisa?"

After giving me a cup of ancho chocolate ice cream—yum—she takes a bite of her roll. "This is good, but Weston's tacos sure do look good, too. I should have had those. Maybe both."

It's like I never asked her a question. Last time I saw the cousins, they were over by the Peruvian food truck arguing over empanadas. Lisa, a health enthusiast despite spending way too many hours in conference and courtrooms, was imploring Naomi not to get the deep-fried delights. Naomi, hardheaded since we were kids, was ordering extras.

I haven't even finished my lobster roll or started on my first cup of ice cream, but I eye a second cup. Surely Lisa won't want hers, and that Bad to the Bone creamy awesomeness is calling my name. Maybe I'm only thirsty.

"West, do you want anything to drink? I'm going to the Shiner booth."

"Yes, definitely. How about I come with?" He pops the last bite of taco into his mouth and stands. "Do you want anything, Diedra?"

"Nah, I'm doing a cleanse."

I open my mouth, then close it just as fast.

Weston only smiles and leans down to Kieran. "How about a lemonade icy?"

Her eyes brighten and she nods.

"Is it okay if I get her one, Diedra?" This is a formality

because Diedra lets Kieran have whatever we'll buy her.

Since her mouth is full of quesadilla, she just shrugs.

When we're out of earshot, I can't hold it any longer. "What sort of cleanse is she on eating all that bread, butter, and ice cream? Please tell me."

Weston laughs and slings an arm around my shoulder, pulling me into his side. Something he's done a million times, but this time is different. Warmth spreads through my arm down through my heart and settles in my belly. I hold my breath until I can exhale without it being noticeable.

To anyone on the outside, strangers passing us by, we have all the markings of a couple. This is the first time I've felt self-conscious about it, so I stop and bend down to fix the strap on my sandal. The one that doesn't need fixing, just to escape Weston's arms.

"I know what you're doing."

Of course he does. We've been friends too long to fool him. "I know. Sorry."

"Don't you dare say sorry. But I hope you know if my touch is unwanted, you only have to tell me." He smiles, but there's hurt in his eyes. "I ought to apologize to you. I should have asked first."

"West."

"No, seriously, Ryan. I'm sorry."

The line is at least ten deep, so we settle at the end and I lean close to him. "Your touch isn't unwanted. I…"

"You what?" His voice raises an octave. "Are you say—"

"There you guys are. Oh, Shiner sounds real good." Naomi wipes a napkin across her forehead.

I forgot about all the heat except what's surging through

my body. "Yeah, I'm getting a Hill Country Peach to cool off some." I hold my hand out for one of Naomi's napkins just to have something to occupy my hands. "Where's Lisa?"

She laughs and lifts an empanada from the tray in her hand, swirling it in the air like a sword. "Probably somewhere sucking on some ice. Your cousin is wound way too tight to be out and about among the general public."

"You know she rarely gets to go anywhere with us. Give her a break."

Weston moves up in the line and reaches for my hand, then snatches his back.

Naomi notices and raises a brow at me.

I frown and shake my head, then move up in the line. "Your sister has ice cream. You should go before it melts. I'll get your beer."

Her other brow levels up to meet the first one. "Okaaay. I'll have a Ruby Redbird if they have it. If not, get me what you're having."

When Naomi's out of earshot, I turn to Weston. "Don't feel like you can't touch me. I don't want it to be like that between us."

"I'm only respecting your boundaries." He says it with conviction, no grudge anywhere in his tone.

"West, we're friends. That's really important to me. More important than just about anything. I don't want to ruin that."

His smile is sad, even with the obvious effort behind it. "Our relationship is the most important one in my life. I would never jeopardize it."

I wrap my arms around his waist and squeeze. Probably

too tight, but he only returns the hug and lays his head on top of mine. We stay that way, exchanging emotions through those simple touch points. I breath in his caramel scent and close my eyes at the familiar comfort.

As much as I'd love to explore these new feelings I have for Weston, I stuff them down instead. It's for the best. There are too many check marks in the *Cons* column. Most of all upsetting our friend group. What if it doesn't work out? Everyone might be uncomfortable around us, and that's even if we stayed friends at all. I can't imagine not having Weston in my life always, and a failed relationship might make that happen. Then there's Flynn's policy against employees dating. He'd blow several gaskets if Weston and I went down that road.

THE FOLLOWING MONDAY when the restaurant's closed, Weston invites me over for dinner. Most of the time Weston either bikes to work, rides his longboard, or uses a scooter, which are the bane of my existence. For obvious reasons. They're parked on every corner downtown and ready for the renting. I don't mind tourists—more than half our business thrives on the tourist economy—but even before the accident I can't count the times I've nearly been plowed into while driving or even while walking. Those things should be outlawed.

I park in Weston's driveway and walk around back to the kitchen entry. His garage is detached and there's a little breezeway connecting the house to the outer building. It basically houses his car, which he drives when absolutely necessary, but his ride doesn't see the sun much. If he can't get there using his own steam, he'll usually catch a ride with me or one of the architect bros.

The kitchen door is unlocked, hopefully because Weston is expecting me. The smell of fresh-made pasta hits me as soon as I open the door. "Is Knox here?"

Weston chuckles, washing his hands in the sink. "I may not be on Knox's level, but we learned from the same mother, you know."

I kiss him on the cheek and place my purse on the island separating the main part of the kitchen from the breakfast nook area. "I didn't mean anything by it. Just, you don't normally cook pasta. I'm not sure if I've ever had your pasta. You seem happy scarfing down mine made from a box."

He flings water at me from his wet hands. "You make an excellent lasagna. And I do not scarf."

I raise my eyebrows.

He grins. "Okay, maybe I scarf a little."

"So what made you decide on pasta tonight?"

He's quiet a moment. "I don't know. I had an interesting tarot pull earlier, so maybe feeling a little nostalgic I guess. I never thought I'd be working at Dad's restaurant without Declan and Knox. I only towed the family line because of Mom and honoring her memory. Plus, my whole life I've been a bridge between my brothers, and..." He shrugs and dries his hands on a towel next to the oven. "I don't know, Ryan. It just felt like the right thing to do, but now I'm not so sure."

I hug him from behind and lie my head on his back.

His breath is a bit ragged, and my heart breaks for him.

He pats my arm wrapped around him, then releases it and walks over to the fridge. "You want wine or something nonalcoholic?"

I'm driving so I shouldn't ask for wine, but after Weston opening up, I feel like we should both have at least a glass. If I can't drive home, I can always stay over. It's not like I haven't done it a thousand times before. "Wine, please."

Weston pours me a glass and places it on the island near my hand.

I climb onto the high barstool and try to get comfortable. "What brought the sentiment on?"

After setting a piling plate of linguine with clam sauce and asparagus in front of me, he goes to fix his own plate, his back to me. "I guess because I texted with Declan earlier." He looks at me over his shoulder. "I can't remember if I told you he's in Italy."

"I don't believe you did. Are they shooting there?"

He lumbers into the seat next to me, fork at the ready. "No, they're vacationing. He wanted Kasi to see where Mom was born and all that. He showed her the tree." He rubs his chest through his T-shirt where the matching tattoo he has with his brothers honoring their mother is located, then smiles and loads his fork with the creamy goodness.

I take the cue to eat. "Oh my gosh, Weston. This is incredible." I stuff another forkful into my mouth.

"Yeah, it's good."

"No, it's excellent. How do you suffer through my dried pasta when you can make this?"

He knocks his shoulder into mine. "I love your cooking.

And spending my free time at your house with you and the twins."

My face flushes, so I turn back to my plate. When he first set it down, I didn't think I'd be able to finish it all. Now I'm thinking about seconds. "This is really good."

"You mentioned that already."

I glance at him in my peripheral and spot the small grin. He knows I'm deflecting. "I'm glad Declan was able to take Kasi there."

"Maybe we can go some day."

I inhale a deep breath and release it slowly, then turn to face him. "I'd love to, but I'll never have that kind of time off."

He nods and points a toothless smile my way, his eyes bright. "I suppose you're right, but wouldn't it be incredible?" He purses his lips, looking at the ceiling in thought. "We would visit my family, of course, but then take off through the countryside, eating all the good food and drinking all the wonderful wine."

I watch his mouth while he talks to the rotating fan above our heads. His lips are so plushy and kissable. His skin so tan from all the time he spends at the lake or disc golf course. I don't dare glance lower because it's becoming increasingly more difficult to think of Weston as just my friend.

When I'd first walked into the restaurant for my interview, I spotted Weston right away as Flynn and the manager at the time gave me a tour of the kitchen. He was making my favorite chocolate cake, and although I was tense from my talk with his father, I couldn't help the not-suitable-for-work thoughts passing through my head. Then he turned and spotted me and smiled the brightest smile I'd ever received. He was so open and friendly, walking right up to me and introducing himself, ignoring his father's protests completely.

Flynn introduced me to his other sons, but in my eyes, they were missing what Weston had—sincerity. Both had been nice enough, but they were clearly placating their dad. Eventually I grew closer with all three sons, but Weston and I became true friends. And then I tamped down any lingering attraction considering our close friendship. His sweetness—perpetually sunny and open—spurred sisterly affection, but Weston has depth. His modesty and hesitancy, even with his spectacular talent, endears me to him. He's selfless and always willing to lend a hand to his friends, strangers, me... That has me reaffirming my belief that we could never have the physical without the emotional, too. And that would be disastrous for us both.

"Ryan?"

I blink.

"Did you not hear me?" He cocks his head to the side and studies me. "You were looking at me."

It's difficult to throttle the blush rushing up my neck, but I look away before responding and that helps. "Of course I was looking at you. It would be rude not to while you were speaking."

He places a finger under my chin and coaxes my gaze his way. "You mean like now?" His touch is soft, but his gaze is not. He sucks in his bottom lips with a knowing grin, then lightly brushes my cheek with the back of his hand.

I stare at him a good long while, right in his beautiful, clear eyes. It would be so easy to lean forward just a little. To taste those lush lips. I'm so tired of being everything for everyone but not taking anything for myself. Just this one time… I shutter my eyes, and a moan works its way up my throat before I catch it in my mouth and swallow. I pop open my eyes and turn before our lips make a connection. What was I thinking?

"Ryan?" His face is as serious as I've ever seen it. "You have to know there's nobody else for me."

I close my eyes again because I don't believe I can resist him looking directly at him. I can't face the truth that he's it for me, too. "We can't."

"Why?"

I exhale the deep breath I've been holding. "You know why."

"Hey, can't you look at me?"

I open my eyes enough to form slits, viewing him through blurry vision. "Don't make me choose between my job and having you in my life. Please." The last word comes out as a whimper.

He wraps me up in one of his bear hugs, stroking my back, and resting his nose in the crook between my neck and collar bone. "I hope you know I would never ask that of you. I truly believe Dad would never fire us."

"Yeah, I maybe would have begrudgingly given you that before a couple weeks ago. But Shay was the best of our best, and he didn't blink an eye." I lean back, scurrying away from his familiar touch. "He already hints that he's not super on board with our close friendship. I'm not sure he approves."

Weston actually snorts, then covers his mouth, eyes wide.

"Sorry."

I smile because that lightens the mood a little.

"I don't think he pays close enough attention to know we're best friends."

"You'd be surprised. He's referenced it to me quite a few times. Never confrontational but slipping it into the conversation in a disapproving way."

"I guess I would be surprised." He takes a large gulp of wine and winces. Weston prefers beer. He probably bought it for me. Taking a trip through the Italian countryside drinking wine would be for me.

I shake myself. "Yeah, so dating is definitely off the table. We're probably best off as friends anyway. All those tricky emotions and all. I would never want to jeopardize having you close. Our relationship means too much to me."

He nods, a sudden sad smile creasing his lovely face. "So what you're saying is even if Dad didn't have the *no fraternization* policy, you still wouldn't want me."

I rush out of my chair and throw my arms around his neck, squeezing tighter than I probably should. "I will always want you. I love you. You're my best friend."

He sighs but smiles against my cheek, and hugs me back. He doesn't say anything, but the unspoken *friend* hangs between us. He releases me and quickly pecks my temple with his lips. "I love you, too. Ready for dessert."

"Sure."

Hurting Weston is the last thing I want to do in life. I'm hurting myself, too, but if I'm not strong, we could ruin everything. So I'll continue to ignore my growing feelings for him and somehow figure out how to recapture the friendship we've always had and grow that. Only that.

CHAPTER NINE

I delegate all the time. Whatever.

I'M HAVING MORE and more days in the supply room lately. My responsibilities are weighing on my shoulders more than usual these days with Saron's latest revelation. The ultracool breeze of the air-conditioning shoots out of the vent directly above, chilling me to my core. We don't store dry goods in here, but all the storerooms are kept at this low temperature for consistency. Although I'm slowly moving toward freezing, I can't make myself leave, leaning against the wall behind shelves of bathroom dry towels and soaps, all meticulously labeled. Just like I require.

My phone vibrates in the pocket of my slacks. When I ease it out with numb fingers, there's a text from Weston. *Where are you?*

If I tell him, he'll rush in here to *save* me. I don't want to be saved right now. I want to wallow in the misery of my own making.

If I don't tell him, I won't be able to stay in here much longer anyway. Maybe someone needs me for something. After all, someone always needs me for something. That's probably it because Weston doesn't normally come looking for me in the restaurant. If he's taking a break and comes by the office to sit a minute and I'm not there, he finds some-thing else to occupy his time. Finding me in the office isn't the norm.

My hands shake as I contemplate what to do. Another text comes through. *Tim's having another freak-out and Dad's not too far away. Seriously, where are you?*

I squeeze my eyes tightly and pull myself together, exit-ing the room. My brisk walk to the front of house warms me up quicker than any sweater could. That and the fact that although Tim came to this job with enough experience to serve in a Michelin-star restaurant, at least at the entry level, Flynn has made him nervous since day one. I'm upset all over again that I had to fire my best server.

Anger spurs me on, but I pull it together in front of the customers. Tim is behind the host stand, hiding in the plants decorating that corner. "What's wrong?"

His gaze darts around the room until it lands on Flynn. Then he shoves shaking hands under armpits. "I just need to get a breath. I'll be okay in a second."

I sigh but stop short of rolling my eyes. My fight isn't with Tim but the way grown people cower at Flynn's feet makes me feel some kind of way. Obviously he shouldn't create such a hostile work environment, and I'll speak to him yet again once the restaurant closes—if he's still here—but he doesn't listen to me. He doesn't listen to Kerry in her HR capacity, either. He worries about lawsuits over sexual harassment between employees yet can't see where he's putting his own business at risk with the enormous chip on his shoulder.

I hold out my hand for Tim's notepad and pencil and

survey his section, thankfully the smallest since he's new. Menus are face down on table nineteen, so I head there first. "Good evening. Are you ready to order?" I'm guessing from the position of their menus and the small plates already on the table they've ordered drinks and appetizers.

One of the women takes a sip of her drink and swirls the ice around her glass, all attitude. "We'll have the porterhouse. Unless you don't think we'll get it before the night is over. Our waiter disappeared, so I'm beginning to wonder."

"I apologize for your waiter's abrupt absence. He had an emergency, but I'm happy to get that for you. What temperature would you like your steaks?" I glance at her companion, hoping the other woman might engage because it's obvious from this woman that she's winding up for a confrontation.

The second woman looks down at the table.

The first woman huffs. "This place has some high reviews, but I'm beginning to wonder if you paid for them."

Okay, I don't have time for this. Other tables in my peripheral need checking on, so I need to manage this situation immediately. "I'm certain, but how about I comp your meal for your inconvenience?"

That gets her attention, but she narrows her eyes and looks me up and down. "Maybe you should clear that with your manager, honey."

"No need. I'm fully authorized. Now what else can I get you?"

She sucks her teeth, then picks the menu back up because of course she does. Now that her meal's on the house, why not run up the bill.

By the time I've taken care of all Tim's tables and Flynn has mysteriously disappeared, Tim takes over, and I make rounds to the other tables checking on their evening.

When the last customer leaves, I head back to my empty office to get some work done. Between Tim's meltdown and my own, I've added a couple hours to my shift tonight.

Weston comes in a few minutes later, concern clouding his usually bright eyes. "Hey."

"Hey. Thanks for texting me."

"Sure. Mind if I sit?"

I look up and purse my lips. "Since when do you ask something like that?"

"I'm guessing you have a long night ahead of you. I don't want to be a bother, and I know you won't let me help."

Tears prick my eyes because I need help so desperately, but there's nothing Weston can do. "You did help me. By letting me know about Tim and Flynn." I gesture to the chair so I won't get a crook in my neck. Plus, I want him here.

He sits and rubs hands across his face. "That's not help. Help would have been handling the situation myself. But we both know if I had intervened, Tim would probably be out of a job right now."

"I'll speak to Flynn tomorrow."

"You're off tomorrow, remember? We have Lisa's birthday party."

I groan and sit back in my chair. "That's tomorrow already?" I love my cousin, but I don't feel like being around family right now. And I can't explain why. "I guess I better get myself mentally prepared because no way I can miss it.

Mimi and Papa would come looking for me."

He chuckles but it rings hallow. "Let me help you, Ryan."

"I don't know what's wrong. I don't know what to ask for."

He snaps his fingers and stands. "I'll be right back."

I stare after his retreating back. *What in the world?*

He barrels back in the door, grinning, then sits across from me again and produces a deck of cards. "Can I pull for you?"

I'm not really a witchy, meta-spiritual kinda person, but if pulling a tarot card for me makes Weston feel useful, I'm in. "Sure."

He shuffles the cards in his large hands, long fingers manipulating the deck with ease, then puts them in front of me. "Go ahead and cut as many times as you like."

I separate the cards in half, then a couple more times until one jumps out at me like it was on a spring. "That's weird."

He smiles and turns over the card. "Actually, not at all weird." When he looks up from the card, his eyes are misty.

"That bad, huh? How long do I have to live?"

"Ryan." He reaches across the desk, holding his hand out for mine.

I settle my hand into his but stare at him, a question in my gaze.

"You pulled the Five of Cups. The grief card."

I blink.

He squeezes my hand, offering me comfort. "It's the mourning card."

"But my parents died years ago. I'm not still mourning. I don't have time for that."

"Oh, Ryan. Mourning doesn't have a timestamp. You can't run from it, either." He rubs his chest where the clock tattoo resides.

"I'm not running from it. I just have so many responsibilities and everything falls on my shoulders. Of course you understand what it's like to lose a parent, but you still had one left. And your brothers." My voice hitches on the last sentence. I still have my sisters, but I'm responsible for them.

"Yeah, our situations aren't the same. I'm not trying to compare them, but I want you to know that I'm here for you. I want you to unload on me if that's what you want."

As hard as I try and as fast as I blink, I can't keep tears from falling. I don't want to cry at work. And I have so much to do. Crying won't help me pay the twins' tuition, either.

Weston makes to stand, but I shake my head. "No, I need to pull myself together. We can talk about all this later, okay?"

"Of course, Ryan. Whatever you want. Can you do me a favor, though?"

"Always. Anytime."

"I have an extra journal or fifty." He laughs and shrugs. "Writer's life. Can I give you one? When you pull the Five of Cups, it's a signal to remember you still have things to be grateful for. Write those things in the journal every day."

This isn't the first time someone has suggested capturing my feelings in a journal. Mimi and Papa sent me to a grief counselor when we moved in with them. As a teenager, I didn't want to explore my feelings. Then I got busy with college, then grad school, and my sisters. I can't keep running into the supply closet, so maybe it's time I dig into my feelings.

I can't really speak so I nod my agreement.

CHAPTER TEN

Do you want to win? Nope.

THE BACKYARD AT Mimi and Papa's house is as festive as I've ever seen it with green-and-gold streamers draped through trees, multiple folding tables covered with white cloths, and tricolored balloons attached to chairs. The family has gone all out for the oldest grandchild's milestone birthday. I guess you don't turn thirty every day.

Weston pulls up as my sisters and I take out of my SUV the last of the food we made at home before heading this way. I made pasta primavera and a green salad. Saron made twice-baked potatoes and Meagan raw veggies, cheese, and dried meats for a charcuterie board. Cooking isn't really an interest of hers, but she wanted to contribute to the potluck and thought the birthday girl's health-conscious appetite might appreciate it.

When Weston opens the back seat of his car, we all gasp at the smell whooshing out to greet us. I step closer and peek under a foil-covered pan, then close my eyes and take another deep breath. "Oh my gosh, you made Portuguese sweet bread?" This is definitely my favorite bread in all the world.

He winks at me and lifts the pan out of the car, handing

it to Saron, whose hands are empty.

Her eyes dart skyward in a haze. "This is the best smell ever."

"Just make sure that pan makes it into the kitchen." I stop her and look inside one more time. "I see six loaves."

She flutters her eyes, not quite a roll, and turns toward the house.

Meagan balances her pan of various raw food baggies and follows her sister. She tosses a small smile over her shoulder. "Thanks, Weston. You're the best."

He is the best.

There's a large box in the back seat along with some smaller ones. "What else do you have back there?"

"The big box has the birthday cake. I also brought an Italian ricotta cheesecake and clafouti made with..." He grins and pulls out one of the smaller boxes, then opens it. "Loquats."

"Oh, that looks divine." We don't serve the French dessert, but I've had it at another restaurant, only made with dark cherries. I bet the loquats will be really good. "But when did you have time to make all this?" After Weston gave me the journal last night, he was at the restaurant pretty late. Almost as late as me.

"I got up really early this morning. Mimi wanted apple pies, too." He shrugs and picks up more boxes. "Let's take these inside and see who can help get the rest."

Mimi's surrounded by a couple people, fussing with her makeup and hair, sitting in her favorite recliner. She looks around Diedra as we come through the door. "Oh, what's in the boxes?"

"Oh, Mimi. You are really something."

Weston blows her an air kiss since we can't get near her and continues on to the kitchen with all his boxes.

I try to get a little closer to Mimi to see what all is going on.

Diedra's friend, Jimmy, is styling Mimi's hair. Mimi swears up and down her hair's natural color is red, but we'd never know because she keeps it dyed. I asked Daddy one time if he knew the original color, but he said it was that same dyed red since he was a little boy. A few years ago, we finally convinced her to give up the curl she was getting every six weeks and let her natural hair take over. It was a chore, but she's happy with the transition and her hair is healthier without double the chemicals.

"Hey, Jimmy. That looks really good."

He gives me air kisses around the box I'm still carrying. "Thanks, honey. How have you been?"

The twins pass through the room along with Weston, presumably heading back to his car for the remaining desserts.

"I've been good. How about you?"

"Oh, you know the usual…overworked and underpaid."

I snort and try to cover it with a laugh. There seems to be a lot of that going around. "Hey, Diedra."

"Hey, girl."

"Let me put this pie in the kitchen. I'll be back."

Papa sits at the table with a package of cracklings, chomping away. "Hey there, youngster." I lay a kiss on his forehead and stack my box with the others. "Are you supposed to be eating that?" He hasn't had any major health issues, other than a replacement left hip, but I don't want him to push it.

He slides my way the most beatific grin in the world. "Oh, it's all right, sugar."

"Oh, okay. So you don't mind if I go back out there and let Mimi know, right?"

He huffs and closes the bag. "You're no fun since you moved out."

That brings me up short. He's teasing me, but there's so much truth in his words. Since I've been solely responsible for Meagan and Saron, I haven't been the same. I was never loose or carefree, but I didn't walk around with the weight of the world, either. "Sorry, Papa. I just want you to live forever."

He reaches for my hand and squeezes. "I know, baby. I know."

The gang returns with the remaining boxes, and Naomi trails them in with a hot-dish carrying bag.

"What did you bring?"

"Mac and cheese. What about you?"

I list off what we brought along with what Weston made. Aunt Melissa's in charge of organizing the food, and in true taskmaster fashion, she kept her cards close to the vest. The menu's coming together nicely, though.

Speak of the devil and in she walks. "Hey, everybody." Following her in is Darryl carrying a large roasting pan. Before we can respond, she issues her orders. "Put that over on the counter by the stove and plug it in, nephew." She surveys the counters and tables covered with food and checks her tablet. It's easy to see where Lisa gets her drive. Melissa's the oldest sister, and when Daddy died, that made her the oldest child period. From experience, the oldest carries a heavier weight.

She walks over to Papa and gives him a side hug. "Hey, Daddy. Did that medicine get delivered for Mama?"

"I know your tablet told you it did, daughter."

Weston shoots a barely concealed grin my way and raises his eyebrows.

"That's true, but I want to verify you have it in your hands."

"I got it and gave her the first pill. Thanks for having it sent over."

She pats him on the back and moves her glasses to the top of her head. Her long wig is straight today, and the glasses slide a bit but she grabs them before they fall. "We'll talk about it tomorrow, but I think it's time to see if Ann can work full time. Maybe even live in."

Darryl and the twins exit the room.

I'm seriously contemplating following them. I bug my eyes at Weston. Stuff's getting heavy in here.

Papa waves his hand. "That's not necessary. As long as I'm around."

"Like I said, we can discuss later."

"Aunt Melissa, is there anything you want us to do?" Weston cranks up the charm, and the tension is immediately broken.

"No, honey, but I'd love to see how the cake came out."

They move to the other side of the kitchen where Weston unpacks the larger box and inside protective materials, finally unveiling the cake.

Melissa claps her hands. "Oh, it's perfect. I already know how it tastes."

Weston actually blushes. "Thank you. We'll have to wait until Lisa cuts it to find out." He scrunches his nose and combines it with a huge grin.

That satisfied Melissa, and she taps his shoulder, smiling.

"Anything for me, Aunt Melissa?" Normally I'm in go-mode, but there can't be two cooks in the kitchen, as the saying goes. And Melissa has seniority.

"No, you and Weston go somewhere and relax while we wait for the rest of the food to get here. You've both done plenty already."

We walk back into the living area, but only Jimmy is left, packing up his hair-styling tools.

"Where's Mimi?"

"Diedra took her into her bedroom to change into her outfit for the day. I'm about to head out."

"You're not staying for the party?"

"Girl, no. It's the weekend. I'm lucky to get away this long, but you know I couldn't let my girl down."

"Not even a plate to go?"

"Diedra said she'll drop off something by the shop later." He throws the strap of his large duffel over a shoulder and steps to the door. "It was good seeing y'all."

When he's out the door, only Weston and I remain. He looks at the chess board and raises his eyebrows.

"Fine, why not?"

I'm a decent player, only because Daddy had been phe-nomenal and taught me, just like Papa taught him. Even though he would never recognize it, Weston is exceptional.

On a subconscious level he must know because he rushes to sit on the black side to give me whatever advantage possible.

Weston runs his hands across the marble board and grins. "I love the feel of this."

"It's nice but not as nice as yours."

He's thoughtful a moment, pursing his lips, then smiles. "Oh, you mean the one Declan brought me from Peru."

I nod and return the smile.

"That one's definitely my favorite." He still smiles, but his eyes dim ever so slightly.

I make the first move, setting up the Italian game just because of my opponent. My usual is the Ruy Lopez, but Weston will demolish me inside of ten minutes if I go that route. "It must be difficult to work at the restaurant without your brothers. Even I miss them."

He looks up from the board and offers me a sly grin. "You even miss Declan?"

"Listen, your older brother could certainly throw wrenches in my scheduling with his last-minute *Dad-approved* time off and he was fairly arrogant, but he was a great chef and we have some customer favorites because of him. We can hardly keep up with the farofa demand." I make my next move and sit back in my chair. "You didn't answer."

He scrunches his nose, scanning the board, then makes his move. "Technically, you didn't ask me anything."

"West."

"Yes, of course I miss them, but we're always so busy at the restaurant, I didn't get to spend a lot of time with them anyway. Doing the competition was the closest we've ever been and it was great, but I have Jerome. Even his brothers, although they were a little younger but always around because they idolized their older brother. I love Declan and Knox, but I'm closer with my friends."

"Hmmm."

"Hmmm?"

"I guess I'm wondering why you didn't go into architecture like Jerome and them. I mean, since you were closer to them."

He shrugs. "Jerome was always interested in math and science. That's really how we met. I was pushed into those areas because Dad wanted all of us to have that background to prepare us for culinary school. I would have much rather taken more humanities electives. And as for Jerome's brothers, they would follow him to the moon, so I understand why they would follow in his footsteps."

"So Flynn made you become a chef." I make another move, but I've lost. Probably in three or four moves.

Weston sees it, too. His next move should be to take my queen. "I would say *strongly encouraged* more than *made*. He navigated all three of us in that direction. Dad groomed and molded us to work for him." Instead of taking my queen, he shuffles the pieces and stands. "You want to go outside and see if anyone needs help setting up?"

"I can't believe you did that."

He bites his lip and looks around the room. Anywhere but at me. "What?"

"You were about to win. Why wouldn't you finish the game?"

"It's no big deal, Ryan. We were just playing for fun.

Who knows what the outcome would have been." He reaches out his hand. "Let's go see if Melissa needs anything."

Weston would rather bow out than compete. I'm no therapist, but even I know Weston isn't a risk-taker. Even poised to win, he gives up.

I stand and put my hand in his. "Fine, let's go."

CHAPTER ELEVEN

Did Weston shoot his shot? Yup.

WE LEFT THE birthday party and Weston convinced me to hit a hole-in-the-wall he discovered with the architect bros. We walk into the dim eatery, more club atmosphere than restaurant, with a bar right up front. Not a modern, lit-up bar or typical restaurant bar, even. An old-fashioned wooden bar like you see in old Westerns. I lean into Weston. "I don't know how I let you talk me into this."

A sixtyish bottle-blond woman comes over with two menus and hands them to us. "You can sit wherever."

Weston shoots her his warm smile. "Thank you."

She brightens a fraction. It's difficult to stay stern with Weston's sunny disposition. "I'll be right over with some water."

We seat ourselves around the corner in the very back, near five televisions tuned to the same tennis game. Only one has the volume turned up and not very high.

I look at the menu and blink. "Are you serious, West?"

"You have to trust me on this. You do trust me, right?" He's smiling with mischievous eyes, leaning my way, so close his exhales brush my lips.

All I want to do is meet him the rest of the way. But I

can't. Too many people depend on me. At least until I get the twins settled. Instead, I turn my head and look at the menu again. "Of course I do, but this seems a little extreme. Do you have a recommendation?"

His soft chuckle is barely audible, but it reaches my ears. He's not deterred in the least and he knows me so well. I'm too close to giving in to my feelings. "I think for your first time, maybe stick with the big baller regular hamburger, which is really good. I've had the cubano, and it was very tasty. Maybe this time I'll try the Saucy Cock." He lifts his eyebrows slightly and bites back a smile.

I stretch my eyes his way because this is as overt as I've seen him. "Are you flirting?"

"Is it working?" He glances my way, probably gauging my reaction.

It's so working. "I guess I'm surprised. You spent a lot of time with Lisa today."

He laughs. "It was her birthday party." Then his expression grows more serious, the smile gone, and a sudden smolder swirls his eyes. "You know there's only one Landry I have eyes for."

I don't fix my face fast enough because my lips have involuntarily raised at the edges. Dang it.

"Hmmm."

"There's no 'hmmm,' and you know why." I've known my friend for years now, but only recently have his words and touch affected me this way. When his palm caresses my arm through the thin silk of my shirt, a shiver runs down my spine. Even more so because that touch means something more to Weston, too.

I like Weston. A lot. But we're not meant to be.

"Because of Dad's strict *no fraternization* policy." Weston says this in the most monotone inflection I've ever heard out of his mouth.

"Well, yes. I need my job. Even more so with Saron's recent revelation. Even without that, the twins are headed to college next year. I'm already just scraping by."

"He would never fire you. We need you too much."

"He would never fire you because you're his son. You're the only one with job security around there."

He whispers, "Barely."

My heart hurts for him. I don't believe for a second that Flynn would ever fire Weston, but he's right he's an afterthought compared to his brothers when it comes to their father. It's such a shame Flynn doesn't treat them the same. And ironic Weston is the only one who stayed.

"I just can't take the chance. Our lives are so intertwined even outside the restaurant. Our friends, my family..." I wave my hand back and forth between our hearts. "Us."

The hurt in Weston's eyes comes through full blast, but in the end, I need my job to support my sisters and no matter how much Flynn may value me, he would let me go in a heartbeat if I fooled around with the one son he still employs.

"What if I quit?"

That catches me off guard and my stomach clenches. My feelings are all over the place. "You can't be serious. I know you're financially secure, but isn't that because you have a really good job?"

"Sure, but at this point, I only stick around to be closer

to you. I love creating confections, but I can still do that. Your family alone has enough gatherings to keep me from getting bored." He laughs and knocks his shoulder into mine, but it doesn't loosen the knot in my stomach.

"West."

"If nothing else, Declan stayed on top of both me and Knox to invest. How and where so I can afford not to work for a while. That would free me up to write more, too."

"I hear you, but I don't believe you. You can't quit, West. Even though your father would never admit it, he needs you. I need you." I sit back in the booth and rest my head in my hands. If he's willing to give up his job to give us a chance, can't I meet him part of the way? I turn to him and put my hand on a hard bicep. "Let's give it a go, but we can't tell anyone. Not until we're sure."

His eyes light up brighter than I've ever seen them, but his face is still serious. He leans forward, placing his forehead on mine and whispers, "Do you mean it?"

"Yes, I mean it. I want it, too, West."

We both move toward each other, our lips a breath from touching.

"Okay, who had the Saucy Cock?"

I snap my head back so quick, I nearly get a crook in it.

Weston only smiles and raises his hand. "That would be me. Thanks."

A young man sets the plate down in front of Weston, then sets the other one in front of me."

"Enjoy."

"Thank you." I stare at the hamburger on my plate with donuts for buns and shake my head. "This should be interesting."

"You said you trust me."

"I do, but goodness, this is different."

"Since you trust me, why not rent out the house and move in with me? You take care of everyone else. Let me take care of you, at least for a little while."

That would certainly solve all my immediate problems but would likely cause others. "As tempting as that is, I can't uproot my sisters at the beginning of their senior year. You live the opposite direction of their high school, so a much longer drive." There are so many other reasons why moving in with Weston wouldn't be a good idea, like his father would never believe it was platonic, but I'll lead with this one. It's also the toughest to argue against.

"Yeah, I guess that makes sense. Let's hope you get into the contest."

I cross my fingers, then pick up my knife to cut the donut burger in half.

Weston watches me, but I don't turn his way. We were about to have the most awkward kiss in the world before the waiter interrupted us, and now I'm scared. How will we navigate this new relationship step?

He doesn't seem as worried because he eats with vigor, then wipes his mouth on a napkin because the cock is indeed saucy. "Oh, I almost forgot. I finished the manuscript."

"No way."

He nods and takes a smaller bite of his chicken-donut sandwich. "Talking it out with you really loosened something inside. The words started pouring out again, and then I was finished. Can I send it to you?"

"Of course. I've been on pins and needles waiting to find out what happens with Sasha."

He grins, then knocks his knee against mine under the table. His demeanor has lightened so much.

I wish I had his sureness in this new step we're about to take with our relationship.

THE HOUSE IS dark when Weston and I pull up. Makes sense that my sisters haven't come home yet. Although Mimi and Papa retired to their room right after they ate and my aunts and uncles had pretty much cleared out, when I left with Weston, my cousins were still hanging on the outside patio. The spades tournament was heating up on one table, and on the other, Lisa slammed a domino so hard it almost broke the card table they were playing on. Darryl and the twins went inside to the family room to play video games. Who knows how late they'll be?

I let Weston convince me to try the donut burgers, and I can't lie—they were surprisingly delicious even if the ambiance left a little to be desired. We were the only customers there, which is never a good sign, but it could have been because we went well past the dinner hour.

Sitting in Weston's car in front of the house, the air-conditioning blowing at full blast and the moon gleaming down illuminating the car, I should feel the romance in the air. Instead, my hands are clammy and I can't stop myself from running fingers through my short curls.

Weston doesn't turn off the car but turns to look at me

and reaches for my hand. "Are you okay? You barely spoke the entire way back."

I jump as if he'd bitten me. "Oh, goodness. I'm okay, maybe overcaffeinated or something."

He brings my hand to his mouth but doesn't kiss it. Just holds my palm against his lips and closes his eyes. When he opens them, he moves his mouth away and smiles. "We'll take our time, okay?"

"Well, yeah. Sure. Of course. We'll take our time." I look away from embarrassment. *Come on, Ryan. It's Weston.* When I glance back, he's only staring at me with his usual sunny smile. "I, uh. Jeesh. Do you want to come in for a little while?"

"I'd love to? I mean, only if you feel comfortable."

I slip my hand out of his and open the door to his car. "Of course I feel comfortable." I almost say *we're friends*, but that isn't the mood I'm trying to set right now. The fact is, if we were only friends, I wouldn't be nervous and he would have turned off the car as soon as we pulled up.

"I can't believe I forgot to turn on the porch light."

"I'm off day after tomorrow. I could set up some motion-sensor lights. I guess I never realized you don't have them."

My keys fall out of my hands before I can unlock the front door.

Weston slips his in the lock before bending to pick mine up. "Oh, do you want this back now because..." His voice trails off.

"No, of course not. You keep it." We always had an agreement we wouldn't use the other's key willy-nilly. I don't expect that to change just because we're trying to, uh, whatever it is we're trying to do. Explore feelings, I suppose would be the best way to describe it. "Oh, do you want yours?"

"No." He pitches the door open, and I walk through, switching on lights as I go. By the time I set my purse on the kitchen counter, the house is lit up like a Christmas tree.

Weston laughs as he walks down the hall to the powder room.

I take that moment to race to the bathroom inside my bedroom and brush my teeth real quick. I splash some cold water on my face and the back of my neck, too.

I'm quick but not quick enough to feign nonchalance. Weston is perched on the couch, long legs stretched out before him, arms behind his head. I don't think he's faking. How can he be so relaxed?

"Hey."

He sits forward, resting his arms on his thighs. "Hey. I emailed you the book. I can't wait for you to read it."

I search my disjointed brain for a moment, trying to remember if I loaned him a book. Oh. "Right. Let me check."

I turn on my phone, and the notification is front and center so I open it and scan a few lines: *Sasha stretched beside him on the freshly cut grass, her brown skin shining in the dewy early morning, her curvy ass pressed against his crotch. Transportation during the night had been a breeze, not the usual queasiness after intergalactic travel, and Ian was grateful.*

"Got it. I can't wait to finish it, too."

"Do you want to get something? Or do you want me to get you something?"

After closing my eyes for a moment and taking a couple

of deep breaths, I ease onto the couch next to Weston. Not too far to be weird, but not close enough we're touching. "I'm really nervous, and I'm not sure why."

He turns his whole body to me, reaching out but stops short, raising his eyebrows.

"Yes, of course, West."

"Okay." He rubs a strong hand up and down my arm, ever so slowly. "Let's talk about boundaries. Parameters of what we want and don't want."

I relax into his touch and lean closer, my head near his shoulder. "I love when you touch me. I always want you to touch me."

He grins. "I love touching you, too, but I'll always ask just in case you change your mind."

"I can't imagine I ever would."

"I hope not, but still."

"What about you, West? What do you want or not want?" My voice is just above a whisper as his touch heats my skin.

He looks up at the ceiling and huffs a breath of air. "I want it all, Ryan. I want us together, in love, forever." He looks down at me, scanning my face.

I've gone rigid and can hardly take a breath in.

"I told myself I wouldn't do this, but I can never lie to you. I know it's too soon? It's too soon, and now I've scared you."

I shake my head and finally suck in some air. "I was already scared. You know how much you mean to me. I'm so afraid of messing that up. Of us not being together forever."

"Yeah, I get it. I'm not going to try to change your mind. I will love you as long as you let me." He stops stroking my arm and sits back.

I miss his touch as soon as it's removed, so I reach out to him and scoot closer so my body is flush against his, my face angled up to his. I'm so close, I only need to lean in. "That sounds like an excellent plan, Weston Everheart." Then I touch my lips to his.

He returns the kiss eagerly, pressing is soft lips to mine, but tempers it, pulling back.

I hiss against his mouth. "Don't hesitate. You won't scare me off."

"Are you sure? What changed your mind?"

I shrug. "I want this. And when you offered to leave the restaurant to give us a shot, I thought maybe it was time for me to stop being so frightened."

This time our lips meet with more urgency, and although it's Weston and I'm still not out of my head about kissing my best friend, I part my lips to let him in.

He cups a large palm around the back of my neck, and I wrap my arms around his waist, moving halfway into his lap. "Yes, Ryan." Then he explores my mouth, our tongues tangling together on the journey.

I'm floating, seriously untethered with Weston's hands on me in this new way. With his mouth on mine. I move his free hand to my breast, inconveniently clothed in a summer T-shirt. Suddenly I want him everywhere, my need driving my hands under his tank to his chest, rubbing his nipples, then stroking down to his stomach.

The sound of a key in the lock of the front door has me scrambling off his lap, huffing for breath in the far corner of the couch.

Weston grabs up a throw pillow to cover his erection.

We wait until the door swings open and my sisters come through, Meagan giggling at something on her phone and Saron scoping us out with sharp eyes.

Saron smirks. "Did we come home at a bad time?"

I don't dare look at Weston, but I take a quick survey of my clothes which are all still in place. "Did you guys have fun? Everyone gone?"

Meagan lifts her face to finally appraise the scene. Then she slaps a hand across her mouth to suppress a loud bark of laughter. Then stares at us with wide eyes.

"Fine. We're exploring something. You know, together."

Meagan laughs. "Oh, we know."

Saron only tilts her head, then walks through the living room, grabbing her sister's hand. "About time" floats back to us from down the hallway.

I still can't look at Weston, discomfort heating my face.

He reaches over, palm up. "You okay?"

I rest my hand in his and finally look at him.

His huge smile belies his quiet voice.

I can't help but smile back. Those extra endorphins surging through my body haven't quite escaped. "I'm fine. Only embarrassed."

"We should have gone to my house."

I snort. "Obviously. But it's okay. The twins seemed to have taken it well. I definitely have no intention of hiding anything from them." I squeeze his hand and stand. "See you at work tomorrow."

No matter how good my body was feeling before the girls walked in, the mood has definitely gone. I'm just happy we were able to get past the awkward stage.

CHAPTER TWELVE

Let's take this car out for a test drive. Okay?

WHEN I WALK into Everheart's, my first instinct is to run. Weston is in the hallway, studying the calendar on the wall. So much for the awkwardness leaving. "Hi, Chef."

He turns and walks my way, smiling, and reaches out to me.

My eyes go super wide.

He pats me on the shoulder. "Hi." Then he whispers, "People are going to think something's up, the way you look right now."

I blink a couple times to decrease the width of my eyes, then take a couple breaths. "I better get in my office."

He waves as I turn to go. "Okay, see you later?"

I throw my hand up and rush to my office. I never thought Weston's sunny disposition would get on my nerves. It's not him but my reaction to him that's truly on my nerves. Maybe it's him a little, too. He's so normal while I'm a hot mess.

"Hi, boss."

I do my best to fix my face and greet my staff. All three are inside this office at the same time—a rarity. Normally at least one person is out doing who knows what. "Hi, every-one. All must be calm for now."

Kerry looks up from her computer. "Don't speak too soon. I just got a notification from Gelson's that the driver is running late. Apparently there was flash flooding in Bastrop and he got stuck."

Another tick against Austin, flash-flood alley. That's actually a well-known moniker around here. Just as much as live music capital of the world. "How late?"

"I'm monitoring the situation with their DC director of operations. I don't think we need to worry, but probably should have a backup plan just in case."

I haven't even set down my laptop and purse yet.

We all run around for the next two hours surrounding the shipment delay and solve it in enough time before the restaurant opens.

I finally have a chance to check my email, hoping I might have a message from the contest organizers. My hopes are dashed but not doused completely because there's still a week left before the deadline. I'll have to make time to speak with Flynn again if nothing comes through in the next couple of days.

If I can find him. Our paths haven't crossed a lot in the past few days. He's taken more time off as of late, which is his prerogative considering this is his restaurant, but it's out of character. Which is another reason I'm sitting at my desk, tapping my foot on the floor. Adding a nervous tick to my suitcase of feels is not something I'm interested in, so I clamp down my foot and concentrate on not moving it. Thankfully the floor is carpeted, and I keep my anxiety from my coworkers. I just don't understand what has brought on this change of behavior in Flynn. I don't like wondering about him.

I pick up my phone and send off a message to Cynthia. Mom's best friend usually has some great advice. *I'm toying with the idea of selling the house so I'll have the cash for tuition. Thoughts?*

Mimi and Papa used a good part of the life insurance money and equity in the house our parents owned to raise us. They weren't expecting to die and hadn't planned as well as they should have considering how young the twins were. I sunk everything left into our little house and keep up with everything else on my meager salary, putting aside as much as I could for their college funds. I tried to ensure plans were in place for this eventual day, but it's difficult making something out of nothing. I need a backup if Flynn doesn't enter me in the contest. Even if he does, I still need to win it.

My phone pings with a text from Cynthia. *Let's discuss when I visit next weekend.*

Oh my goodness. How in the world did I forget she was coming down for a couple days? *Okay, sounds good.*

I'll worry about that later because it's showtime and I need to be out front.

Weston approaches me before I can get past the kitchen, and my skin gets all tingly, my breath shallow. I look around to see if anyone's watching.

"Do you want to go to the beach tomorrow?"

"What beach? Galveston?" I really hope not. Besides being four hours away, it's basically gray water. Water I wouldn't step into even as a child when my parents and I would make the hour drive down. If I can't see down a couple feet, I'm not going in.

He laughs and shakes his head. "Definitely not. It's a place I hang out a lot because the water is super clear and warm. The path down is a little rocky, so you'll need water shoes getting down to the shore."

"That sounds really cool. I wonder why I've never heard about this place. What's the name?"

He leans in closer and lowers his voice. "Hippie Hollow."

"Oh yeah, you go there all the time, right? To kayak and stuff with the guys?"

"Yes, same place. Do you know anything about it?"

I search his eyes, which have a playful lilt. "Not really. Just whatever you've told me. Why are you whispering?"

"I don't want you to be surprised, but it's a nude beach." He grins even wider.

I gasp.

MY BEACH BAG is bundled and ready to go, next to the door. While Weston installs the new security lights out front, I pack some sandwiches and fruit to take with us since we plan on spending a few hours at Hippie Hollow.

Did I ever imagine Weston is an exhibitionist? Not really, but it's not shocking, I guess. His favorite clothes are shorts and tank tops when it's even remotely cool outside. And he's never seemed particularly modest.

Did I ever imagine I'd be heading out to a nude beach? Never in a million years, but after Weston assured me it's clothing optional and there's nothing wild going on out there, I made up my mind to try something new for once. I won't be stripping down, and Weston promised not to, either, this time, but it should be fun hanging out in warm, clear water. I also have his manuscript queued up on my tablet while we're relaxing.

That reminds me to pick up the journal Weston gave me out of my bedroom. I've only written a few pages in it but want to dig deeper.

Weston comes in through the back sliding glass door in the kitchen. "All done."

"Oh, wow, that was fast."

He shrugs and walks over to the sink to wash his hands.

"Was something wrong in the back?"

"It can't hurt to have a couple out there, too. You'll have to figure out when you want them on because if a raccoon or squirrel comes through, it'll trip the light, which will shine directly in your, um, bedroom."

I glance at him before sealing the small ice chest. Was that a blush on his cheeks? "Thanks for installing the lights. I feel better already. I didn't even know those things existed."

He dries his hands on the dry towel hanging from the oven door, then whips it over one strong shoulder like the chef he is. "Oops." He places it back on the oven door. "Can I help with anything?"

"No, I think I'm ready to go. I just need to text the girls." I drop my phone, then bend over, exposing quite a bit of cleavage in the process.

Weston looks at me and grins. "You sure you don't want to stay home instead?" He waggles his eyebrows my way.

"Are you flirting with me?"

He walks over to me, standing really close. "Definitely."

I close the gap and wrap my arms around his waist, looking up a smile to see his expression. His smile is there, but there's a heat in his eyes.

He returns the hug and pulls me close into his warm body.

I lie my head on his chest and close my eyes, breathing in his cinnamon scent. A comfort for all these years, but something more now. Under the cinnamon is a smell uniquely Weston that has always called to me. Just now it's calling me by a different name. *Girlfriend.* "We better go." I back up and grab up the cooler.

Weston takes it from me and kisses me on the forehead. "Okay."

WHEN WE GET to Hippie Hallow, it's nothing like I expected. The sign we pass on the way into the parking lot reads that it's actually a county park. There's another sign warning about nudity in the huge but nearly vacant parking lot. "Is it normally this empty?"

Weston holds out a twenty-dollar bill to the guy at the gate house. "On the weekends, especially holiday weekends, it closes when it reaches capacity, so you have to get here really early or you don't get in. We're coming at the perfect time."

"You really do come here a lot, huh?"

He grins and shrugs, turning his car into a parking spot

near a trail. "Enough. I rarely come on the weekends, though. Way too crowded; people get drunk, do some other things they aren't supposed to do...you get the picture?"

Indeed I do. "They let you drink alcohol here? Seems like a bad combination."

"Technically no. You can drink as long as you don't make a big display of it. We've definitely brought beers out, and as long as you're relaxing, it's fine." He unclicks his seat belt and grabs my hand. "Ready?"

"As I'll ever be."

He kisses my hand before letting go and hopping out of the car, circling around to the back to get our stuff.

I sludge out of the car, looking around at my surroundings to ground myself. It's just a normal parking lot with green trees and water in the distance. I shake myself and take some breaths to relax.

Weston hands me one of the packs, and we head to the trail. We pass another sign reminding us nude swimming or sunbathing may occur at anytime, anywhere past this point. My eyes widen a bit, but I try not to appear bothered. Weston slings the cooler under one of his strong arms so he ends up with everything he's carrying on one side, then picks up my hand with his free one.

I turn his way and smile. "I'm good, I promise."

"You'll let me know the minute you're not, right?" He squeezes my hand. "Up that way is a trail that goes the length of the park. You can also go closer to the shoreline and there's another path, but it's harder to navigate. We won't go too far today, though. Watch your step."

I nod and take in the scenery as we walk down the uneven steps that remind me of the ones going up to Mount Bonnell, but not quite as steep. The trees are so dense here, it's difficult to remember it's midmorning. "Do you ever take the trail up here?"

"Sometimes I come out here just to hike. It's a great trail."

"I guess that's one thing I can give Austin over Houston—the hiking and hills." It was completely flat where I grew up but lots of trails nonetheless.

"Houston's nice, too. My uncle has a house on the lake there."

"Oh, wow. You've been?"

He nods and smiles. "You seem surprised."

My foot catches on a split between the stones, and I nearly topple but Weston has his arm firmly around my waist in seconds. "Oof, thanks for saving me from tumbling down the hill."

"Not on my watch, Ryan." He smiles and moves his hand back to mine and waits for me to right myself completely. "Do you want me to carry the pack?"

"No, because then you'd have to let go of my hand." I look up to him and smile.

The puppy-dog smile he returns is so endearing. Not that I need anything else to endear me to this wonderful man. "Thank you."

I want to tell him not to be grateful when I show him affection, but we both know this has been a struggle for me so far. I can't quite move out of the friend zone all the way, but I'm determined to try. I lift his hand and kiss the back. "Back to your uncle. I was under the impression none of you had a relationship with the Everheart side of the family."

"We're much closer to Mom's side of the family, that's true. Dad refuses to speak to any of them, so it's awkward but we're usually invited to events, and I've taken them up on it sometimes. Knox and Declan, too, but rarely."

You could knock me over with a feather right now. "Wow. I had no idea. I mean, I know the story behind Flynn falling out with his parents because he didn't want to be a doctor, but I just figured he left the family and you all never knew them."

The foliage thins out some so we must be getting close.

"I haven't seen them in ages. I probably wouldn't know any of them if they passed me on the street. Mom was much better keeping us connected to them. She really believed in family. Dad…" He shrugs and gives me a sad smile. "Not so much." He points to the upcoming rocks. "We're here."

I scan the area, wondering exactly where *here* is. "When you said rocky, you weren't kidding." A lone couple has a blanket spread across some flat rocks below, and a couple of boats aren't too far offshore.

"Well, there's dirt, too." He laughs and leads me down another path parallel to the shore until we find a bit of a clearing and set down all of our stuff. "Come look."

We ease closer to the water, and when I look in, I gasp. "I've never seen the lake this clear. Wow."

"It's great, right? Wait until you get in. So warm."

I take a deep breath and inhale the familiar lake scent. "Are you sure?"

He smiles and walks back to our stuff, then takes a blanket out and spreads it over the area. Then he removes his shirt over his head and tosses it into one of the packs. Next come the shorts with one hook of his thumb.

I throw my hands over my eyes, then peek between my fingers.

More shorts are underneath. I sigh with relief because although I'm not adverse to seeing Weston naked—actually looking forward to it—out here is not where I wanted to witness him unclothed for the first time.

I shrug and pull my own top over my head. I wore a one-piece suit but may still leave my shorts on. I haven't made up my mind about the water yet.

Weston has his back to me, digging through the cooler for water. "Do you want a bottle, Ryan?" He calls to me over his shoulder without looking back, holding up a bottle of water.

"Not yet." While he's occupied, I take the time to have a good look at him in swim shorts. He's fit, of course. How could he not be with all of the activity he does? At six four, he's so tall that the result is the lengthening of his muscles instead of bulk. He's soft in places but mostly toned overall, especially his arms and legs. The more I stare, a warm feeling fills my belly. I bite my lip and look away.

When I turn back, Weston is gazing my way, eyes big.

I look down and remember the top in my hands. Although I wore a one-piece, it's by no means modest. There are cutouts revealing plenty of side boob and cleavage.

"You are so beautiful."

I look down at myself, then back at Weston's adoring eyes. That warm feeling trails up from my stomach to my heart. "You think?"

He smiles and shakes his head, then stands. "Yes, I think very much."

I slip an arm around his waist and look up at him. "I think you're beautiful, too."

The tips of his ears pinken, and he grins. "Thanks."

After carefully sitting down on the blanket, I reach in the cooler for the grapes I packed. "Want some?"

"Sure."

Weston sits beside me, his nearly naked body almost touching mine. I bite my lip, thinking about removing my shorts after all. I glance at the other couple who, I think from this distance, aren't wearing anything at all, then back to Weston with hooded eyes.

"I'm going to stop you right there." He grins and picks a few grapes out of the container I'm holding.

"What?"

"Making out here is not a good idea. You think nobody's watching, but somehow, they know. I've seen several couples get arrested." He pops a grape into his mouth, grinning. "*Handcuffed naked* may sound like a good time, but not so much when there's lots of people gawking."

"I was not thinking that at all, Weston Alessandro Everheart."

He cocks his head to the side and lifts his eyebrows. "Okay?"

"I mean. I was thinking a little kissing, not getting naked."

He lies back on the blanket and reaches for me.

I snuggle into his side, skin dewy with the humidity in the air, and lie my head on his firm chest.

"I'd love to kiss you right now, but I wouldn't want to stop there. Let's save it for when we're alone."

I twist my head up to look at him. "Are you saying you couldn't control yourself?"

His face turns serious. "Losing control isn't an option. I'm only talking about what I would want. I would never want what you don't want."

"I was only teasing, West. I didn't mean it like that." I sit up and look out at the water. Of course he would never go that far. "I hope I didn't offend you."

Weston's breath is on the back of my neck. "How about a kiss here?"

I nod and close my eyes.

He brings his lips to the back of my neck, then trails kisses down my back, between my shoulder blades. Heat blooms once again in my belly but travels decidedly south until all I want to do is turn around and pull those stupid swim trunks down. Oh. "Oh." I move away before I'm the one losing control. "I get it." I turn my head to see him.

He's still serious, but a sly grin creases his pretty face. "Want to swim?" He stands and reaches a hand down, but all I can see is the erection threatening to bulge out of his swimwear.

I barely croak, "Maybe later."

He leans down and kisses my forehead and heads down to the shore, then wades into the water, no embarrassment evident anywhere in his movements.

My face is heated with embarrassment, though, and I look around for any voyeurs. Weston was so right. Kissing can wait until we get home. I watch him for a little while, then lie back and pull out my tablet to pick up where I left off on his manuscript: *The sparks flew through the air, and Ian and Sasha ran down the long tunnel carved through the space station's underbelly. "Hurry, Ian." He was moving as fast as possible, but the Gorsocs were gaining ground. He reached into the pouch of his jumpsuit and grasped the ball of hinger, then activated it with one hand and hurled it backward. Sasha whistled her approval but never let up the pace as the Gorsocs fell from the narrow ledge.*

I look up for a moment and watch Weston's powerful arms slice through the water, counting down the time until we can be completely alone.

I BACK WESTON up against the stove in my kitchen because after being with him all afternoon and not being able to touch him, I have worked myself up into a fairly lustful frenzy.

He smiles but his breaths come faster than when we first walked in the house and unpacked. "Won't Meagan and Saron be home soon?" He bends to touch my lips quickly with his own. Not a peck, but a promise.

I'm nearly breathless myself as I reach around him and grab the glorious behind I've been watching all day. "Yes, but at least we won't be arrested for grinding on each other before they get here."

He smiles against my lips, then licks the seam and lifts me off the floor to straddle him. My bended knees balance on the counter, and he supports me easily with his large hands under my thighs. "This okay?"

"Absolutely." I kiss him open mouthed and coax his tongue inside.

His erection comes up full force between us, and he's unabashed as he pushes it against the crease of my shorts.

A groan escapes my mouth as I return the movement and add a circular motion, getting as close as I can. I don't close my eyes at the kiss because I want to see Weston in this light, as a sensual man I'm severely attracted to instead of my best friend who I love with all my heart.

He kisses down my jawline and nips my earlobe, then trails slow, languid kisses down my neck to my exposed collarbone.

I throw my head back for easier access and nearly topple us both, but Weston keeps us upright. "Careful, love."

I almost giggle, but he squeezes the backs of my thighs, pulling me to him again, and his hardness hits me just right. "Yes, right there, West. Don't move."

He stills and allows me to grind against him, working myself toward climax. And then I feel it full force. The pull at my clit and the tingling below my navel. Then the clamping of my walls squeezing the orgasm from me. I tighten my grip on Weston's shoulders until the final release. "Jeesh. Wow."

Weston is breathing hard against my neck but still as can be, his rock-hard erection still settled between my legs, his heart beating wildly against my own.

"Oh, do you want me to, uh…"

He shakes his head and whispers, "Just give me a second."

"I could—"

He shakes his head ever so slightly.

I'm not sure why, but I'm hurt for some reason. It almost feels like a rejection, even though that's ridiculous.

Weston finally lifts his face and kisses me hard. "Maybe we can go back to my house after dinner. The twins will be here any minute. I'm going to the bathroom real quick."

Oh, of course he would be thinking about the family situation instead of his own needs. "Thanks. I better, too."

We take off down the hallway, him to the powder room and me to my bedroom, and sure enough, the front door slams open. Both sisters' voices are raised, but I'm not sure if it's against each other or together against someone unknown.

I hurriedly clean up and change out of my swimsuit and pull a sundress over my head, then race back to the living room where the twins are still arguing.

Saron rolls her eyes. "You're being ridiculous."

Meagan drops her backpack on the floor and puts her hands on her hips. "You're being ridiculous." She singsongs it, mocking her sister.

"What in the world is going on with you two?"

Weston enters but sits on the couch on the other side of the room.

"Saron scheduled her Howard visit. She's really going."

I blink, a little stunned. "Why didn't you consult with me, Saron? I want to go with you."

She snorts, but it's filled with bewilderment. "Good Lord, Ryan. If I wait for you to take a day off from your precious Everheart restaurant..." She twists to look at Weston. "No offense." Then turns back my way. "I'll be a senior in a nursing home instead of high school."

A lump grows in my throat and there's an unfamiliar sting in my eyes.

Weston jumps up from his seat and walks over to put an arm around my shoulders.

"That's so unfair, Saron. You could at least give me a chance." I never throw it in their faces that the reason I work so hard and rarely take a vacation is because I'm trying to give them the best life possible. It's not their faults, but a little gratitude sometimes wouldn't be the worst thing in the world.

Weston squeezes my shoulder. "I should go."

I only nod because here's another sacrifice I'm making for my sisters they won't even appreciate.

He moves to kiss me, then stops.

"I'll walk you out."

When we're outside, I fall into his waiting arms but hold the tears back. I still have to face my sisters and I need to be strong.

Weston hums and rubs circles into my back, then kisses the top of my forehead and lets me go. "What do you and the twins want for dinner? I'll have something delivered." He pulls out his phone and navigates to the Austin local delivery app.

I smile up at him. "You're too good to me. Anything is fine. I appreciate it because I'm so mad at Saron, I can hardly think straight, less known cook, but they still need to eat."

He makes a few clicks, then pockets his phone. "I'm only as good to you as you deserve. I'm sorry they're so upset."

"Honestly, I was so surprised Meagan was taking it so

well. Especially as cavalier at Saron's been about abandoning us to go halfway across the country." I slap a hand over my mouth in disbelief. "I shouldn't have said that."

Weston wraps me up in another tight hug, then releases me. "Food should be here in a half hour. I'll see you at the restaurant tomorrow, okay?"

"I'm really sorry about tonight. Thanks for being so understanding."

"I know how important your sisters are to you. You don't need to apologize in the least." He bends to kiss me one last time and heads down the sidewalk to the driveway, then into his car. He waves as he drives off.

I hold up a hand, wishing I could run after him.

CHAPTER THIRTEEN

Almost caught. Probably.

A LTHOUGH CHEF IS on the schedule today, he called in to say he wouldn't be here until dinner prep. I have my issues with Flynn, goodness knows I do, but the way he's been disappearing from the restaurant is completely out of character. I'm really concerned at this change in behavior.

I review the plans for the upcoming engagement party and ensure everything's been checked off, including the inventory ordered. Then flip over to my email, which grew to over a hundred messages while the restaurant was closed yesterday. I can't win.

One message conspicuously missing from my inbox is something from the contest committee. Only a few days left, and Flynn still hasn't submitted me. Today is the day we'll have to hash it out because after the commotion with my sisters yesterday, there's no doubt Saron will be headed to DC next year. I need to figure out how to pay for it soon.

My phone buzzes on my desk, and when I check it out, there's a message from Weston. *Meet me in the storage supply room.*

I frown at the phone but stand nonetheless. This is an unusual request from Weston, and my mind immediately goes to trouble. Maybe it's something to do with Flynn not being here.

When I make it into the supply room, the chilly air hits me right away. It's welcome considering the near run I made to get here. "Chef?"

Weston steps out from my favorite hiding place near the bathroom supplies. "Hey."

"Hey?"

He reaches a hand out to lead me back into the darkness behind the shelves. "Sorry, but I really missed you. Do you mind?"

"Um, sort of. We really shouldn't be in here. Anyone could see us."

He nods and an almost frown mars his exquisite face. "You're right. I shouldn't have."

"Hey, I missed you, too." I step closer to him and wrap my arms around his waist. "Just don't make it a habit." I stand on my tippy toes to reach for his lips. So far we haven't been able to just keep our kisses simple, but considering where we are, we should be safe from ourselves.

Weston deepens the kiss and places his hands on either side of my face, and suddenly I want to climb him like a tree but manage to control myself.

"Ryan?"

I whip around, but Weston pulls me close to his chest and whispers in my ear. "Shhhh." My heart pounds a mile a minute.

"Ryan, I saw you come in here. Where are you?"

I take a couple breaths and step from behind the shelf, hoping to keep Flynn from discovering Weston back there, too. "What can I do for you, Chef?" My throat is dry, but I manage to squeak out those few words.

"What were you doing back there?" He leans around me to look, but I start walking toward the door, hoping he'll follow.

"I was taking inventory of the bathroom towels. Do you need something?"

He looks back at me with a confused expression, lips pursed, and eyebrows drawn together. He clears his throat. "I'm here now. You can call Chef Sinclair and let her know she doesn't need to come in after all."

"Okay, Chef." My hands are slick as I open the door and the handle slides out of my grip.

Flynn crosses his arms and narrows his eyes.

I look away and try for the door again, finally getting it open and racing back to my office. When I get there, I nearly cry, but Ace is there watching me closely. Instead, I nod at him and pick up my desk phone to make the call to Chef Sinclair, hoping Ace doesn't notice the way my hands shake when I pick up the receiver.

Weston slips in by the time I hang up the phone. His face is blank, which makes me want to sob.

There's really no conversation we can have here with Ace sitting a few feet away. If Flynn saw us, I will lose my job for sure, never mind the contest.

"Hey, Ace. How's it going?"

"Good, Chef. Everything okay?"

Weston smiles and it transforms his face completely back to his normal sunny self. "Yeah, I'm good." Weston turns my way. "Ryan, could I talk to you a minute?"

Ace clears his throat, then stands. "Boss, I'm going to go out and check on the staff."

"Thanks." I take a couple shaky breaths while watching Ace walk through the door and close it behind him. Tears prick my eyes, so I blink a few times before looking at Weston.

"I'm so sorry, Ryan. Obviously this is all my fault."

I'm shaking my head before he can finish. "No, it's mine. I knew more than anyone the stakes to having a relationship with someone I work with. This is why I didn't want to explore it." I put my face in my hands and concentrate on holding back the tears. "Did he see you?"

"I'm pretty sure he did. He looked right at me but looked over me at the same time. The usual, basically."

I want to reach out to Weston to comfort him about his father's lack of attention, but right now I don't have anything left in the tank to give. This is absolutely a problem of my own making and I should have known better, but I can't let my sisters down. "I'm going to his office to talk to him. To beg for my job if I have to."

"I'll come with you. It's as much my fault, if not more."

"I don't think that's a good idea." I stand and steel myself, readying myself for any result Flynn will throw my way. "I'll let you know what happens."

"Ryan." Weston reaches for me, but I slip out of his reach.

"It's better this way. I'll talk to you later, Chef."

IT'S OBVIOUS WHEN I step across the threshold of the open door into Flynn's office that he's waiting for me. He sits behind his big desk with his arms folded over his chest. A vein throbs on the side of his next and he wears a tight smile.

Bravado is my first instinct since it's what I usually display with him, but I lower my jutted-out chin and relax my hands at my side. I broke his rule and he's well within his rights to fire me without the least bit of guilt. The decisions I made leading up to this moment are the reasons why I'm in this situation. "Chef, I want to—"

"Ryan, I'd like to discuss your application to the National Restaurant Executive of the Year contest."

"My what? But what about—"

"We can talk about anything you would prefer, but if there are topics acknowledged, then consequences will be necessary." He spreads his arms wide, palms up. His sly smile widens. "Hypothetically speaking, of course."

I nod. "Of course." My stomach unclenches a fraction. Flynn isn't benevolent. I need to know his angle, but I can't ask or the worms will be out of the proverbial can.

"Have a seat."

Sitting across from him like this, I'm a scolded child in front of the principal. Being beholden to Flynn is not the position I want to be in. Anger boils in my chest, threatening to gush up my throat. Or slide into my stomach to sicken me where it belongs. I'm the one to blame.

"I'm not inclined to submit your application."

My face heats from embarrassment because we both know I don't have a leg to stand on anymore. I can't leverage making a stink about my compensation if he doesn't submit me because at this moment, in this situation of my own making, he has the complete upper hand. "But—"

He raises a hand. "I'm not turning you down completely, but I'd like to have a discussion before I make a decision."

I slide back in my chair, waiting for whatever he has to say. Knowing I'll have to sit back like this and take it.

"You've done a good job since you've been employed here."

I want to open my mouth to protest, to stand up for myself and yell how I've done an exceedingly excellent job. Instead I slink farther into my seat.

"First as the assistant executive administrator under Edgar as he groomed you to take over. You absorbed most of his teaching except for one extremely important lesson." He raises his eyebrows as if waiting for me to ask. Or volunteer the information he thinks I should know.

I sit up and lean forward slightly. Then let out a huff of breath even though I'm trying to control my breathing. "And that is?"

"You can't release."

"I don't understand. What?"

"Delegate. You don't delegate. A good manager hires trustworthy people and gives them the space to do their jobs. I'm not sure how you made that decision to hire your assistant, but…"

"Ace came highly recommended from another Michelin-star restaurant. He's good at his job."

He barks a mirthless laugh. "If my entire job was to surf the internet all day and play dice with the dishwashers, I'd be superior at it, too."

I frown and give myself a headache drawing down my eyebrows. "None of that is true."

"The fact that you don't know that is a problem. And on top of having nothing to do, you raised his salary to meet yours. No wonder he doesn't have any respect for you."

No way I can just sit here and listen to this. I pop up and pace the floor, trying hard to keep my composure. "I raised his salary because he deserved a raise. He makes the same as me because I'm severely undervalued."

"You're a hard worker, Ryan. I'll give you that. But you're not a manager. Managers achieve through others. You achieve plenty—but all through yourself."

I look out the window of his office because I can't even face him right now. Some of this is hitting a little too close to home. "I know I can depend on me. I know I'll be here to take care of what needs to be taken care of." A sob escapes my throat, and before I can catch it, the sound tears out of my mouth.

Flynn sighs. "Do you have a therapist? I have a great one I've been seeing lately."

I spin on him, eyes stretched to maximum capacity, tears now freely flowing.

His posture is more relaxed, his face open.

"Why?"

"I know what grief is like, Ryan. It's been eating me up inside for over twenty years. I recognize it in you, too."

"Is that why you've been disappearing so much?"

He grumbles, resembling his usual self. "No, that's something else. But related in a way. I can give you her phone number if you want."

I sit back down in the chair across from him and reach into my pocket for a napkin. "I did grief counseling when I moved here. I'm fine."

"Listen, I can't force you to go. But if you're unable to extend me a commitment you'll make a serious effort to delegate, I can't submit your name in good conscience. One of the questions is about delegation, and the answers you gave were…maybe not fabricated but certainly told through a rose-colored lens."

There's no arguing my way out of this. I don't agree with him, and it would be dishonest for me to give my word on something I don't believe is an issue. I stand and nod. "I understand." I turn and walk to the door.

"And Ryan." His tone is stiff.

"Yes?"

"If that hypothetical situation doesn't resolve itself, all of this would have been a moot point."

I don't bother to turn around because he isn't telling me anything I don't already know.

CHAPTER FOURTEEN

Is it over? Uncertain.

WESTON PACES OUTSIDE my office when I return from Flynn's. "I'm still employed. He didn't want to acknowledge seeing you."

He places a hand over his heart. "That's such a relief." He opens my office door for me to pass through.

"That part is. He also basically said I was a terrible manager and don't know how to delegate." My chest tightens again, and I look around for some water.

"Can I get you something?"

"I'm just looking for... Oh, here's a bottle." I unscrew the top on the bottle I retrieved from the small corner table we sometimes use to confer around. "Did you hear what I said?"

He pulls his lips inside his mouth and places a hand on the back of his neck, then looks around the office. Anywhere but me. "Um, yeah?"

I blink.

When he looks back at me, he's biting the side of his bottom lip.

"I take that to mean you agree with your father. Perfect time for that to happen." The sarcasm on my tongue doesn't feel right, but nothing about this situation does.

"Ryan, I think you're phenomenal." He puts a hand up as if swearing. "But I've mentioned before that Ace takes advantage of you."

My breathing becomes labored all of a sudden. My best friend turning against me after nearly getting me fired was not on my bingo card today. "I can't believe you're taking Flynn's side. Of all people."

"I'm not at all. I said this weeks ago. You're the one who told me Dad knows everything going on in his restaurant. Of course he would know if Ace was actually putting in the work." He shrugs. "In for a penny... Why are you always doing inventory? Isn't that Kerry's job?"

"I, uh..." The air thickens, choking my breath. I take a gulp of my water, then drop onto my chair. "She handles the ordering."

"Right, based on what you tell her to order. She only needs to click on the order button."

"Why are you doing this?"

He steps around the desk and reaches for me, but I roll my chair out of his grasp.

"I don't think this is a good idea."

After backing up, he slides into the chair across from my desk. "You're right, of course. I just wanted to comfort you. Maybe we should talk about it later, back at my place?"

I shake my head and close my eyes, fortifying myself. "I mean us, West. We should have never gone down the romantic path. If I followed my first mind, we wouldn't be upset with each other right now."

"Ryan, I'm not upset with you at all."

I raise an eyebrow. "Really? Because you never talk to me like this." What he's said isn't mean, but it's very un-Weston. My best friend is super supportive, not judgmental.

"I know. And I'm sorry." He massages his temples. "I shouldn't have said anything, but please don't shut me out now."

A tear slips behind my defenses and I wipe it away. We can't go back, but I don't see a way forward, either. Not if I want to keep my job. This is exactly what I was afraid of to begin with. "I don't see how we can continue seeing each other." My voice catches on the last word. I take a couple shuddering breaths until I can control the tone of my next words. "We'll have to figure out how to repair our friendship, but for now, I need to concentrate of putting things right. It's my duty to my sisters. I need some time."

Weston stands, his expression stoic, and nods. He doesn't speak another word before walking out my door.

WESTON HASN'T BEEN scheduled to work the past couple days, but today he's back in the restaurant, while I'm off for Cynthia's visit. I wouldn't say we are avoiding each other, but neither has made an effort to reach out to the other.

My heart aches every time I think about him, which is almost always. When I awake in the mornings, he's my first thought. Same as when I go to bed.

I walk into the kitchen in a robe and house shoes, the smell of coffee leading the way.

Cynthia pours herself a cup. She's fully dressed in a pretty red jumper, and her long, curly hair hangs over her shoulders. "Good morning, sunshine. I hope I didn't wake you. I'm sure you went to bed very late last night." She sets the cup on the counter and extends her arms for me to step into them.

Seeing her makes me feel some kind of way. Having Mom's best friend's arms around me brings on all the strong emotions I've been burying. I sob into her hair. "I'm so sorry. I can't seem to stop."

She rubs my shoulders and rocks me back and forth. "Just let it all out, baby. Let it go."

And I do. Soaking in the warmth of her neck, the citrus scent from her hair, and the purr reverberating in her throat, I cry until I have no tears left.

She passes me a paper towel from the rack and leads me over to the small kitchen table. "Do you want some coffee?"

"I can get it." I make to stand, but she places a hand on mine.

"Let me, sugar." She returns with her own coffee and a cup for me.

"Thank you. I think I'm just really tired."

She hums and takes a sip of her coffee. "Have you not been sleeping well?"

I swipe at my eyes as they fill with water again. "Not really. Plus I get in really late every night. I didn't even get to see you last night because I was so late."

She nods. "Why do you think you haven't been sleeping well?"

I shrug. "Who knows. I'm worried about my sisters, for one."

"Right. You mentioned you're thinking of selling your house."

My stomach clinches for what I've lost. "I don't think that's really an option anymore. Weston offered for us to move in with him, but…" I sob again and bury my head in the paper towel.

Cynthia waits patiently for me to breathe through this latest teary episode.

"For some reason, Weston and I thought it was a good idea to alter our friendship." I shrug. "To try for a closer relationship."

She nods. "You two were already very close, so by closer, you mean…a sexual relationship?"

I shake my head. "We didn't get that far yet. We already love each other, so we thought we might venture into the romantic kind of love."

She scrunches her face, and I'm reminded of her failed relationship with her best friend before Mama. "And it didn't work?" She asks the question without judgment, though.

"It was working great. We just shouldn't have started it in the first place." I test the heat of my coffee, placing the rim of the cup close to my lips. It's still hot but maybe cool enough. I take a tentative sip. "My boss has a strict *no fraternization* policy."

"Oh, I see. But isn't your boss Weston's father?"

I sigh and take another sip. "It's such a complicated story, but Weston has never garnered his father's attention. He's so special and talented but not the way Flynn respects, so he basically just pretends Weston doesn't exist." The coffee is extra special this morning. Maybe because someone else made it. It's cool enough to take a big swallow. "He wrote a whole novel. And it's so good. I only have a couple chapters left to read, but I already know it's better than most everything I've ever read."

"You sound very proud." She angles her head to the side and smiles. "Weston is a talented pastry chef. Why wouldn't his father admire that?"

"Well, you're the therapist, but my guess is that it has something to do with Weston's deceased mother also being a pastry chef. It's really clicking into place now because Flynn mentioned the other day that he's seeing someone professionally to work through his grief." I set down my cup and lower my voice. "He thinks I should, too."

Cynthia reaches across the table to place her hand on top of mine. "What do you think?"

The front door opens, then closes. I glance at Cynthia, confused.

She mouths, *Saron.*

I move my wet paper towel behind the salt-and-pepper shakers so she can't see.

My sister strolls into the kitchen dressed in running shorts, glistening with sweat. She pulls the wireless earbuds out of her ears. "Told you I wouldn't be gone long, Aunt Cynthia. Good morning, Ryan."

"Hey, good morning. You went running this morning?" The unnecessary question slips from my mouth before I can think better of it.

Saron looks at me and narrows her eyes. "What's going on?"

"Nothing. I just didn't realize you were running this morning."

"I run almost every morning, Ryan." She washes her hands in the kitchen sink, then assembles for the blender a banana, hemp and pumpkin seeds, walnuts, shredded coconut, oat milk, and protein powder.

I sink into my chair, throbbing with misery. The fact I didn't know she runs every morning is a problem. I'm out every night so late that when I wake up in enough time to start the cycle all over again, Saron has run and then gone off to school. "Do you have a marathon coming up I forgot?" I release a mirthless laugh.

"Next month, but this is for cross-country for school."

"Oh, right. I guess it is that time of year."

"Yup." She turns on the blender, which silences any thought of further conversation.

I glance at Cynthia, but her expression is impassive.

When the blender noise stops, Saron grabs a large tumbler out of the cabinet to pour her smoothie into, then moves to put her earbuds back in.

I ask, "Hey, what do you have going on today?"

"Well, for now, I'm going to take a shower, then whenever Meagan drags out of bed, we're going to Barton Springs."

"Oh, okay. I was going to see if you wanted to go to the farmers' market out at Lakeline Mall with us."

She gives me her fake half smile. "Maybe next time."

"Okay, but if either of you want anything from out there, text me."

She barely nods before heading for the shower.

"Teenagers."

Cynthia chuckles. "Is what I'm wearing okay for the market?"

"Definitely. Just make sure to wear some sunscreen on your arms."

She smiles and winks. "Always the mom, huh?"

I take a deep, shuddering breath. "You're leading me back to our conversation before Saron came."

"We don't have to talk about it if you don't want."

"I can't figure it out by myself." I go on to tell her how everything unfolded with Weston, Flynn's ultimatum, and my deepest worries about not being able to take care of my sisters the way they deserve. "So, you asked me before if I need therapy, but I've already had grief counseling and I'm still struggling."

"Grief is a curious emotion. Not only does it manifest differently for everyone but even in a single person, it can ebb and flow. Transform and reshape. Lie dormant, then reappear. There's no quick fix for grief, and while it was wonderful for your grandparents to send you to counseling as a teen, you're an adult now with so many responsibilities."

I stand and take my empty cup over to the sink. "So you think I should go to therapy again."

"Are you asking my opinion—because I don't want to offer you unwanted advice."

I turn around and face her. "Yes, I'm asking for your advice."

"Then yes, I think you should return to therapy. Do you want me to recommend someone here?"

"I suppose so."

"Let me get my tablet." She rises and heads down the hallway to Meagan's room. Meagan slept in Saron's bedroom to make room for Cynthia to stay the weekend.

Making up my mind to return to counseling does bring a sense of peace down on my entire body. Therapy won't fix all my problems, but at least it's a start.

I DON'T WASTE time stopping at my office when I enter the restaurant, bypassing it completely without even looking inside and marching straight to Flynn's. My heart drops when I look inside and he's not there.

After looking all over, I finally find him in the employee break room eating a large bowl of pasta.

I narrow my eyes. "Where did you get that?"

He raises his eyebrows, then picks up the napkin next to his plate and wipes at the corner of his mouth. "I asked Chef Sinclair to make it. I'm thinking of adding a pasta dish to the menu."

My eyes hurt from stretching them so hard and my throat's too dry to speak.

He chuckles. "I'm uncertain if I've ever seen you speechless, Ryan."

"What's happening here? You rebuke anything Italian for the menu."

Flynn tilts his head for a sideways nod as if agreeing I have a point. "As I mentioned the last time we spoke, I'm working through some things." He takes another bite and closes his eyes, appearing to savor his meal. "What can I do for you?"

I take a deep breath and step farther into the room, nearing his table. There's nobody else here, thankfully. "I've been thinking about what we talked about last time."

"Is that so? Which part?"

"All of it. I can see where it would appear I'm not delegating."

He lifts a brow and stares me down.

"Okay, what I mean to say is that I will make a greater effort at delegating."

"Do I have your word, Ryan?"

"Yes, of course. I wouldn't say it if I didn't mean it."

"And what about the therapy?"

Although I do plan to make an appointment with one of the several therapists Cynthia recommended, I have no intention of sharing that with Flynn. "That's none of your business. As my employer, it's against the law to even ask me about something like that."

He nods. "You're right. I agree to submit your application for the award, then."

I fight back a smile because I feel a *but* coming on.

"But I also need you to reestablish a list of duties for your administrative personnel and have individual meetings with them. I'd like you to copy me on the lists."

"You've never interfered with my management of my team before. I'd prefer to handle it myself because this will undercut my authority."

"Do you know why your team calls you 'boss'?"

My stomach clinches because I didn't know Flynn was aware of this particular quirk by my staff. "I assumed that was their way of establishing boundaries. Like the same way I always call you and the other kitchen personnel 'chef.'"

"It's because they want to give you the appearance of authority. I can't undercut something that doesn't exist."

Just when I thought Flynn was softening, he gives me a quick reminder. I put my hands on my hips, readying for a fight.

"Before you get riled up, just do what I ask and you're in the contest. You'll also thank me later when you realize I'm right."

That deflates me. "Fine. I agree."

"Good, but I don't want you to get your hopes up. It's very competitive. Hopefully you're working on a plan B for your financial troubles." He stands with his empty bowl and plows right by me before I have a chance to respond.

It's for the best because what in the world would I say? I don't have a plan B. If I don't win, Saron will have to go to state school and I'll continue to stick it out here with my low pay that ensures more financial aid for them. That's my plan B, and it's one Saron will never go for. It's not anything I want, either.

CHAPTER FIFTEEN

Decisions are made. Good?

B Y THE TIME I pass the theater seats, climbing the steps to the second floor of the Austin Central Library, I'm already winded. One of these days I'm going to get serious about exercise. Maybe Monday.

I stare at the elevator a long moment, but there's no point in taking it if I want to truly find Weston. He would only take the stairs, so if I don't want to miss him in case he's on the move, I'll need to suck it up. But first I inhale the bookish smell and long for days in the future when I can relax in the library with a good book instead of snatching pages where I can: in line at the grocery store, in the break room at work while scarfing down a quick meal, or occasionally in bed on my off days when there's nothing much planned early in the morning or late at night. The way I zipped through Weston's manuscript was a minor miracle, but it was just that good. Plus my best friend wrote it, so of course I made it priority.

After walking through the entry next to the stolen-book detectors, I scan the tables outside the little food stand, but nobody's sitting there, so I turn right and take the first set of stairs to the next floor.

When I reach the top, I grab the railing to catch my breath. A homeless person reclines on a couch overlooking the atrium, and they turn to me with raised eyebrows.

"Hey." I wave, then start my search through the stacks. There are so many places to sit hidden away down the rows of books, I can't just make a sweep around the outskirts.

When I don't find him this time, I take out my phone from my jeans pocket and look at the text from Weston again: *At the library revising.*

That was in response to the first exchange of messages we've had in several days—a message I sent without preamble: *Where are you?*

I could type out another text, but I want to display a grand gesture by showing up and clearing the air. I miss my best friend desperately.

By the time I reach the fifth floor, my longing transforms from friendship into something more. I place my hands on top of my head and squeeze, realizing just how much I care for Weston. I want to be with him as more than friends. I know it's dumb and that I'll pay the higher price if Flynn finds out, so we just need to ensure Flynn never finds out. At least not as long as I work there.

Finally, I step out onto the rooftop garden and search the high tables loaded with library patrons. No Weston, though. I walk over to the edge and view the city from this vantage point. The breeze helped by the rooftop fans blows the smell of the river running through downtown over to me. It's fresh mixed with soil and entirely Austin.

Weston sits on the other side of the garden at a low table made for two people. Thankfully he's alone, and when I slide into the chair opposite him, he looks up, first irritated with a crinkled forehead, then his face transforms as I watch. The skin on his forehead smooths and his eyes brighten, then a smile creases his beautiful face.

"I've missed you so much. And I'm so sorry I took out what happened with your dad on you."

He reaches across the table, and I place my hand in his open one. "I missed you, too. But not just as a friend."

I open my mouth to say something, but he holds up a hand. "Okay if I finish?"

I nod, then brace myself for his next words.

"The last time we spoke, you said we'd figure out how to repair our friendship. Is that what this is?"

I inhale a sizable portion of the rooftop air. "No. Well, yes, but not only that. I know in my brain that we shouldn't explore more than a friendship. Not just because of what happened with your father, but also because I don't ever want to lose you. These past few days have really driven that home." I set my purse on the table and place my cell phone inside. I want Weston to understand he has my undivided attention. "But in my heart and soul, I want to be with you. As more than just friends, so if you still want that, too, let's pick up where we left off."

Weston lets go of my hand, then scoots his chair around the table to be closer to me. "I want that more than any-thing." He picks up my hand again and presses his lips to the palm.

"That makes me extremely happy, but we need to estab-lish some real boundaries this time."

"Like no kissing at work."

"Exactly like that. No kissing at work. No texting me to meet you in a dark room at work. No even looking at me too long at work." I let out a huge cleansing breath.

When I made up my mind to come over to the library, it was with the intention of finding Weston and making up with him as friends. I thought I knew my own mind better than that, or maybe I was in denial.

I place my hand on his thigh and lean in. "Can you keep it strictly professional at work? I don't even want our friendship to steep over into that space anymore."

"Of course, Ryan. Whatever you need."

"It's what I need, but I hope you understand why it's so important to me."

"Of course I do, and I'm so sorry for putting you in that position. I should have waited until we were off work."

"It's not only your fault, West. I need to keep my priorities straight."

The expression on his face crumples, and I put my hand around his neck, playing with the curls at the nape.

"You are my priority, but during business hours, work is my priority. You get that, right?"

"Right. Yes, of course. It would be easier if the only reason I step foot into the restaurant isn't because of you. But I promise you I will remember how important your job is to you. And that Saron and Meagan are counting on you." He grins at me, then lowers his eyes, staring at my lips.

"Do you want to kiss me now?"

"So much yes."

I chuckle but touch my lips to his quickly. "Me, too, but this probably isn't the place. I can imagine they look out closely for this sort of thing."

"You're probably right. Do you want to get out of here?"

"I do, but I also don't want to interrupt your work. New story?"

"Nah, just revising the one you've already read."

"Revising? But it's perfect."

"No story is perfect after the first draft. And this one needs quite a bit of work."

I shrug because I read a lot and this story is as close to perfection as I've ever seen. "It's your book, but I already love it."

His cheeks actually redden ever so slightly. "Thanks, Ryan."

"I'll leave you to it, but I have a couple of other things to tell you. Come over later?"

He grins. "How do you expect me to concentrate now? I'll follow you home and pick this back up tomorrow."

WHEN I WALK through the front door, the first thing I notice is Meagan sitting on the living room couch. I'm not sure I've ever seen her out here by herself. "Hey, what's going on? Where's Saron?"

She barely looks up from her phone before responding. "Cross-country scrimmage or meet or whatever they call them." She goes back to scrolling.

Weston knocks lightly before coming through the cracked door. "Hey, Meagan." His cheerful demeanor is contagious and not easily ignored.

This time, Meagan puts her phone on the coffee table and gives Weston a small smile. "Hi, Weston. I was wondering where you were. Everyone's just disappearing."

Ah, okay. That's what this is about. I sit on the couch and signal Weston with my eyes to sit as well.

"Sorry I haven't been around. Ryan and I had to work some stuff out, but I'm not going anywhere. You can count on that."

She lifts one shoulder, then picks up her phone again.

I lean down to catch her eye. "What's so important on your phone?"

"Just looking at the UT website, trying to figure out my life. What I'm gonna do to amuse myself."

"We'll still see her. She's not leaving forever." I scoot a little closer to her and shore myself up against the sad feelings creeping through my veins before they seep out of my eyes and mouth. Meagan needs me to be strong, but I'm struggling. Then again, maybe she needs to share her grief with someone. "I'll miss her, too."

She shrugs, then stands. "I've got homework." She's down the hall and to her room before I can respond.

Weston moves over right next to me and puts a strong arm around my shoulders, then kisses the side of my head. He doesn't say anything, but he doesn't need to. His presence is enough.

"I'm going to start therapy again. I probably should ask Meagan if she'll go, too."

"Sounds like a great idea. Is there anything I can do?"

"Just continue to be your normal supportive self. I've been fighting against the thoughts of seeing someone, but between Cynthia and your father, I finally see I need to go."

"My, uh, father. Really?"

I turn to face him and nod. "Yeah. He made some good points last we spoke. The whole thing about me delegating, and he thinks I'm still grieving, needing to control everything because I don't trust anyone else to be there. I've got to let go, though. If one thing the accident with Naomi taught me, it's that the girls need to stretch their wings and live."

"My father, huh? That's out of character."

I offer Weston a sad smile. "I'm sorry, West. I know he hasn't been the best dad."

He snorts.

"Right. He's been a terrible father and I'm definitely not taking up for him, but just like we both said, he knows his restaurant and everything that goes on within. Including how my staff doesn't respect me."

"Ryan, that's not—"

"It is. You don't have to make me feel better. It was harsh hearing it from Flynn, but that's my fault. You've been trying to tell me in your sweet way, and I didn't listen. I'm sorry."

"You're an excellent manager. You just haven't hired the best people."

"We'll see how they respond to the new me. That will tell the real deal. It'll be a struggle, but I've got to learn to let some things go." I move in closer to him and lean into his side. "Since your father has an extra radar level where his business is concerned, let's reaffirm that we won't interact while we're at the restaurant."

"I promise, Ryan. I won't even drop by your office anymore. Instead, I'll just hang out in the break room and work on my revisions."

"I still don't think you need to revise."

He wraps his arms around me and pulls me tighter against his body, then nuzzles his nose behind my ear, breathing warm air against my neck. "I missed you so much."

My breathing suddenly becomes labored, my body responding to his small touches. I turn my head just enough to line my mouth up with his. "Me, too, West. So very much."

Weston captures my lips with a quickness, sliding his tongue against the seam.

I open for him and taste the cinnamon on his tongue.

He grunts ever so slightly in response and positions his hands on my waist, pulling me even closer, which doesn't seem possible. His cinnamon scent fills my nose, and I get lost in the kiss, in him.

When he pulls back, I nearly fall forward. "Hey."

"We better stop before…you know… Meagan's here."

I lay my head on his shoulder in shame. One kiss from Weston and I forgot about my sister just that quick. "I'm the worst."

He puts a hand under my chin, lifting my gaze to his. "You're the absolute best. You've done so much for your sisters—still doing so much for them. Please don't beat yourself up for snatching a moment of joy for yourself."

"Your mom must have been an angel because you are the sweetest person in the entire world."

He laughs, a real belly laugh. "That was so corny."

I join him in laughing because it absolutely was, but

something about Weston's openness makes me want to just say anything to make him smile. A real smile. "It may have been, but it's true. You're perfect."

His laughter dies down, but the smile is still wide on his face. "Nobody's perfect, but I appreciate you saying it."

I grin at him, then press my lips against his again. This time the kiss is chaste but no less intense. I tamp down the need to say *I love you*, even though that's everything I feel. I've loved Weston for a long time, but I want to ensure this is romantic love before I say it.

When I pull back, it's written all over his face, too.

We smile at each other and nod, an understanding passing between our linked gazes.

CHAPTER SIXTEEN

He's a super freak. Surprise!

THE RESTAURANT IS busier than I've ever seen it. A shipment of dragon beans is late, which means that one of the only two vegetarian dishes Everheart serves is in danger of not having its main ingredient for dinner tonight. Three of the waitstaff have called in sick, and there was a last-minute cancelation of a corporate event.

I find Ace in the dishwashing area, leaning over a counter stacked with glassware ready for the machine. He starts when he sees me, eyes wide.

"Ace, I need you to check with Nancy on the backup list and replace the three staff who called in."

His face creases in confusion. "Uh, don't you normally handle that, boss?" He shines a megawatt smile my way.

I can feel Flynn's gaze on the side of my face. Or maybe it's just my shame heating my profile, guilt from not realizing Ace has been manipulating me all this time.

"Report back to me once you've handled it. Also, check with Kerry on the missing beans and find out what her backup plan is."

"But you usually tell her how to handle it."

I ignore the pleading in his eyes, but everything in me

wants to tell him never mind, I will handle it. I take a steadying breath. "Thanks, Ace. Let me know what you come up with."

I walk off without a backward glance, however Flynn is in my path as I walk through the kitchen. He steps to the side ever so slightly and crosses his arms, his stern regard firmly in place. There's a small smile barely turning up the corner of one side of his mouth. I was looking for it, otherwise I would have missed it.

Before I break out into a smile myself, I race past him and concentrate on the remaining lunch crowd, stopping at the first table past the empty chef's table. Reservations for it have been sparse since the leading Everheart brothers left the restaurant. Weston is just as handsome—if not more, in my biased opinion—but he was never one to perform for the customers, preferring to concentrate on his baking and rarely looking up.

A young Black couple is enjoying the prix-fixe menu options.

"Good afternoon. I'm Ryan Landry, the manager here. How is everything?"

The woman speaks up, hazel eyes sparkling. "Everything has been absolutely delicious. Last time I was here, I wasn't feeling super well, so I'm happy I was able to make it back."

"So happy to hear, and we're happy to have you back." I make a move to go to the next table, but she speaks again.

"Is Weston here, by any chance?"

I blink. Then look at her companion. He's a mountain of a man with a friendly face. I guess he could be her brother instead of a lover, but why is she asking about my man? I blink again, then chuckle to myself at my ridiculousness. "Sorry, no. He's off today."

"Oh, that's too bad. We're friends of his brother." She shrugs. "Well, really, his girlfriend, but we love him now, too."

The butterflies in my stomach stop twittering around down there, and I smile. "Oh, okay. Knox and Rowan?"

"I should have just led with that, huh? No, we grew up with Kasi. I'm Joy, and this is Tariq."

Tariq gives me a wave and a smile. "Hi."

"Hi, it's nice to meet you both. Weston will be sad he missed you. How long will you be here?"

"We're heading back tomorrow morning early."

"That's too bad. I'll definitely tell him you were here. What are Declan and Kasi up to these days? Still traveling?"

Joy laughs, nodding. "You know them. They stay on one adventure after another, but actually they're back in LA doing post on their series."

I don't really know Kasi that well, but she's been great for Declan. "Please tell them I said hello." I smile at them both. "I should probably make my rounds. Again, it was great meeting you. I'll give Weston your regards."

I make my way around the restaurant, checking on our guests, and when I return to the office, Ace is there, sweating and scrambling around between Kerry's desk and his, phone in one hand up to his ear and a tablet in the other, frantically scrolling. I could take over as I usually do—Lord knows I'm itching to handle this myself—but we all have to start somewhere, and while it would be a disappointment to not have the vegetarian dish, it wouldn't be a tragedy. Calling backups from the waitlist list is easy peasy, so I'm sure Ace could at least handle that with ease.

After making myself comfortable behind my desk, I switch on my laptop and the monitor and scan my email. My stomach does little flips and I have to bite back a smile when I spot the email from the contest coordinators. It's the confirmation I've been waiting for, and it takes everything in me to not stand up and dance. Not that I doubted Flynn—well not much, at least—but it's great to see the confirmation in writing.

Even though the office is in chaos, I take a moment for myself to relish this small victory. Next I text Weston. *Got the contest confirmation! Also, delegating my ass off.* That may be a slight exaggeration, but I definitely am trying to get on the right track. Not bad for my first time out the gate.

The response comes before I can put the phone back on the desk. *That's awesome! On both counts.*

Oh yeah, I almost forgot. Kasi's friends were in for lunch. I'll tell you about it later.

Sounds good. Do you think you'll be off early enough for me to see you later?

Doubtful. There are disasters popping up everywhere, and while I am truly delegating, I can't let Ace do everything. I'll let you know.

Okay. He inserts a red heart emoji.

This time I allow myself a small smile before I jump into the fray.

WHEN THE RESTAURANT finally winds down and I'm sitting

in the parking lot in my car, I check the time on my phone. Two in the morning is really late, just as I expected, but I also yearn to see Weston. I'll text, and if he doesn't answer, so be it. *You up?*

Gawd, that sounded like the booty call it is. I look around at the empty lot and vow to myself this will be the last time I'm in this lot alone. I've got a long way to go before I completely trust my staff to take care of their tasks, but wanting to have a real life outside this restaurant is a good motivator.

I wait five minutes, but no text greets me, so I crank my car and tamp down my disappointment.

Before I exit the parking lot, my phone chimes. *Come over?*

On my way.

A few minutes later, Weston greets me at the kitchen door, pulling me into his warm body, then bending to snuggle against my neck. He smells of deep sleep, and his bare skin is soft against my cheek. He's only wearing boxer briefs, which are a bit twisted like he just threw them on haphazardly.

"You were asleep, huh? I'm sorry for texting so late."

He straightens and closes the door behind me. "It's never too late to see you." His tired eyes tell a different story, but I don't argue.

Instead, I smile and glide my thumb across his lips.

He nips at it with his teeth, then pulls it deep in his mouth.

That simple action puts my nipples on high alert, and my head falls back involuntarily, a groan escaping my throat.

Weston cups the back of my thighs, gripping with urgency.

I throw my arms around his neck and brace for his next move.

He swoops me up and backs me against the wall next to the door, pressing his hardness against my core. I wrap my legs around his waist and rock against him, then stretch my neck to capture his lips.

A low rumbling builds in Weston's throat, and I swoop in and seize the sound with my mouth when he parts his lips. Our tongues tangle and slide against each other, and his cinnamon taste fills my throat.

He pulls back slightly and looks me in the eyes. "Everything okay? This okay?"

"For sure. Come here." I bite his bottom lip and smile when he grunts. He doesn't waste any time, pressing his body against me once again. This time I reach between us and rub the head of his erection, which has escaped the top of his underwear.

"Oh G-d." He slides his big hands up my thighs and fills them with generous handfuls of my butt, squeezing through my underwear, then breaks the kiss and lifts me easily, placing my legs on his shoulders.

I brace my hands on the ceiling after helping Weston push up my skirt around my waist.

He yanks my underwear to the side with his teeth, then delves his tongue inside me, assuaging the ache that started about two minutes after I stepped through the door. He laps up the wetness that flows the more he applies his intimate touch. When he swipes his tongue across my clit, I'm already close.

I chance removing a hand from the ceiling and ease it toward my breast.

"I've got you." And he does have me so thoroughly, both with sucking on my clit and balancing me on his shoulders against the wall. I watch him as I release my breasts from the bra that's been binding them all day for work. He glances up and smiles against my cleft as I rub the hardened nipples, sending a cable directly to my clit.

He knows I'm close and quickens the pace, applying a little more pressure.

"Yes, West, don't stop." I rock against his tongue and relish the building pressure in my belly that turns into a tug on my core, then sweet release, my orgasm pulsating in his mouth.

When I'm done, Weston eases me to the floor and pulls me tightly against him, enveloping me in his warm body. His breathing is labored, though, and this time when I reach for him between our bodies, he backs up a little. He chuckles in my ear, "I'm done, too."

"Oh." I'm not sure what to say and am suddenly shy.

"Yeah, and it was really good coming the same time as you. Trust me." He captures my gaze with his. "Is something wrong?"

"No, not at all. I just, um…" I smooth my skirt back down but don't bother with my panties still wedged to one side. I'll fix those later. "This isn't a little… I don't know. Different. You know, for us?" Of course he has to know, but he doesn't bail me out, only waits for me to finish stumbling around through my feelings.

He smiles and kisses me again, chaste but long and sensual.

My eyes fall closed as I relish the kiss.

When he releases my lips, he places quick kisses along my jaw leading to my ear. "Yes, different. But do you think a good different?" He moves his head back to gauge my reaction, his eyebrows pulled together.

"A wonderful different, West. The best different."

CHAPTER SEVENTEEN

Family's everything. Periodt.

M Y PHONE HAS been blowing up in the pocket of my trousers for at least the past half hour, but I was working the tables during the lunch rush. At some point, I'll delegate this to Ace to handle at least occasionally.

When I step into my office, I pull out the offending device and check the notifications. Looks like most are from the family group chat. When I click on the chat, I realize it's the pared-down cousin group chat instead of the full one with Mimi and Papa and the generation above us.

> **Diedra:** *All I'm saying is that you need a man and Jerome is running up on you so hard, it's a wonder he hasn't given you a concussion.*

Ugh, inappropriate as ever.

> **Lisa:** *I'm a new associate. Now is not the time for a love life, no matter how fine that man is.*

> **Naomi:** *I thought they were too busy to hang out because of the new project. How does Jerome still have time to try to talk to you?*

> **Lisa:** *It's an effort, believe me. Both of our schedules are packed as hell. Why bother right now? I can't get him to*

see that, though.

Naomi: *Have you actually said that to him? Is he crossing boundaries?*

Darryl: *Someone said Lisa's leading Jerome on. Now, can we talk about something else? Jeesh.*

Lisa: *No you didn't just drop that bomb and try to change the subject. Who is "someone"?*

Diedra: *Yeah, Darryl. Spill all the tea.*

Darryl: *Hey, that's all I know. They said obviously you're not interested but keeping his nose open for some reason. Don't worry about who my source is. That's not important.*

Diedra: *Wait, whose nose?*

Lisa: *Obviously he means Jerome.*

Diedra: *Don't get mad at me just because you don't know how to talk to a man. Send him my way and I'll show you how it's done.*

Naomi: *Okay, sister. That's enough of that. Lisa, do you like Jerome?*

There's been no response since I've been sitting here catching up.

Me: *Hey, just reading this. Everyone gone?*

Diedra: *Nah, we are still here waiting on your big-headed cousin to fess up.*

Me: *Maybe she's working through her feelings. Let's give her a break.*

Diedra: *And Mama Ryan has entered the chat tryna run things. Girl, please.*

My face heats to an unhealthy degree, and I look around

the office. Everyone's out taking care of the business like they should have been doing all along. No wonder I was rarely alone in here.

> **Me:** *What are you talking about? I would love to not run things. You volunteer me every single time because you don't want to. When have I ever inserted myself?*
>
> **Diedra:** *Remember when y'all moved here and you started dating that boy. Damn, what's his name?*
>
> **Lisa:** *Gregory.*
>
> **Diedra:** *Right, Gregory. All he wanted to do was play football. But that wasn't good enough for our dear cousin. No, she had to turn him into a blerd. Had him wearing suspenders and dressing like Carlton. He nearly had a nervous breakdown trying to keep up with your demands.*

I slam the phone down and cross my arms over my chest. He wanted to be more studious. I just helped him.

Instead of giving Diedra the satisfaction of leaving the chat, I turn off my notifications and click on my laptop. What I really want to do is talk it out with Weston, but that's impossible with both of us in the restaurant today.

I scroll my email and reread the confirmation message from the contest organizers:

> *Congratulations! You've been nominated by Chef Flynn Everheart for the National Restaurant Executive of the Year. The responses to the entry form questions will be judged by a panel of industry experts and sponsors. First round finalists will move to the second round, announced by September 15th, and invited to compete in the semifinals and live finals starting on October 1st in New York.*

Great, two days before my birthday. Let's hope I'll have a great present this year.

Semifinal: The first set of competitions will include an interview with industry professionals, including verbal testing on your executive management skills listed in the attachments.

I survey the attachment, which is basically a replica of the questions Flynn "responded to" when he submitted me. I continue reading, getting more excited as I go.

Three candidates will move to the final round, which will replicate a live scenario relying on your executive management skills. This will be judged by a panel of top industry professionals.

I bet this is where Chef Buccola comes in. I tap my chin, taking a moment to wonder who else might be a judge. I'm sorely tempted to ask Knox if he knows, but although I need to win this desperately, I don't want to cheat my way there. I'm an excellent executive and only need to rely on my skills, education, and experience.

The following evening will be the awards dinner, where the winner and two runners-up will receive their awards.

I sit back and take a deep breath, reminding myself what's at stake. I don't have time for pettiness with Diedra, that's for sure.

THIS TIME I vacate the parking lot before Ace, leaving him there to put out a fire with one of the dishwashers. That seems to be who he hung out with most anyway, so this should be a piece of cake for him. I didn't see Weston leave since we're actively avoiding each other at work, but we already made plans for me to head his way after work.

When I turn onto his street, I spot Weston a few houses down from his, riding a longboard, his large bag strapped over his back. I pass him but don't honk since it's late and I can almost guarantee his neighbors won't appreciate the noise. Instead, I pull into his driveway and cut the engine, leaving everything in the car except my purse and phone.

Weston skids to a halt right next to me, executing some kind of kick with the board where it lands in his hand, and grins. "You beat me." He leans in, then pulls back. "I should probably shower first."

I grab the collar of his chef's jacket and pull him back down, then press my lips to his for a long moment before releasing him. "You smell like baked goods. I can't imagine that's ever a negative."

He laughs and takes my hand, leading me through the low gate and up the path to the back door.

"When did you leave?" I place my purse on the island but keep my phone. Although I vowed to ignore Diedra, shamefully I haven't been able to stop checking the chat.

"About fifteen minutes ago. I must have just missed you." He leaves the board outside, then locks the door and places his bag on the counter next to mine. "You thirsty? Or hungry?"

"I'll get some water while you shower." I absently look at

my phone again, and when I look up, he's still watching me. "What?"

"Is everything okay?"

"Yeah, of course." I move to the cabinet and take a glass down. "Do you want something to drink?"

He shrugs, then unbuttons his jacket. "Nah, I'll get something when I'm done. Be right back?"

"I'll be here." I fill my glass with what looks to be fresh-made lavender lemonade and take a big gulp. It's still so hot outside, and even that short walk from the car to inside the house overheated me. I glance at my phone and check the notification.

> **Diedra:** Just stating facts, cousin. No need to get butt hurt. But you do you, babes. I just hope Weston doesn't end up in a smoking jacket by a roaring fire reading a classic book. That man is way too fine to be cooped up like that.

Anger pulses through my veins with a quickness, and my fingers hover over the keys. There's so much I could type out right now. Like how she doesn't contribute anything to our grandparents' care. Or that she lives off child support payments from her ex and doesn't even try to get a job. Or how...

"Ryan? What's happening?" Weston reaches for me, tentatively as if approaching a scared animal. He's dressed in khaki shorts and a tank, water glistening from his black hair, all wavy and long.

"You showered fast."

He glances at the microwave clock. "If twenty minutes is

fast, I guess?"

I lean into him, and he wraps me up in a strong embrace. My heart pounds in my head, my breathing labored. I can't believe I lost track of time seething about Diedra. It's almost like I blacked out, but with terrible thoughts.

Weston strokes my back and rubs his cheek back and forth across the top of my head. "You want to tell me what happened?"

I sigh, somewhat calmer from Weston's touch, and step back, then sit in one of the high island chairs.

Instead of sitting, Weston stands in front of me, trapping my legs between his, then picks up one of my hands and kisses it.

I relate the family chat exchange, mostly. I may have been a little light on the Gregory details and Diedra's criticism. Why, I'm not sure because I know Greg asked me to help him.

"She said I was fine?" He doesn't whither under the look I toss his way, only laughs, then covers his mouth. "Sorry. I know you're upset and it isn't funny?"

"So you don't care she thinks you're that malleable that I could change you into a boring househusband."

He shrugs, then rounds me, circling me with his arms from behind. He places one forearm under my breasts and the other across my belly, then nuzzles his nose against my neck. "If I can be your husband, I don't care what kind it will be."

I stiffen, then lean away from him so I can see his face. We've barely started actually dating and definitely haven't talked about marriage in any abstract way.

"I'm not proposing, Ryan."

I release my breath. "No, I know. But we haven't ever talked about anything like that. You want to get married someday?"

He bites the side of his lip and his eyes droop ever so slightly. "You don't?"

"Yes, of course I want to get married someday. And have children, too."

His eyes brighten and a grin creases his face. "How many children? Like ten?"

I snort laugh. "No, definitely not that many. But maybe two, no more than three. Do you want ten children?"

He sits in the chair next to mine but still connects himself to me through his hands. "Diedra wasn't too far off. Maybe not the smoking jacket or sitting by the fire, but I'd love to be a househusband with as many kids as possible, but two, maybe three sounds good, too."

"Seriously? What about your job?"

"What? At the restaurant?" He pulls his eyebrows together. As close to a frown as I've ever seen on his face.

"Not exactly there maybe, but I mean as a chef?"

"I could cook for my kids." He reaches up and smooths the curls near my ear. "And my wife, of course. That would satisfy any lingering itch I might have."

I lay my hand on top of his, both pressed to my cheek. "What about your writing?" I close my eyes because I'm not sure I can look at him while he gives me his reply. Weston is fun-loving and laid-back and talented, but until tonight, I didn't realize he doesn't have any drive at all. I'm not certain how I feel about that.

KELLY CAIN

"I love writing. I don't believe I'd have to give that up, right? I can craft stories from anywhere, if you haven't noticed."

Writing has been Weston's passion as long as I've known him. Maybe that's why I'm confused about his grind. I'm not totally informed with creative spaces. I make a mental note to talk with Naomi later. I open my eyes and smile at him. "That's true."

He returns my smile, easy as ever, then leans in for a kiss.

I meet him halfway and try to lose myself in the kiss, but I'm still unsettled.

Weston gives me a peck, then leans back with furrowed brows.

"I guess I'm still upset by what Diedra said. It's great that you're aligned with her conversion for you, but not so great that she implied I'm the one who'll cause it. Like I'm some big, bad task master who tells everyone how to be. Even if you had a gaggle of kids, I can't imagine you'd be sitting in the house all day. You'd have them out disc golfing as soon as they could take some steps."

He's laughing before I can finish my little diatribe. "For sure."

"So you don't care?"

"Do I care what she thinks of me? Not really? She's entitled to her opinion."

I let out a groan before catching myself. "I love how nice you are, but sometimes you have to…" I think of what I want to say. Actually, I know what I want to say. He needs to take a stand sometimes, for goodness' sake. "I guess what I'm saying is to not let people mistreat you. I get that you're

178

confrontation averse, but that doesn't always work."

He actually frowns. "Do you enjoy confrontations?"

He knows I don't. That's why it's been so difficult for me at work. The only person on Earth I enjoy sparring with is my boss, who happens to be Weston's dad. And a truly awful person who doesn't have feelings, so it's okay to wrestle with him when needed. I sigh. "No, but sometimes, especially with family…" I look at him pointedly. "You have to stand up to them."

"Are we still talking about you and Diedra?"

"Do you think if you told your father how you feel, things would be different with him? And your brothers?"

He turns in his chair, facing the counter instead of me.

I pick up my lemonade and take a deep drink.

Weston doesn't turn back my way but does glance at me from the side of his eye. "How do you think I feel, Ryan?"

"I think that you're upset your father has never paid any attention to you. That he favored Knox ever since your mom died. And spent most of his time with Declan because they were so similar."

"He favored Knox long before Mom died. But that never bothered me. I had my friends, and they were my family. I didn't miss the ones at home."

Even though I'm hot as fish grease with Diedra right now, she's still my cousin and I love her. My family means everything to me, and I can't imagine going out and finding another one. Long before my parents were killed in that terrible car accident, we were close with our people. Having to move in with Mimi and Papa wasn't some dreadful undertaking. Sure, I was hurt over leaving my friends in

Houston, but falling into my grandmother's bosom made it bearable. I'm not sure how I would have survived losing Mama and Daddy without my family's embrace. "I know Knox is busy with opening Rowan's restaurant soon, but do you ever talk to him? He's right here in town."

He shrugs. "I love both of my brothers, Ryan, but the closest we've ever been was during the competition in San Francisco. I've never spent that much time with them before." Then he turns his whole body to me. "Is this going to be an issue between us?"

Is it? Weston finds families. He found mine, and they love him as their own. He'd never ask me to distance myself from them. I know that in my heart. But can I create a lifetime with him and never see his family? Would our children not have uncles who they spend summers with? Would my family be enough?

I lean my forehead on his. "No."

CHAPTER EIGHTEEN

Breakfast with Weston? Anytime.

WHEN I WAKE, the first thing I do is check my phone. Relief floods my body. There's a text message.

Weston: *I hardly slept last night. Can I make you breakfast?*

I smile and tap out a reply.

Me: *Me, either. That sounds great. I'll be over as soon as my sisters get off to school.*

We didn't leave things great last night. I was still uneasy, and who knows what was on Weston's mind because if he had any doubts, he probably wouldn't even register them. I sigh and fall back onto my pillows. I'm already diving back into the spiral, and that's the last thing I want this morning. Instead, I pick up the journal on my bedside table and write a few lines.

I check the clock on my phone, then pad into the bathroom to wash my face and brush my teeth, then slip my robe on and head to the kitchen.

Meagan's playing music in her bedroom. That's her usual routine while dressing for school. Saron's is quiet, of course.

Hopefully I've timed it right and can put together Saron's smoothie so she can grab it when she comes in from practice. Or whatever they call it for cross-country.

When I turn off the blender, a hand reaches in the cupboard next to my head and I jump and nearly fall over.

"You scared me to death."

Saron pulls an earbud out and fake-grimaces. "Is that for me?"

"Girl, yes."

She pours the green liquid into her cup and gives my shoulders a quick squeeze. "Thanks, Ryan." Then she's gone as quickly as she appeared.

Next I toast an English muffin, scramble some eggs, and heat up a couple premade frozen sausages for Meagan. Guilt twists my insides, but then I take a deep breath and release it. At least this breakfast is better than the cereal or bar she has when I'm sleeping in after a late night at the restaurant. Hopefully my new schedule will be better for making decent breakfast in the future. If only I could get her to take an interest in cooking. Without Saron around, I would worry for Meagan next year, but luckily there's plenty of dining halls on campus. I only need to figure out how to pay for them.

Once my sisters are out the door, I jump into the shower and put on my prettiest sundress. I have several in my beloved shade of green, but this time I pick one in purple, Weston's favorite color. I feel bad how we left things last night but okay with it at the same time. If we don't have the hard conversations, we can't grow together as a couple. But we need to figure out how to have those talks without putting us in such a mood we don't want to touch each other.

When I get to Weston's, the glorious scents greet me at the door before I can knock and enter.

He stands in front of the stove, moving strong muscles on display with such efficiency, flipping something in a pan without using utensils, then turning to me as if in slow motion. His hair is wet again, freshly showered, strands curling around his ears. The huge smile on his face gives me all the feels, but I don't linger there because my gaze involuntarily travels down that long, powerful body hidden only by a small apron and dark green boxer briefs.

All my senses leave except sight. I don't smell the wonderful breakfast laid out before me anymore, and my blood is pounding in my ears so hard, I miss what Weston said just now. His lips move but nothing comes out. Then he quirks his head to the side and frowns.

I tear my stare away from him to steady my lust. When I look back, he's close to me and I can breathe again when he pulls me into his chest. "Hi."

"You worried me for a minute."

"What can I say—I was overwhelmed by your full beauty on display."

He kisses the top of my head and releases me.

"Hey, that felt good."

"Yup, too good. If I kiss you properly, all my efforts in the kitchen this morning go to waste." He laughs and goes to pick up the pan from the stove, sliding onto a plate a perfectly cooked omelet, then looks my way, blue eyes piercing and filled with want. "Unless you want to skip breakfast."

I shake myself and look away again. That seems to be the only way I can keep my brain functioning this morning. "No, let's eat. I need the energy. Everything smells wonderful. What do we have?"

He pours a faded orange liquid from a pitcher into champagne flutes.

"Mimosas? Or Bellinis?"

"No, it's only peach juice with Topo. The first time I get to worship your body properly, I want to have a clear head."

For some reason, that sends an embarrassing heat up my neck. He's already had his tongue in my most intimate places, so I'm not sure why his words make me blush. Maybe I'm still not quite past the *friends* part of our relationship, but hopefully this morning will push that over the edge. "I think you worshipped it plenty last time, but I'm looking forward to what your idea of adoration is." Before I give him a chance to change my mind about breakfast, I make the short walk down the hallway to the powder room and wash my hands and splash a little cool water on my hot face and neck.

When I return to the kitchen, Weston is sitting at the island with platters of food laid out.

"Wow, West, this looks incredible." I think back to our conversation the day before, and although neither of us specified if those future kids would belong to both of us, I could totally imagine Weston making yummy food for our children and caring for them with immense love.

He shrugs as if indicating it's no big deal. "Thanks. To answer your earlier question, we have lemon-ricotta pancakes, because I know how much you love citrus, a French omelet, and your favorite sausage."

"Wow, West. You made those sausages from scratch? This morning? How long have you been up?"

He takes my hand in his and kisses it. "I didn't sleep much last night." He slices the omelet in half and puts a piece on both our plates.

I follow his lead and load our plates with pancakes and sausage. When I take a bite of the pancake, I close my eyes in ecstasy. "So good."

"I'm happy they turned out okay."

"Okay? These are the best pancakes I've ever had in my entire life. West, you are an incredible chef. I wish you knew that."

He laughs, evidently trying to lighten the mood. "You're a little biased. Do you want to do anything else today? Disc golf, maybe?"

I put down my fork and turn to him in my chair. "I know what you're trying to do, but I don't want to avoid anymore, okay? I want us to speak freely and share our souls with each other. That's what I need from a relationship. Can you do that?"

He bites his lip, barely meeting my gaze. "I can try, but it's not natural for me. I just want everyone to be happy."

"And me complimenting you makes you unhappy? Or me disagreeing with your self-assessment does?"

He sighs and puts his own fork down. "Both, I guess. You think of me as being a lot better at things than I actually am. It makes me uncomfortable because I know it isn't true."

"You think I'm blowing smoke up your ass?" My eyes

prick. I did not intend to go in this direction.

He grabs up my hands and moves closer to me. "I know you believe what you're saying. Like I said, you're a little biased with your rose-colored glasses. But I've lived with myself over thirty years. I'm just an average guy who lucked into a wealthy family."

"West. I—"

"It's okay, Ryan. I settled into that truth a long time ago. Everyone can't be a spectacular chef like Knox, who is also supersmart and comes up with the most incredibly successful ideas. Or Declan, who has charisma coming out of every pore of his body and creates on the fly something out of nothing." He shrugs and picks up his fork again. "Let's eat."

I'm speechless, but I do pick up a piece of sausage and shove it into my mouth because although I want nothing more than to jump on the counter and yell at Weston how wonderful he truly is, that won't convince him. Although he was born into wealth, that doesn't mean he didn't work hard in culinary school to become an exceptional pastry chef. And even though he works in his father's restaurant, he could go anywhere and be the head pastry chef, no questions asked. I suppose having the last name *Everheart* has a lot to do with that. I'm beginning to understand why Weston may have this impression of himself.

No, he needs to figure it out for himself, and all I can do at this point is support him. Starting with this beautiful breakfast he made us, even though I've lost my appetite. Maybe I'll nudge him where I can. Like passing along the best manuscript I've ever read in my life to someone who can do something about it.

WITH FULL BELLIES, we relax in comfortable silence upstairs in the game room on a huge sectional couch with built-in recliners. From my limited knowledge, there seems to be every gaming system created along with a huge television screen installed into the wall. There's a large mini fridge behind the wet bar area with a microwave. I've never spent any time in this room probably because it screams *man cave*.

I groan when Weston pulls my feet in his lap, and he pushes a button for the seat to shift and lay back. "So full."

"Same." He laughs and pats his belly. "I may not have planned this out so well."

My eyelids suddenly become very heavy, so I sit up on my elbows, remembering I needed to tell Weston something. "So I reviewed the contest agenda again last night, and I should know if I made it to the next round by next Wednesday."

"That'll be a nice birthday present." He narrows his brows and sets his blue gaze on me.

"I was thinking the same thing. That's all I want for my birthday this year."

He releases an exasperated sigh and rubs the soles of my feet. "You never want anyone to acknowledge your birthday. This year will be a double cause for celebration."

"I never celebrate because it's too much of an indulgence. I have stuff to get done and people to raise."

"And those people are raised, so why not this year? You're doing a great job delegating. Mostly. So you don't have to worry about the restaurant."

I shove his shoulder and immediately regret it, holding my full stomach. "Mostly, huh? Well this year I need to get ready for the contest."

"If I remember correctly, you said there were questions you'll have to answer in an interview and then perform for the judges when you make the finals. You've already answered the questions and you know how to run a restaurant. What's to get ready?"

I don't have a comeback because he's right. There's nothing I can do to prepare because I'm already doing it. The last piece fell into place when Flynn forced me to be a better manager rather than doing everything myself. And while I haven't conquered it completely, I know the goal I'm working toward. And what I need to do to accomplish it. "Do you have something in mind, West? Please don't say another birthday bash like we did for Lisa. I have another year before I reach that milestone birthday."

"Well." He sets my feet on the floor and holds out his arms.

I slide into them and rest my head on his chest.

"I was thinking we could rent a house on Canyon Lake. Do some kayaking, maybe let me finally teach you to paddleboard. Some jet skiing. That sort of thing."

"That does sound lovely. Just the two of us?"

"Unless you want to invite the twins along."

I don't, but that sounds selfish of me.

"You know it's okay if you don't, right? Or maybe just ask them how they would feel about you going away without them?"

"No, I'll let them know we're going and they'll be on

their own overnight. They'll be in school anyway, so that'll be a good reason not to ask them to come. Plus Saron has cross-country."

"I think I forgot to tell you but I went to her meet my last off day. She's really good, Ryan. Did you know?"

I know she's a great competitor and was constantly topping her personal best in the marathons she's run, but I didn't realize her school cross-country stuff was so important to her. "I guess not. She usually excels in everything she puts her mind to, though, so I'm not surprised." I shift so I can look at him. "Thank you for going. I should have been there to support her."

He lays a long kiss on my forehead. "You support her every day, Ryan. She knows that. Plus, Papa was there, too. He's the one who told me about it. He goes all the time."

That doesn't ease my guilt, though. I've been paying more attention to supporting them financially than I have emotionally. "I'm glad."

Weston rubs my arms, and I think about how I want to be a better sister.

CHAPTER NINETEEN

She looks hot up there. Yeah.

WHEN WESTON JERKS, my eyes fly open. "What happened?"

He swipes at his eyes, then looks at his fitness watch. "We've been asleep nearly three hours. Sorry for waking you."

I stretch and sit up, wiping the drool from my mouth, then look at his chest, thankfully dry. "I'm glad you did. I had no idea I was asleep."

"Me, either. I was so disoriented for a minute." He laughs and runs a hand through his hair, now perfectly dry and beautifully wavy.

I stare because tousled, nearly naked Weston is very sexy. The blood in my veins thickens and my breaths become more shallow.

He sees me watching, and the smile drops from his face, desire clouding his eyes.

We reach for each other at the same time. All hands and lips and tongues. Weston's smooth skin heats under my touch. His mouth is hot when I reach for his tongue with my own, tasting of lemon and vanilla. His erection grows until it strains the limits of his boxer briefs, and I straddle him on his recliner, rubbing against the object of my lust.

Weston glides his fingers through my short curls, scraping his nails against my scalp, sending electric energy down my spine. I grind against him in response. He breaks our kiss, trailing licks and pecks down my throat to my collarbone, where he nips and rubs his lips across my skin.

I put my hands on his chest to steady myself as I crush my core against him, sliding back and forth, relishing in every touch of his lips and tongue to my body. My breathing becomes labored, but I spare a moment to think how lucky I am. That this beautiful soul is really my partner and I get to be this close to him.

Looking down at him on his quest to worship my body has me way in my feelings, so I close my eyes and heighten the sensations Weston is gifting me. It's almost too much, and I shove my breasts forward, needing him to devour me there before remembering I'm still fully dressed.

"You have way too many clothes on." His voice is clear but raspy, clearly on the same wavelength as me.

"I was just thinking the same." I reach behind me to pull at the zipper there, but Weston beats me to it, unzipping the dress with ease. I pull the strapless bra over my head and toss it to the floor where my dress soon follows.

Weston just stares, his eyes going slightly unfocused.

I pick up where I left off before the dress fiasco and lean my nipple near his mouth, which he takes greedily. The spark to my clit is instant, renewing my grinding against his ever-hardening erection. I look down, wishing to see it, but Weston's head is in the way, worshiping one nipple after the other. They both respond to him, pebbling into large brown discs with lengthening peaks, and he takes full advantage.

I'm impatient, though, and want to see him, to touch him so I reach between us and grasp at the band of his underwear, pulling until his cock springs free into my hand. His skin is silky and slightly wet but hard and throbbing at the same time.

He lies back hard, his chest rising and falling at an unhealthy pace, his pupils blown out, but somehow helps me with his boxers and throws them to the side while I rid myself of my own panties.

He tries to pull me closer, but I shake my head. "I really want to taste you."

His eyes close and he groans. "You're going to kill me today."

"I hope not. I still want you inside me, too."

I crawl up his legs that go on for days until I'm comfortable. Weston puts his hands in my hair before my lips even touch him. I smile against his shaft, then lick the wetness from the slit, and he groans again. I circle the fat head with my tongue, relishing the salty-and-sweet taste and the rubbery feel against my lips. Then I lick down and up the back of the shaft before finally sliding him into my mouth. He doesn't push my head, but the constraint he exercises while massaging my scalp isn't lost on me. I continue the rhythmic sucking and hollowing out of my cheeks, then cup his balls.

Weston grabs the couch and bucks his hips. I glance up to watch him come undone, but he isn't looking at me at all. I'm unsure if his eyes are even open, but he yanks back and grabs his cock, pumping and spilling all over his stomach.

"Good Lord, Ryan."

I wipe at the side of my mouth and grin, feeling pretty triumphant but still super horny. Dang it, that was poor planning.

Weston jumps up and kisses me. "Don't move—be right back."

I watch his firm backside and strong legs walk down the hallway to his bedroom. He returns a few minutes later, cleaned up and carrying a handful of condoms. "Ambitious, huh?"

"Did you have somewhere else to be today?"

I laugh and fall back against the couch. "There's no place I'd rather be, doll."

"Cheeky all of a sudden, hmm?"

I stretch, trailing my hands up my body. "Am I?"

He watches me the whole way, and his dick absolutely twitches, coming back to life. Then he kneels on the floor next to me and throws the packs onto the coffee table. I reach my hands out for him and he gladly comes, easing himself next to me. The heat in his eyes broadcasts his desire, and I melt under his stare. "I'm ready for you to tear open one of those packages. Are you?"

He nods and shifts, pressing his hardening erection against my leg. I kiss him, sucking his tongue into my mouth. Connecting with Weston is urgent now, and I want more than his tongue inside me.

"Do you want to move into my bedroom, or are you comfortable here?"

His sectional is more like a couple of full-size beds pushed together, so I don't see the point in wasting time walking down the hallway. "Here. Now." I grunt out my response, pulling Weston on top of me, rubbing my legs against his, yearning for the friction of our bodies joining.

"Okay." He smiles against my mouth and reaches for the condom, moving away from me just long enough to sheath himself. I make room for him to fit between my legs, and when he nudges against my opening, I sink my teeth into my lip. His gaze is steady on my face. "Still ready?"

I push against him, trying to suck him within.

"Tell me, Ryan."

"Please get inside me right this minute, Weston Alessandro Everheart."

He grins and eases himself in ever so slowly, stretching me as he goes. I widen my legs to aid his introduction inside me. It's slow going at first, but when he's seated all the way inside, we only stare at each other. Tears prick my eyes because I never thought this would happen. I never imagined my best friend would become my love. "What are you thinking?"

"That I have everything I want." Then he kisses me and moves his hips. I match his movements and cup my hands around his neck, pulling the waves of his hair at the nape. Our movements are slow at first, maybe a little tentative. I would imagine Weston is making sure he doesn't hurt me by allowing my body to adjust to his. This friction is what I've been craving. He breaks the kiss and moves his mouth near my ear, his breath heavy on my neck. "Are you okay?"

I'm filled to capacity, but it feels good. "Very."

"Good." He quickens the pace, varying the rhythm, and sucks a nipple deep in his mouth.

I buck under him, taking him as deep as possible.

"I love your nipples." He squeezes my breasts in both hands, never breaking his stride.

As much as I love Weston's heavy body on top of me, I want to switch. "Let me on top."

He slows, painfully so, and finally withdraws because although the sofa is huge, it's not big enough for the two of us to change positions while connected. He lies back, and with his hands on my hips, I descend onto his hard cock straining toward me. I take my time until I'm comfortable, then when I move against him, my core clenches him, pulling him in for more.

"You look so hot up there, Ryan."

I try to grin, but I'm too horny and filled with lust. My arousal is maxed out looking for a release. Weston must understand because he sits up and our bodies shift, placing my clit right against him. He wraps his arms around me, pulling him flush against me, and it only take a second before I come, grunting and clawing at his back. He waits until I'm coming down before delivering a couple quick pumps and going still deep inside me.

He pulls me back down with him, and our hearts pound against each other. He kisses my forehead, then coaxes my face up. I angle up so he can kiss me, and I get lost in it so easily. He squeezes me, then puts a firm hand on the side of my head and drags his index finger lazily through my curls. "I could lie here with your forever."

I smile against his chest. "Same, West. Same."

I ONLY HAVE a moment to celebrate because we are super busy tonight, but I click off my laptop and execute a little shimmy behind my desk, hoping neither Kerry nor Nancy see me. Ace is working the front of house tonight, checking on customers and ensuring the waitstaff is running okay. I've already reviewed next week's schedule with Nancy and the monthly inventory report with Kerry. Now, I need to check on the back of house, especially since Flynn isn't here. Again.

Instead, I do the thing I'm not supposed to do because Weston is working tonight, too—I text him to meet me in the supply closet. As innocently as I can, I get up and slip my phone into my pocket. "I'm going to check on Andre and the others. I'll be back."

Nancy waves while gathering up her stuff. She's been here almost an hour past her usual time and not happy about it, considering the frown on her face and the pace in which she's packing her bag.

Kerry looks up from her spreadsheet. "Okay, uh, Ryan."

I can almost hear the *boss* she wanted to say, but since I've turned over a new leaf and ensure they're doing the duties they were hired for, I haven't heard the moniker much. I chuckle to myself as I walk down the hallway to the supply closet. This time last month, I would have been working through the schedule with Nancy, doing the bulk of the work, instead of reviewing it like today.

Patting myself on the back can wait because I'm going to smother Weston in kisses when he meets me. I slip through the door and make my way around the corner into the dark depths of the room behind the paper products.

Weston comes in two minutes later, creeping through

the space. We act like we're robbing the place. Or maybe sneaking around because we're not only breaking Flynn's rule, we're breaking the one I set when we decided to do this thing full throttle. If Flynn were working tonight, I wouldn't even chance it.

I stage-whisper, "Hey, over here."

He spots me and moves into the tight space, studying my face in the dim light. "Everything okay?"

"Yes, everything's great."

"Hmmmm." He draws his brows together and narrows his eyes. "If we get caught, you're not going to end things, are you?"

"That's fair." I stand on my tippy toes and kiss him full on the mouth, savoring his soft lips and strawberry taste. Vanilla and sugar whirl around me, pulling me closer. "Dang, I could eat you up right now."

"Not that I'm complaining—at all—but what are we doing here?"

I tamp down a squeal and raise my shoulders somewhere around my ears. "I made it to the semifinals. I'm going to New York."

Weston grabs my shoulders, and we jump up and down in the small space. "Oh my gosh, that's wonderful. I knew it, though."

I tap his shoulder. "Me, too." Then I giggle my butt off.

"Do you think, um…" He sort of shrugs, suddenly shy. "I could come with?"

"West, of course I want you to go with me." I jump up and wrap my arms around his shoulders.

He catches me and squeezes me so tight. "You're going

to kill it. I'm so happy for you."

I snuggle in his neck. "Thanks." I slide down his body, allowing my hands to trail over his chest and down his stomach. I remember where I am and stop my next move before I take it way too far up in here.

He places a hand over mine and squeezes it against his stomach, staring at me with want in his eyes.

I raise up to kiss him again, cupping a hand around his neck, my blood pumping fast through my veins.

He matches my heat, enveloping my mouth, his tongue tangling with mine before he abruptly steps back. "We better get out of here."

I blink a couple times, refocusing the reality around us. "I can't believe I lost my whole mind. Thanks for saving my job. Jeesh." I wipe the corner of my mouth and reach into my pocket for some lip gloss. Then wipe my finger across Weston's lips to ensure I haven't left any behind.

Weston clears his throat. "You go ahead. I'm going to stay here a minute before I go to Dad's bathroom to clean up."

I purse my lips. "You're not going to, uh…"

"Of course not, Ryan." He barks it in a harsh whisper but laughs to take the edge off, then shrugs. "I understand why you might think that, though."

"Your place later?"

He's nodding before I finish my sentence. "Definitely."

CHAPTER TWENTY

Birthday at Canyon Lake. Woo-hoo!

F OR THE FIRST time all summer, I'm actually happy about the heat. Weston introduces me to another Austin-area first—Canyon Lake. I've heard of it because one of our servers got married out here, but I really had no idea it was so huge. And nice. It probably puts Lake Conroe to shame, and I'm actually okay with that. Because now I'm making new memories with my best friend who's also my boyfriend.

Canyon Lake boasts being one of the cleanest lakes in Texas. That's something I've noticed about Weston—he usually picks the cleaner lakes, like Hippie Hollow. Maybe that has something to do with the fact that he loves being one with nature. I glance at him coming down the walkway—buck naked—and laugh under my breath. He makes me feel like my tankini swimsuit is a winter coat.

When he gets closer, I shade my eyes and look up from my perch on a reading bench right next to the water. "Aren't you afraid someone will see you?" Now I understand why he wanted such a big house with a quarter mile of private riverfront for just the two of us. I balked at the price when he booked it, but he convinced me by combining celebrations of advancing in the contest and my birthday. It still seems extravagant, though.

He leans down, and I meet him midway for a kiss. "That is never even on my radar. However, I do realize everywhere is not clothing optional, and I heed the surroundings." He purses his lips in thought—or maybe regret at streaking not being the norm.

"Are you sure you aren't part Dutch?"

"As far as I know, but Dad's side can be a mystery, so you never know. Supposedly the Everhearts are Irish and Welsh." He picks up two boards and waggles his eyebrows. "I think you're stalling. Tell me if you changed your mind. I'm not trying to force you into this motherlode of enjoyment."

"No, no. I want to learn, but I'm happy we brought the kayaks, too, though. That seems so much easier."

He looks at the boards, then hands me one. "I'm not going to lie, kayaking is a lot easier because of the fatigue factor, but we won't go long and definitely will quit if you get too tired."

I survey the huge board taking both my hands and arms to hold it, and frown. "Why's mine heavier looking than yours?"

"I bought you a beginner one. It's more stable."

"Wow, no pressure. Now I have to love it since you bought me a whole special board."

He laughs and shakes his head, then wades into the water with his board. "Nah, if you don't like it, we'll store it in the garage for when I teach our kids." He raises his brows in challenge, a wide grin splitting his face.

I don't even argue because in all honesty, that's what I

want with Weston, too. We just need to give it some time. Yeah, we've been friends forever, but testing the romance connection is important before we dive in. "Sure."

He cocks his head to the side and narrows his eyes, then his grin widens. "Give me that board. Don't forget your paddle. I've already sized your SUP paddle."

"My what paddle?"

"Your stand-up paddleboard paddle." He splashes a little water my way, totally giddy. I can't tell if it's for doing his favorite sport or my acquiescence to the kids comment. I'm inclined to believe the latter.

"Do you like this more than disc golf?" I wade out with my board balanced on the water and my paddle in hand.

Weston grimaces. "Please don't make me choose."

"So like a one A and one B, I guess. What's next, teach?"

He stands behind me, pressing all his nakedness against my back, and wraps his arms around me, nuzzling in my neck.

My knees go weak.

"What's next is let's just admire our surroundings for a moment. How beautiful is this?"

The lake isn't too wide here, and the landscape across from us belongs to someone else's private section because it's completely manicured and green. The trees are beautifully trimmed and a family of deer graze underneath. They must be accustomed to people because they don't pay us any mind. Or maybe they know it would take a bit of time to cross the lake to get to them.

It's morning and not too humid yet. Weston wanted to start early while the water is calm so I wouldn't be spooked.

I'm sure that's the best strategy, but who knows if it'll make a difference. "It's extremely beautiful and so peaceful. I know I was mad about the cost, but having all this to ourselves is amazing." I turn in his arms and raise my mouth to his, savoring the connection of our lips and our bodies.

Weston's cock makes itself known just a little, and he steps back. "Nudity might be acceptable if someone does wander down here, but we should probably go back to the house before starting anything else."

As tempting as that sounds, I want my lesson. Mostly because Weston has gone through the trouble of getting the board and setting everything up just perfect. Plus he's so excited about teaching me, I wouldn't want to steal that joy from him. "Don't try to get out of teaching me how to paddleboard, buddy."

He grins and kisses me again, then wades over to the board, giddy with excitement.

I CLEARLY WAS not made for paddleboarding.

Weston ices my sore biceps while we lounge on the porch swing. "You did great, Ryan. It's a lot more effort than people realize."

"Sure, okay. But we were only out there, like, ten minutes and my arms turned to noodles." I eye his strong arms, then frown. "Now I know why your arms are so cut. All this time, I thought you liked to paddleboard because it was fun."

"I do like it because it's fun, but yeah, it's a great

workout, too. If you do it enough, you won't even notice you're exercising."

I shrug, then wince.

Weston kisses me on the temple and hops up. "Let me get you an Advil."

I make a puppy-dog frown and droop my eyes. "Thanks, love."

He chuckles and strolls through the screen door.

I gingerly relax against cushions lining the back of the long swing. Three people could fit on here comfortably, which is nice because I'm able to stretch out a bit and still leave enough room for Weston. I take a look at the hammock strung up about halfway down to the lake and imagine what sort of wildness Weston and I could get up to. Then again, it probably can't hold that type of activity. I shrug and lie my head back because this house is billed as a three-bedroom, four-bathroom luxury lodge, which leaves plenty of places for us to let loose inside the house.

Weston returns with my pill and a glass of water. "What were you thinking about just now? You have a very naughty look on your face."

"Do I now?" I lift my brows aiming for seduction. The gesture probably falls somewhere around mild temptation.

If Weston notices, he doesn't show it. Instead he waits for me to swallow the pill, then strokes a thumb across my cheek, eyes dim with desire. "How long do you think that'll take to kick in?"

"Who needs arms?"

He laughs and leans in for a kiss, careful not to jostle me. I close the gap and pull his bottom lip into my mouth and suck. This sends a zing straight to my clit, and I've surprised myself. I open my eyes and giggle a bit, but the pure lust on Weston's face sobers me quickly. I taste his mouth again, coaxing his tongue inside, licking and nipping.

Weston breaks our kiss and swiftly moves from the swing to his knees, his dick at full attention.

I lay back and open my legs, lifting my butt in the air so he can remove the bottom of my swimsuit. "Hurry."

He makes quick work of it and settles his face between my thighs. "What do you want, Ryan?"

"I want you inside me."

He shakes his head. "You're sore."

"Okay, then I want you to eat me like that chocolate cake you made for my birthday dinner tonight."

He grins, a lopsided crease of his mouth, then touches the tip of his tongue to my clit. It's barely contact but enough for me to buck my hips. "Jaysus."

He hums near my core, then makes a languid lick through my slit. I want to reach for him, to grab fistfuls of his gorgeous hair, but he's right—my arms are sore. Instead I grind against his mouth as he sucks and licks down to my core. When he inserts two fingers and sucks my clit with intention, I'm undone. My belly tightens with anticipation and my breathing comes faster, a shallow pant. Weston holds on to my thigh and pumps his fingers faster until my orgasm shoots through me, gripping his fingers like a vice.

He holds on to me as I quiver, then finally calm and get my breathing under control. He sits back up on the bench and puts my legs on his lap but grips his rock-hard dick in his hand, then strokes, watching me the entire time. I lick my lips in anticipation as if I were hovering over his erection, waiting for it to erupt. It doesn't take him long to come, and it's glorious to watch him unravel.

When I release my lip, it's pained and creased. "Jeesh, that was intense. You are so amazing."

He barks a quick burst of laughter. "Why do you sound surprised?"

My cheeks flush with embarrassment. "Oh, West, I honestly never thought about it before. I mean, of course I thought about *it* before, but not really how you'd be. You're so incredibly sweet and kind and gentle."

He smiles but it's not his usual light-up-the-room face. "Thank you?"

"I'm sorry I'm so clumsy at this. Honestly, I'm giving you praise even if it doesn't sound like it. You are completely uninhibited and freaky deaky, and I love that about you."

This time he does laugh unabashedly, and that sound truly lights up my soul. I hope I'm never the cause of anything less than joy coming from Weston Everheart. We have to make this work because I would never forgive myself if it didn't.

FOR MY BIRTHDAY dinner, we feast on pizza and pasta from a local restaurant because I begged Weston not to make a big deal. All I really wanted from him was his famous chocolate-mousse cake, which I haven't seen since we arrived this morning and he took it out of my car in a special cake box.

I pick up one more slice of pizza because although I'm

saving room for dessert, it's so tasty and I never have pizza.

Weston frowns and shakes his head, swallowing a bite of his I-lost-count slice of pizza. "My ancestors are watching us right now and wondering how their blood could end up with someone who intentionally puts pineapple on her pizza."

"Is pizza really Italian?"

He sighs and allows his head to fall forward until his chin rests on his chest. "You're trying to kill me. Listen, I've heard pizza has been attributed elsewhere, but the way you think of pizza is all Italian, baby."

"Well, all right, *baby*. Hopefully that includes pineapple." I take another bite and grin around all that salty pepperoni and sweet goodness.

Weston shakes his head and removes the last piece from his box and folds it over and basically inhales it. Then he gets up and brings back two small but elegant plates and dessert spoons.

"You must have brought those from home."

"I did. Guess what else I brought from home?" He goes behind the counter and brings out a small gift bag and sets it on the table, then heads back into the kitchen.

I ponder the bag for a moment. It's too big for jewelry— thank goodness because I'm not a huge jewelry person. Although I would cherish anything from Weston. It's a tall-but-skinny bag like for wine almost. Hmmmm.

Weston comes back with the cake lit up with a jillion candles.

"Dang, how old do you think I am?"

He sets the cake down before me and shrugs. "I know. I just couldn't help myself." Then he claps his hands with glee.

"It's your birthday."

I just laugh and reach for his hand. "Thanks, West. I appreciate you so much."

He kisses me, then moves back. "I think you better hurry and make a wish before we set this place on fire."

I'm a little rushed, but there's only one wish that comes to mind. *I wish Weston and I will be in love forever.* Then I blow out the candles. It takes me three tries, but I hope that doesn't invalidate my wish. "Let's dig in."

"You aren't going to tell me your wish?"

I tilt my head and smile, then reach for his hand again and kiss the back. "Soon."

He cuts each of us a piece, and it's simply delicious. It's always good but somehow tastes even better knowing Weston made it special for me. "I love it, West. Thank you."

He pecks my lips quickly, then slides the gift bag over to me. "You ready to open your birthday gift?"

I release a long-suffering sigh. "I told you not to make a big deal. You already rented this amazing house and baked me my favorite cake. That's more than enough."

"It'll never be enough for you. Open." He smiles and rubs his hands together.

I reach in the box and my hand hits a box. I slide it out and draw my eyebrows in confusion. It appears to be some sort of doll. I glance at Weston, but he only shrugs, biting his lip. I open the box and pull out the...bobblehead? When I study it, there's something familiar about it. I sit it up, and that's when I realize it's me. "What in the world?"

"It's you in your usual ensemble you wear to work. It's a boss lady but custom made to look like you."

I blink. "Oh, wow. That's um amazing." Okay, I guess this means Weston is flawed. He's a shitty gift-giver, but that's okay because it truly is the thought that counts. "Thanks, West." I kiss his cheek, which quivers under my lips.

When I pull back, the laugh he was trying to hold in bursts through his lips. "Oh my goodness, your face."

"Wait. What?"

He reaches under the table and pulls out a bigger gift bag. "Sorry, I just couldn't resist messing with you. I still think the bobblehead will be perfect on your desk, but here's your real gift." He sobers and swipes the tears of laughter from his eyes. "I hope you like it."

My palms are slick when I reach for the new, bigger bag. I'm absolutely terrified to open it, but I look up to him and smile. "I'll love anything from you, West."

He grins and leans forward, elbows on his thighs, hands steepled.

Again when I reach into this new bag, my hand hits another box. It's much larger and flatter, though, and when I pull it out, it's a perfect square, but there's nothing on the outside to give away its contents. I separate the tape on one end, then slide out another box. Only this one has a transparent top and there's a gold disc underneath. The record label reads *Happy Birthday, Ryan! Love always, Weston.* My eyes prick with tears, and I look up to him.

He smiles at me, a toothless grin, with eyes filled with love. "I made you a mixtape."

There're five songs—all my favorites, and I think back to all the times Weston and I jammed together, danced together, relaxed together. All those moments as friends, but this is something special. Tears streak down my face, and I reach for him. "It's perfect, West."

He wraps me up in a gentle hug, rubbing my back, and kissing away my tears.

"Thank you so much." Then a thought occurs to me. "Oh, I'll need to buy a record player."

"Already taken care of. I texted the twins to pick it up from my garage, and they've already set it up and been blasting it. It's Bluetooth as well as an old-fashioned record player. I hope your neighbors don't get mad."

"How am I going to top this in just three weeks for your birthday?"

"I thought Virgos always had a plan?"

"I will before then."

"Just tell me what your wish was, and that's gift enough for me."

"I'll tell you, but that's not your birthday gift." I lean forward until our faces are nearly touching. "I wished that we'll love each other forever." I kiss him until I taste his salty tears. "I love you, Weston. So much."

"I love you, Ryan."

And of course I know. I've always known.

CHAPTER TWENTY-ONE

It's for Weston's own good. Maybe.

WHEN I PULL up to Mimi and Papa's house, I frown from the lack of parking. There sure are a lot of cars here considering Papa wanted me to help him set up the new Fire Stick Lisa gave him. They finally cut cable loose after we've all been after them for at least a year.

After driving past their house, I finally find a spot on the street that isn't in front of someone's mailbox or trash can. I side eye their neighbor setting the trash out so early when they know it won't be picked up until early in the morning.

The driveway is stacked two deep, and I notice Meagan and Saron's car near the garage. What are they doing here? I check the time on my watch and realize school's out. Maybe they stopped by for a visit. If I had known, I would've let one of the twins set up the streaming device.

There's music coming from out back, so I unlatch the gate and go through to the backyard, passing Papa's newly planted garden. There's a row with a picture of Swiss chard at the beginning, and I shake my head. I'm still not completely over what Diedra said about Weston. She doesn't deserve all these greens.

When I make it around the house, several pairs of eyes

turn my way. Then there's so much chatter and whoops and people rushing me, I hardly have time to get my bearings.

Darryl squeezes me and lifts me off the ground, turning in a circle. "Congrats, cuz."

I laugh and slap at his shoulders. "Boy, put me down."

When he does set me back on the ground, more cousins and aunts and uncles are there to take his place with plenty of hugs and taps on my back.

Naomi finally makes it through the thrash of bodies and hugs my neck. "We're so proud of you."

"For what?"

"Girl, what? For making the finals in New York."

"That's what's happening? Oh my gosh, it's only the semifinals."

Diedra slaps me on the back, a little harder than called for, and grins. "Same difference. We know you'll win it all, fam."

My eyes gain a little moisture out of nowhere. No matter our occasional differences, my family always shows up for me. "I can't believe you're all here. Thank you so much."

"Y'all let the girl breathe. Come on in the house and fix your plates." Papa hangs out the screen door waving the crowd in.

Naomi links my arm through hers, and we follow our family into the house.

"Who cooked?"

She bumps my arm. "Everheart's catered."

I grin. "I have the best boyfriend ever."

"That may be true, but this was his father."

I stop midstride before we get to where Papa's standing.

"You're kidding." To say I'm shocked would be an understatement. I figured Flynn knew I made it in because the contest organizers would have notified him since he submitted me, but I found out nearly a week ago and have seen him twice and he didn't mention a word. So I didn't, either.

"I'm not kidding."

Papa clears his throat.

"Sorry, Papa." We say it in stereo and walk through the door.

He kisses me on the cheek as I pass. "Congratulations, baby."

"Thanks." My voice catches in my throat, and I have to clear it. "You really didn't need your Fire Stick set up, huh?"

"Sure I did, but Darryl took care of it."

"That was nice of him." I glance around at everyone fixing their plates, not waiting for the guest of honor, then chuckle. That's my family for you.

Naomi pulls on my arms again, and we head through the kitchen to the living room. Mimi sits in her comfy chair looking like the queen she is, dressed in a gold housedress. I bend down and kiss her cheek. "Hey, Mimi. You look beautiful as usual."

She pats her hair and grins. "Oh, shucks."

Aunt Mavis brings in a plate and sets up Mimi's TV tray.

Naomi tugs on me again. "Let's wash our hands. I'm starved."

Suddenly I am, too. "What's for dinner?"

"Mmmm, there's crab cakes, steak salad, mashed potatoes, creamed spinach, king salmon, and filets."

I release a low whistle. "Wow, that's the elite level for

catering. Not the highest level, but close." I'd love to know how Kerry hid the extra inventory from me. Then again, I've been letting them do their jobs, so I guess that's how.

"Huh, I'd hate to see the highest level."

"Girl, you really wouldn't. I still can't believe Flynn Everheart did this. Color me shocked, for sure."

We walk back through the living room and Mimi is savoring a bite of food with her eyes closed. She was always such a great cook but hasn't made a meal in some years now. I'm happy she still enjoys food, though.

When we get back to the kitchen, mostly everyone has cleared out to the backyard, but there's plenty of food left for us. "Wow, people will be able to take some home for later."

"He sure knows how to congratulate someone."

I snort.

"Oh, and Weston did send you a little something special. It's in the fridge, and I gave strict instructions for nobody to touch it."

"Oh, yum. I know it'll be decadent. I hate that he's working and can't be here."

Naomi hands me a plate and starts loading up her own. "That is too bad. I can't even tell you how happy I am that you two finally got it together."

"Finally?" I pick up a garlic roll and inhale the buttery goodness. Weston definitely made these.

"Yes, finally. Weston is a very patient man. That should work well for you in the future." She giggles and bumps my shoulder, still piling more food on her plate.

I'm sure there's an insult in there for me somewhere, but she's right. Weston has the best temperament for me—we just click—but there's just that one small puzzle piece missing.

I pick up the tongs and lift one of the filets onto my plate joining a piece of salmon and spinach. I nibble at the roll while thinking if I want to jump into the deep end or not. "So, Naomi."

She raises her eyebrows, then picks up silverware and a napkin. "Yes?"

We take our full plates over to the kitchen table instead of going in the backyard with the rest of the family. I want to talk to Naomi alone away from prying ears. Before I answer her, I walk back to the living room and look in on Mimi and Papa. "Do you need something to drink, or do you have everything you need?"

Papa lifts up a glass filled with a red liquid, mouth full and chewing.

I sit down at the table with Naomi and cut a piece of meat. "Remember when we talked a few weeks ago about Weston's manuscript?"

She stuffs a forkful of salmon in her mouth but nods.

"Well, I want to send it to you—unofficially, of course— so you could give me your honest opinion on it. I think it's fresh and the writing is incredible, but of course you'd know better than I would. I'm just a reader, and you're a big-time editor."

She nearly spits her food out. As it is, she picks up her napkins and wipes her mouth. "Laying it on a little thick, huh?"

"Not at all. I haven't told any lies."

"Mmmm."

"So, what do you think?"

"Personally I think you should get Weston's permission first, but if you truly mean unofficially, then I'll take a look. But on my personal time, off the books."

"Exactly. I just feel like if he had someone else's validation—someone's other than mine—he would have the confidence to pursue writing. I thought he was a talented pastry chef, but he may have missed his calling."

She swallows a sip of water, then puts another bite of food in her mouth, this time a piece of her garlic roll. Her eyes roll to the back of her head. "I can't imagine he'd be better at anything than this, but I'll let you know what I think."

"Thanks, Naomi. That's all I'm asking."

We enjoy the rest of our meal, and it's extra tasty because one, Flynn was thoughtful for once in his life, and two, Weston's words will finally be in someone's hands who can convince him of his higher purpose.

I smile to myself on how much of a great girlfriend I am.

I ANSWER THE video call as soon as I see Cynthia's smiling face. "Hey there. You've been on my mind."

She grins and nods vigorously. "Same. I thought to myself, *Let me drop everything now and call.* How's everything been? How are the girls?" A twinkle lights her eyes. "And Weston?"

"We're all great. Weston's at work and the girls are at school. I'm just getting some pre-packing for New York because I won't have time after today."

"Great idea." She squeals and shimmies her shoulders. "I'm so excited for you. How do you feel about all of it?"

Forever the therapist. She sounds just like Dr. Okoner. *How do you feel when your cousin makes accusations you try to change those you love?* I chuckle. I feel like kicking Diedra's booty, but I couldn't say that. "I feel good. I'm at peace that if I don't win, I have support and we'll figure it out as a family. I'm gonna win it, though."

"I'm so happy to hear that, Ryan. But what do you mean by 'we'll figure it out'?"

"I've been working with my therapist, as you know, and I'm coming to realize I can ask for help sometimes."

She strokes her chin in thought. "So if, for instance, Lisa or Naomi offered to pay for the gap in tuition and room and board, you'd allow it."

I bite my lip, thinking how I want to respond. I wouldn't accept money from my cousins—they do enough already. I won't accept money from Weston, either, for obvious reasons. "I mean that if I don't win the money to cover the gap, I'll talk with the girls about options."

She smiles but raises her brows.

"More than likely the twins will need to get jobs. It was a pain when I was in grad school, but I made it through. They will, too, if necessary. And if Saron really wants to go to Howard, she may have to take out a student loan to pay the difference. I'll help her pay it back."

"Wow, baby. You've only been seeing Dr. Okoner a few weeks and this is wonderful progress. I had a feeling she'd be good for you."

I beam under her praise. All I ever want is to take care of my family and friends, but now realize I can't put them all on my shoulders. Most of them don't want to be there anyway. I think back to handing over Weston's manuscript to Naomi and wonder if I've made a mistake.

"She is. I'm glad you recommended her." It helps she can do video sessions and even text when needed. That's part of the reason I'd gone without therapy so long despite knowing deep in my heart I needed it desperately. It wasn't very convenient.

"So you've worked through everyone isn't your responsibility. Have you gotten to the root of that yet?"

Cynthia throws out that question ever so slickly, almost like she really doesn't care about the answer. I smirk. "You almost sound like a therapist. Oh, wait…"

She laughs and shakes her head.

"I think that I'm a nurturer by nature and maybe believe I know it all and am the *it won't get done right unless I do it* type. But I think we both know when Mama and Daddy died, that activated those underlying tendencies. And my guilt took over big-time."

She gives me a sad smile and wipes at the corner of her eye.

Mention of my parents brings tears to my eyes as well, but I blink them back.

"Do you still harbor the guilt?"

I'm quiet a moment, surveying my feelings. "Sometimes. Intellectually I understand it isn't my fault. I truly understand that. But then there are times the memories creep in of that night. It's so vivid. Mom standing by the breakfast bar in the kitchen looking through her purse and me begging her to drive me to the game." I allow the tears to fall now because I've never really told anyone the next part. "She actually started crying because she was so tired and still needed to make dinner, but that didn't move me at all. Then Daddy came through the door and saw what was happening. He put gentle arms around Mama and said he'd take her to dinner while I was at the game as long as you could watch the girls." I suck in a ragged breath. "You know the rest."

"Oh, Ryan. I wish I were there to give you a big hug. Sometimes teenagers can be self-centered. It comes with the territory I'm afraid."

I snort. "Oh, you don't have to tell me. The twins have been my change. They've given it back to me in spades."

"Well, sounds like you truly are making progress, and I know you're going to be a superstar at that competition." She looks away from the camera again, wiping her eyes. When she comes back, she has a bright smile plastered on. "Now tell me all about Weston."

"I'm not sure what you want to know. You've already been around him a ton. You know how kind he is. He's a wonderful human. And a super-talented writer." I feel the pang about that manuscript again.

"Yes, what I meant is tell me all about Weston and you."

I wipe my eyes with the heel of my hand, then look up at Cynthia through the phone, hesitating.

"You know what happened between me and Connie is ancient history. And it was a different time and circumstance than you and Weston. She had to choose between me and her family, and she chose them even though they only wanted to 'cure' her." She shrugs and takes a deep breath, then smiles. "Tell me."

I smile and lift my shoulders to somewhere around my ears. "I love him. Completely."

She clasps her hands and grins, tears flowing again.

And I know exactly how she feels.

CHAPTER TWENTY-TWO

I'm in it to win it. Facts.

WHEN WE STEP through the door of the hotel, the first thing I spot is the coffee shop. "Oh, thank goodness."

Weston swivels his head my way. "What?"

"Coffee right here in the lobby."

He grins at me and shakes his head. "Ryan, there's, like, ten levels of conference rooms and restaurants. I'm sure there's coffee everywhere."

I shrug because technically he's right, but this is a familiar coffee shop and New York is a bustling place with everything shiny. And metal. And loud. I'll take a comfort of home where I can get it. "We all can't be world travelers like you, dear."

"Awww." He kisses me on the temple, then walks over to the information desk.

The woman behind the desk is dressed in the black uniform of the hotel with a name tag that reads *Sharon*.

I recognize the moment she spots Weston coming her way because she pushes her breasts out and sucks her stomach in, plastering a huge smile on her face. "Welcome. How may I help you?"

Weston, as cheerful and friendly as ever, gives her a wide

smile. Poor woman. "Hi, Sharon. I'm Weston, and we're looking for the registration desk."

"We?" She looks around, and when she spots me, I wave and grin. Her posture deflates to normal. "Yes, Mr., er, Weston, please take these elevators to the third floor. Make sure you take the ones on the left because the others are express."

"Thank you so much, Sharon. You've been a huge help." He flashes her another megawatt smile and comes back to me and grasps my hand. "Third floor, my lady."

I only laugh and thread my fingers through his. I adjust my overnight bag on my shoulder, and we step onto the elevator. Weston carries the bulk of our luggage, which isn't a whole lot since we'll only be here two nights and neither of us are clothes horses. I did have to bring a couple of nice outfits for the competition, though. And a fancy evening dress for the awards banquet.

When we step off the elevator, there's a line leading to the registration desk which spans two walls. At least seven or eight employees dressed the same as Sharon man the computers behind the desk.

Weston sets our biggest bag at his feet and turns to me. "What do you think of New York so far?"

"Well, the airport was fine. A lot bigger than Austin's, of course." I flew out of Houston a few times, but only from terminal C when we visited my uncle on Mama's side in Chicago, so I can't really compare. "And it was really neat driving through Queens, which I've only heard about in television shows. It's a lot different than I expected."

He nods. "Wait until we get out and explore tomorrow

after the morning competition."

The hustle and bustle of the city is already wearing on me, but I don't want to bust Weston's bubble. He seems intent on showing me a good time here, even though my mind is solely on the competition. If it makes him happy, though, I'll roll with it.

Once we've checked in, we wait for an express elevator to take us up to the fifty-sixth floor. Only these elevators are in no way express because it takes nearly ten minutes for us to get on a free one. I watch him over the head of a woman who wedged herself between us in the full box.

He smiles and shrugs.

When we step off, Weston leads me down a long hall, a turn, then another long hall until we finally step in front of our room. I slide the card key in front of the screen and the door clicks open. We step through, and I...don't really do anything. Even though we're in a skyscraper hotel next to the theater playing *Hamilton*, it's just a regular hotel room. There's a small bathroom to the right and an even smaller closet to the left, where I deposit the bag I'm holding.

Weston moves the remainder of our luggage into the closet, then looks around the rest of the room.

There's a huge bed centered on the right wall and a mini fridge, dresser, and desk on the left wall. Another sofa chair sits next to the huge picture window.

Weston pulls the drapes back and gasps, as he is known to do. "Ryan, come see?"

The view is incredible. It extends all the way down to the river with tree-lined cozy streets connecting us. It's hard to believe that where we are, with concrete and tall buildings all around, borders a quaint neighborhood of row houses and small restaurants. "It's amazing. Seriously."

He clasps his hands, practically vibrating with excitement and anticipation. "I was hoping to be able to see the park, but this seems so much better." Then he pulls me into a hug and rubs his cheek on the top of my head. "I'm so excited for you."

I laugh against his chest. "I believe you but think you may be a little excited for yourself, too."

He leans back, still connected to me. "I am, but mostly because this trip is for you. I know it's work related and you're doing it for your sisters, but you get to see New York. I hope it'll be a special trip because you deserve it and so much more."

Mist clouds my eyes at the way he looks at me, sincere and loving. He wants the best for me, and I'm finally discovering that maybe what I thought was my best—making enough money to care for my sisters, working hard to excel in my career, and keeping my family close to be there for them—may not be all there is to life. Maybe, just maybe, I can take a little for myself.

I reach up to cup the back of his neck and stretch against his body. "I love you so much." Then I put my lips to his and glide my tongue across his mouth. He opens readily, capturing my tongue in his mouth and sucking it inside. I grab at his T-shirt and try to remove it, but he's much too tall for me to get it over his head. He laughs and pulls it over in one swoop. Then shucks his shorts before I can back up good.

Weston's in front of the window in all his naked glory.

"Hey, come here. Can't people see you?"

He shrugs, then looks over his shoulder. "Maybe, but I'm in my room, so if they're looking, that's their business."

I shake my head and back up some more, then turn and head to the bathroom to turn on the shower. Even though it isn't a huge room, the shower is a nice size and I want to wash the plane off before we go any further. I strip off my pants and call to Weston out the door. "I think we can both fit, if you want."

He appears a second later, hard dick in hand. "I definitely want."

"You always want. And I'm not mad about it." I unbutton my blouse and toss it to the floor with my pants. "Condom?"

He snaps his fingers, then rummages through the luggage and returns with a strip. He laughs at the expression on my face. "For later."

"Okay because I'm starved." I hook my finger, beckoning him to follow me into the shower.

He grins. "Me, too." Then accompanies me in.

I TAKE THE elevator down to the sixth floor, then the escalator the remainder of the way because the only elevators available didn't go to the fourth floor, where the first set of competitions are being held. There's plenty of bustle in the area with several doors leading to conference rooms. More than likely, there's a multitude of other conferences and events going on, considering the size of this hotel.

After a quick trip to the bathroom to adjust my blazer and ensure my pants are zipped and all hairs in place, I check my welcome packet one last time, then glance around to find the meeting room. I open the heavy door and enter the cavernous room. There are several people milling about and chatting between about ten large rounds.

Although we had a room-service breakfast with coffee, I walk over to the carafes for more just to have something to do. I don't know anyone here, and all the others are men. Not one single woman in sight and only one other person of color, who's alone at one of the tables.

I make my way over to his table and sit across from him. The table is large enough that we wouldn't have to even speak but we could if we choose to.

He looks up and smiles, then looks around and back to me, tilting his head as if to acknowledge the lack of diversity in the room. He stands and comes around the table, hand outstretched. "Hi, William Green. Nice to meet you."

I stand and accept the handshake. "Ryan Landry. It's great to meet you as well."

"I'm in from Seattle. First time in New York."

"Same. I mean, my first time in New York, too. I'm from Austin."

He nods. "I've heard it's a great town. Live music capital, right?"

"Exactly that. It's the best feature, although I don't get to enjoy it as much as I'd like."

"I understand that too well." He gestures his hand toward my chair. "Please, have a seat. Do you mind if I move a little closer so we can chat?"

"Not at all."

William goes back to his seat to pick up his welcome packet and a bottle of water. There are pads with pens scattered around the table, which is handy but I brought my laptop just in case. There's also glasses filled with cold water. Also handy because I didn't think to bring any, unlike William.

When he sits next to me, he leans in. "Not too much diversity, is it?"

I chuckle. "Not at all, but reflective of our industry unfortunately." If I had to guess, I'd put William at around forty. "How long have you been managing?"

"Only about five years at this level. I've been in the service industry about ten years. Before that, I was a CPA." He shudders. "That didn't last long. Just wasn't a good fit, but I love what I do now. Mixing with all different types of people, the hustle and bustle of the day-to-day. It's exciting." He takes a sip of water. "Please excuse me. As you can see, I'll talk you under the table if you let me."

"Not at all. It's great hearing the enthusiasm in your voice."

"Yeah. Do you not love it?"

I thought I did, but after Flynn pointed out my major flaw, it's been a bit of a struggle to not let my natural inclination take over. That part hasn't been fun, but I'm getting used to it. "I enjoy the work, but I'm not sure I love it as much as you."

He nods. "Understand. It's not for everybody. Lots of long hours, cranky chefs, missing waitstaff, and unappreciative customers." He chuckles. "Wait, why do I like this again?"

"There's also satisfaction of keeping everyone on track toward a collective goal, joining in the creation of something fantastic, and relishing the compliments of those customers who keep coming back." I have a tingle in my veins, a reminder why I wanted to do this to begin with.

"Ah, sounds like you remembered why you do this."

"Pretty much. I'm bossy and want to run everything, so this job works out well. I'm not a fan of the long hours, though."

He takes a long pull of his water and sighs. "It can be a hardship. Do you have a family?"

"Twin sisters. They're about to graduate from high school and leave me, though. You?"

He reaches for his phone and turns it on swiping a couple times, then shows it to me. "That's my wife, Rebecca, and our daughters, Abigail and Eleanor. They're in middle school."

"Oh, beautiful family. I bet they miss you."

"Rebecca is upstairs. We're lucky enough that our parents live close by, so they're watching over the girls. I'm thankful they're able to help out so much, or this job may not have been an option."

"I bet your wife was excited for the trip."

"Very much so. I can't wait until we can take in the city together. She's been before and has family in Queens, so we'll drop by there, too. Are you on your own? You mentioned your sisters, but I imagine they're in school."

"They are." Then I smile, thinking about Weston waiting for me upstairs. I left him stuffing down a huge stack of pancakes but ignoring the croissants. He said they weren't right, although they tasted fine to me. He'd know, though. "Actually my boyfriend came with me. He's been here before, too, and has a whole agenda of things he wants to show me once we wrap up today." I get a little tingle because I'm not a hundred percent sure but I think that's the first time I've ever called Weston my boyfriend to a stranger before.

William opens his mouth to speak, but several men and two women come through another door and seat themselves at the long table in the front of the room. He rubs his hands together and picks up a pen. If they give away prizes for enthusiasm, William is definitely their man.

The other occupants find seats around the various tables, but nobody joins us at ours. It's unfortunate because as much as I'm here to compete with these men, it's always good to network. Perhaps later.

One of the new arrivals, a stout older man with a shaved head, approaches the microphone in the middle of their head table. "Good morning, everyone. I'm Jonathan Miller, and I'd like to welcome you to the first round of competition." He goes on to outline the agenda for the morning.

I look at my paper to note which room I should go to and what time.

William appears to be doing the same. "Looks like I'm up."

"Me, too."

We ride the escalator together, and I check in on my feelings. I should be nervous, considering what's riding on this, but I'm not. I perform for people on the daily. Not just our customers but our staff, too. If I show nervousness, that doesn't bode well for getting what we need accomplished. Besides, I've been told I'm akin to a duck: Calm above the surface but furiously paddling below. I smile at the comparison and step off the escalator.

"Good luck, Ryan."

"Good luck to you, William."

CHAPTER TWENTY-THREE

The city that never sleeps. Yawn.

WITH ROUND ONE in the books and my golden ticket punched, I'm ready to hit the town. William made it through as well, and I found myself genuinely happy for him. Tomorrow morning will be the final competition, then the awards ceremony that evening. There's nothing I can do to prepare, so I plan to enjoy the rest of the day with my love and get to bed early.

When Weston and I step off onto the busy sidewalk, I back up into the hotel.

"What's wrong, Ryan?"

"There are so many people out there. Do you know where we're going?"

He squeezes my hand and moves us over to the wall near the coffee shop. He strokes my cheek with the back of his hand and smiles. "I'm sorry."

"Goodness, for what?"

"I'm doing the thing where I think I know what's best and just do it instead of checking in with you. We don't have to go anywhere. We can stay in our room all day, and I'll be just as happy as long as I'm with you."

I kiss him on the cheek. "You're too good for this world,

West." I grab his hand and stiffen my spine. "Let's have a look at this little city."

This time when we walk on the sidewalk, I take in my surroundings—but only what's right around me instead of looking down the block. "Okay, I have my tennis shoes on and these shoes are made for walking. Where to?"

Weston actually groans and puts his hands over his ears.

I tap him on the shoulder. "It wasn't that bad."

He raises one brow and dips his chin, then grimaces. "If you say so." He takes my hand in his. "This way. We can have a little Cuban food, then walk over to Rockefeller Center, then over to the park. I really want you to see Belvedere Castle. You can see where they perform Shakespeare in the Park from there."

Whew, I wasn't kidding. I'm happy I wore my tennis shoes because that sounds like a lot of walking. "Sounds great. As long as we're back for an early bedtime."

"We'll be back in plenty of time. There's a place on our street going toward the river that has great dumplings."

We wait at the light, and I notice a grandstand with bunches of people sitting on it. "What's going on over there?"

"They release theater tickets, so people are waiting to see if they can get into the show they want last minute."

"Oh, cool." We cross the street, and I look up at the iconic sky-high monitors broadcasting movies, music, and clothes. "Neat."

Weston follows my gaze and smiles. "The restaurant is right across the street. It's touristy, but they have great food."

After a lunch with assorted filled *tostones* cups, *costillas glaseadas con salsa de guayaba*, *pimientos rellenos*, and *arroz con camarones*, we stroll to Rockefeller Center and hunt for the Jacques Torres chocolate chip cookies I read about in a young adult book. We circle the building where we think it's supposed to be, but the phone GPS is vague.

There so many people milling about, window shopping, or eating on benches, so I sit down on one while Weston shades his eyes and looks up. "It has to be that building, but it looks like a concert hall or something." He looks down at his phone again and shrugs. "Let's just go in."

"Okay." We have to cross a bit of a plaza, then back up the steps to the same building we've passed fifty-leven times and ruled out. But when we do step in, it seems to be some sort of office building. Then we walk in farther, and it transforms into a shopping center. "Wow, who woulda thunk it?"

Weston shakes his head, then holds out his hand for mine. "I can't believe this was in here the whole time. Okay, let's find this cookie shop next."

It takes us a couple of false starts up and down stairs, down hallways that end in nothing, before we descend to the basement level where there are several food shops. We finally find the store with all things chocolate, and I'm a bit...underwhelmed. It's super small, with a limited eating area on one side and on the other, a display case with different treats lined up. In the open area, there are shelves of packaged goods. I pick up a couple tins of hot chocolate mix for the twins.

When we check out and make it back onto the plaza, I reach into my bag and pull out one of the cookies, then take a bite. I close my eyes, waiting for the nirvana to hit me, but the sensation never comes. When I open my eyes, Weston is waiting expectantly. "They're not even half as good as yours. You could bake this guy under the table."

He grins and puts his arm around my shoulder. "I'm sorry you're disappointed. I don't think they make the cookies there. More than likely, they're made at the main store and brought over. You probably didn't get a fresh batch."

"Seriously, West. You could set up shop and make millions of dollars because your pastries are otherworldly."

"If only that were my goal in life." He pulls me in for a hug and then we walk down the sidewalk toward the park arm in arm.

I'm tempted to ask Weston what his goal in life is, but I'm a coward. I want everything in the world for him. Not just because I love him but because he's talented and such a good person. I wish he had the confidence to know that about himself, but I'm afraid he doesn't. Not even close.

When we reach the park, there's more zigzagging and false starts to find the castle. We happen upon the Tavern on the Green restaurant, and there appears to be a wedding reception happening because a carriage pulls up and a woman dressed in a ball-gown-style wedding dress stands and her supposed husband dressed in a tux helps her down. I turn to Weston and grin. "Can you imagine?"

He laughs and nods.

"Pretentious." We both say at the same time, then fall out giggling.

Weston puts an arm around my shoulder, and we stand there gawking. He leans down near my ear. "Very romantic, though. You have to admit."

"Begrudgingly." I pull out of his grasp and reach for his hand. "Let's blow this Popsicle stand. You promised me a castle."

"For you, milady, the world."

He lets me lead him while still checking his phone for the right direction. We stop at a fork in the path, and Weston places his hands on his hips, looking both ways.

A couple walks near us, and I raise a hand and wave. "Hi, excuse us. Do you know the way to Belvedere Castle?"

The man looks at his companion, and they shake their heads. "Never heard of it."

"Oh, okay. Thanks." I turn to Weston then with raised brows. "Are you sure this is a real place? I haven't seen any signs for it."

His face is creased in confusion. "I...I mean, of course it is. I've actually been there before." He lets out a huff of a laugh. "These people have me doubting myself. Surely they haven't moved the entire castle. It's a real weather station, for crying out loud."

I shrug and pick a course. I'm guessing, with my luck, up is the way to go because G-d forbid I take the easy route. "Come on, West." I grumble under my breath, "This place better be spectacular."

"I heard that, love."

I grin back at him.

After another twenty minutes of walking, a sign points up a steep staircase—*Belvedere Castle*. I don't even turn around but grind it out up these stairs until we get to the top, then lean forward with my hands on my thighs, breathing hard.

Weston stands next to me, rubbing my back, and taking pictures with his phone. He's not even winded.

When I stand, there's another set of steps for us to conquer, and we walk over to the wall, overlooking water and beyond that, bleachers for the outside theater. The city stretches out all around us. I turn and marvel at the building we came to see. "Wow, it's a real castle."

Weston bumps my arm. "Of course. What did you think it'd be?"

"I just figured it was a facade for people to take pictures or something."

He scratches his chin, glancing up. "Now that you mention it, I think when I was here last time, I read they initially meant to build something like that but then changed it to serve the weather station." He spins and pulls me back into his chest. "You want to take some pictures?"

"Definitely."

I fumble with my cell phone, and because his arms are so much longer, I hand it over so he can take some selfies of us. I look at the photos while he bends to tie his shoe. We're both so...happy. Smiling eyes and wide grins. And in one, Weston looks down at me and any stranger could see he loves me. I look at him while he rises out of his crouch. "I love you, West."

He tilts his head and smiles. "I love you. So much." Then he wraps me up in a tight hug and the city falls away around us. There's just the two of us, hearts pounding against each other. His natural vanilla-and-sugar scent envelopes me in joy and affection, and I realize that while I may not deserve him, I'm happy I have him.

THIS MORNING'S FINAL round begins earlier than yesterday's, and when I walk into the main conference room, it's been transformed. They've created a restaurant since yesterday morning's interviews and announcement of the finalists. It's a shell of a restaurant but set up to replicate a fine-dining establishment with front-of-house seating and back-of-house kitchen. There's even facades of a storage room and walk-in freezer.

The judges are gathered in the front. Although we didn't meet them formally yesterday, we learned who the three finalist judges would be. Chef Buccola is the first to greet us with a warm handshake. An older man nods at us, and a third man about Flynn's age actually hugs us in turn. His personality is almost bigger than the entire room. He finally introduces himself as Chef Kessler.

They've set up a breakfast buffet in the corner since it's so early. William meets me near the plates and leans near me, lowering his voice. "The quiet man is Chef Cornwell. Brilliant chef, but not big on personality."

I laugh, sure to keep my movements behind a raised plate. "I hadn't noticed." Ah, sarcasm, like the warm blanket of my youth. I'm certain if my parents are able to see me nowadays, they're extremely happy I lost my touch for it. It ruled supreme during my teenage years. For the first time in a long while, my eyes don't mist when thinking of them. "What do you know about Chef Kessler? His name is so familiar."

"I believe he has a restaurant in Napa. Have you heard anything about Chef Buccola? I watched him on that TV show over the summer. What's it called?" He snaps his fingers. "*Restaurant Feud.*"

I laugh again. Being with William totally takes my mind off the competition coming up. Not that I was really nervous to begin with, but I'm definitely more relaxed now. "It's called *Restaurant Family Feud*, and my boyfriend was on it this season."

He claps his hands together, then looks around. "I thought Everheart sounded familiar when you said where you work, but I didn't make the connection." His eyes widen and he grimaces. "So the father who replaced the son who left is your boss."

I add some fruit to my plate and turkey sausages and eggs plus a piece of wheat toast. I want plenty of energy this morning, so I load up with more than I usually do for the first meal of the day. "He's not as bad as the show portrayed him. There was some creative editing." I want to *donk* myself on the head for defending Flynn. I guess it's a case of *I can talk about him, but nobody else can*. The truth is the show did do a bit of editing, but he gave them plenty material to work with.

William chuckles and pours himself a glass of orange juice. "I hope so, for your sake. Which son is your boyfriend? The one who left?" He holds up the carafe, asking a question.

I nod and grab a glass from the table. "No, he's the pastry chef. Weston."

"I remember him. A strapping fellow towering over everyone. He looked as though he could go a few rounds with Tyson but was so kind. He really treated everyone so well. At least that's how the show cut it."

"No, that's very much Weston's personality. He's the best."

We walk over to the table they've set up for the three of us. Our third, Andre, hasn't made it here yet.

"Well, did he give you any good intel on Chef Buccola?"

There's no need telling him all about the drama between Flynn, Knox, and Chef Buccola. It's mostly on Flynn's part anyway and doesn't apply for this competition. "I've only heard really nice things about Chef Buccola. Weston's brother, Knox, works for him as a consultant, and he enjoys his job. I hadn't met him before today, though."

He nods, and we eat our food in mostly silence because we don't have a lot of time before we get started. Andre makes it just as we're finishing up and grabs a Danish and coffee as we're led to another staging room.

Andre takes a big gulp of his coffee. "Morning."

William and I nod and both mumble, "Morning," at the same time.

One of the contest organizers comes in and lays down the events for this morning. We've already been prepped from yesterday, but this serves as a reminder. We'll each have a separate turn back in the "restaurant" dealing with obstacles that normally arise during the course of a service.

William is up first, so that leaves me and Andre in the small room alone. We haven't spoken more than three words to each other. Yesterday, he was in the *it* group who didn't pay a lot of attention to me and William. I have no interest in getting to know him, and there's nothing else I can do to prepare for what's to come other than what I've been doing the past few years, so I pull a book out of my bag and read.

The next time I look up is when they come for me. I pack my book away and follow the organizer back to the main conference room. I have to keep my mouth from falling over when we walk through the door because I'm met with absolute chaos.

I recognize the other contestants from yesterday who are playing characters in this make-believe restaurant. Some are chefs, others are customers and waitstaff. I set down my bag and take a quick survey of the situation then spring into action.

"Manager, we're two waitstaff short. They called in sick." Instead of doing what I would have done six months ago—picked up an apron and taken orders—I identify the assistant managers and put them to work, one to call the backup roster of staff and the other to take orders.

"Manager, table six says their food had a hair in the soup." This one I take myself.

They hit me with one scenario after the other, sometimes two at a time, but I tackle them like the pro I am. There's always some emergency to take care of at Everheart's, but this is certainly on another level.

By the time my turn is over, I'm exhausted and ready to fall into the bed with Weston and rest up for tonight's award banquet.

CHAPTER TWENTY-FOUR

What's that journal? Grief?

M Y SLINKY DRESS hangs on the closet door, waiting for me to slip into it. My palms sweat, and I have to go back into the bathroom and wash them once again.

Weston stands in front of the mirror styling his hair. He hasn't put on his jacket yet but already is devastatingly handsome. I think back to all the years I've known him and can't capture a memory of him this tailored and put together. Sure, he's been suited and booted before, but nothing like tonight.

I blink back the moisture in my eyes before ruining my mascara.

"What's wrong, sweetheart?" Weston's concern transforms his handsome features.

"I'm fine, just feeling a little emotional." To be safe, I swipe my eyes with a tissue. "Thank you for dressing up for my, uh, thing. I know it's not your favorite."

He reaches for me but can't figure out where to put his hands. My hair is in the normal short curls I wear daily, but I took extra care to style them with more definition. Makeup is almost a must for my job, but tonight, I've stepped it up a notch with smoky eyes and a red lip to match my dress. My black, strappy heels lay on the floor below my dress. Maybe I'll win tonight or maybe I won't, but I'll definitely look good doing it. *Lord, I hope I win.*

After eyeing my shapewear, he finally settles on stroking my arm. "I hope you know by now, this…" He sweeps his free hand up and down his body. "This is a minor sacrifice for supporting you and all your greatness."

I stand on my tippy toes and give him the slightest peck on the lips. "You're truly the best, West. I hope it's not all for nothing."

"Don't talk like that."

"What if I don't win?"

"Then we'll figure it out."

I take a deep breath, then let it out slowly. "Yes, we'll figure it out. I better get dressed."

While I slip on my dress, Weston washes his hands in the bathroom sink, then pulls something down from the shelf in the closet. "Um, I guess I have something for you?"

Hmmm, statement as a question means Weston's flustered. But what about? I glance at the box in his hand as I secure the buttons on one side of my dress. "You do? What is it?"

The deep breath he takes is audible and visual as well—his big shoulders rise up to around his ears and his chest puffs out to an unhealthy degree before finally deflating back to normal.

He hands me the box with trembling hands.

Sweat pops out on my brow and I'm suddenly nervous because he's so nervous. Weston doesn't get nervous. Like ever. I take a breath to steady my own hands before reaching for the box. When I open it, my eyes stretch in amazement. "My oh my, these are absolutely gorgeous, West. Oh my goodness." I press myself to him as carefully as possible. "They're perfect."

"You really like them?"

I nod and remove the heart-shaped ruby earrings and put one in each ear. Then I take the necklace from the box and admire it in my hands, the cold metal of the platinum chain slinking through my fingers. This heart-shaped ruby is twice as large as the ones on the earrings and set in an infinity symbol surrounded by small diamonds just like the earrings.

Blinking back tears, I try to clasp the necklace around my neck, standing in front of the full-length mirror.

Weston must see my struggle, and he steps behind me, then gently removes the chain from my hand and winds it around my neck, trailing light touches of his fingers as he secures the necklace in place. He stares at me in the mirror, then places sweet kisses down the length of my neck, never breaking eye contact.

Heat radiates from wherever he touches or kisses me, and I close my eyes to raise the sensation, my nipples tightening under my dress. But I also feel an immense love for this man who has probably never bought a piece of jewelry in his life paying such close attention to me that he picked the perfect accessory. Something that I will always cherish as long as I live. I am loved. And loved well. "Thank you. This is perfection."

He catches my gaze when I open my eyes, and grins. "Declan helped."

The fact that he enlisted his fashion-forward brother to

pick something for me doesn't diminish the gesture in the least. "This is definitely Declan's wheelhouse, but the intention is all yours. You're as perfect as this gift, West."

His grin grows wider into a smile. "I love you, Ryan."

I turn in his arms and place my hands on his shoulders, wishing I could just squeeze him. Desiring even more that we could just shuck out of these clothes and blow off the awards. If only that were an option. "Same, West. Hard same."

He kisses me quickly, thankfully before any heat releases from our lips. "We better get downstairs."

"Yes, of course, you're right." I grab my clutch and look at myself one last time in the mirror, admiring the new addition to my outfit tonight. Then I look at West. As beautiful as my ruby earrings and necklace are, they don't hold a candle to the man standing in front of me. I sigh. "Let's go."

We make it to our table just as the lights dim in the large conference room. A huge video displays on the wall playing video and pictures from the past two days' events, including from this morning and our head-to-head competition.

I lean over to Weston and whisper in his ear, "That's impressive how quickly they pulled this together."

He nods, gaze glued to the screen. "You are so badass." He doesn't grin or change his awed expression, just stares and nods.

Tingles run over my skin at the generous accolades Weston haphazardly throws my way. His opinion has come to mean so much to me over the years. I wonder if he even understands that. I take a sip of water and turn back to the video.

Once they've finished the play-by-play recap, they launch into the history of the contest complete with photos of past winners. Then mini commercials of each of the sponsors. And finally, the judges' photos and bios.

The lights in the room brighten again and everyone politely claps—the nervous energy is palatable throughout the many tables filled with contestants and their plus-ones, sponsors and their families, judges, and contest organizers—all in black-tie attire, sparkling and rich. I finger the ruby hanging between my breasts, then look over at a grinning Weston.

My skin tingles again.

One of the contest officials steps up to the microphone at the head table. He's the same man who greeted us the first day. Jonathan. Was that only yesterday?

I lean forward in anticipation.

"Thank you for coming this evening. I hope you enjoyed that video presentation. Thank you to Carla King for putting it together. I'm sure you're excited for the awards presentation—and so am I—but first, we have some other business to attend to. If you unfold the parchment on your plates, you'll find the order of events tonight. As you'll see, first up is dinner." He chuckles at his own importance, making us wait through a whole meal before we find out the winners.

Weston squeezes my hand under the table. "I know."

I sigh and squeeze back. Neither of us lets go.

Course after course of probably spectacular food passes before us. Weston relishes his with his usual gusto, but mine tastes like dust on my tongue. I cough uncontrollably to drive home the point.

Weston is there with a pat on the back and a glass of water to my lips before I choke completely and pass out. "Are you okay, Ryan?"

I nod as vigorously as I can, considering I'm still fighting the drop of water that went down the wrong pipe. I wheeze, then dab at my eyes with my napkin. "I'm okay."

"Okay." He surveys me completely before turning back to his dessert of some sort of lemon pie. He has a piece of cake lined up next. I push mine over to him, and he raises an eyebrow, then shrugs and accepts my offering. "Can I get you anything?"

"Yes."

He puts down his spoon, leans in, and glances around the room, his eyes narrowed in all seriousness. "What?"

"You can get them to hurry up and give out the awards."

Weston comes within an inch of rolling his eyes. I don't think his eyes work that way, unlike his brothers, but he definitely displays his version. "If only I could, darling. I would make it happen in a heartbeat." He picks up his spoon. "Hopefully it won't be too long."

I don't bother to answer because there's nothing I could say but the obvious. I, too, hope it won't be much longer. I glance at tonight's agenda again for probably the sixtieth time and note what else is left before the actual announcements I care about.

We suffer through more sponsor content and explainers of the events, then finally the panel of judges step to the front and crowd the microphone.

Weston reaches under the table and places a heavy, warm

hand on the top of my thighs.

I lean into him and breathe.

Chef Buccola speaks first. "I speak for all of the judges tonight that it has been a pleasure to be a part of witnessing firsthand the talent our industry has to offer." He clears his throat. "But I know you didn't come to hear me drone on about the state of the restaurant business, and you already know how important you are to sustaining excellence." He gestures to the older man on his left, sweeping his hand toward the front.

The man, Chef Cornwell, steps to the microphone next. "As you know, we will present three awards tonight. A grand prize and two runners-up. Good luck to all our contestants." He gestures to the next man, and this time I want to roll *my* eyes. There's no luck involved in this. Only skill and experience.

Chef Kessler steps up next. Since yesterday, I did some digging because his name was so familiar and discovered although he and Flynn aren't friends, they are acquaintances. I'm pretty sure they may have gone to school together but weren't close.

He leans down to adjust the microphone. It's not attached to a stand, so he simply plucks it from the mount and stand up straight again, a mischievous grin pasted on his face. It's apparent why he and Flynn were never friends. This guy is all swagger and good looks, and while Flynn may be handsome, he's older-man handsome with zero swagger. He taps the mic and laughs. "Yes, it's still working. As my colleagues have been hinting at, we're ready to announce the award winner of this year's National Restaurant Executive of the Year. But first, we will ask the three finalists to join us at the front." He points at the floor space in front of the table where they're standing, then glances down at the card in his hand and back up.

I stop breathing because any minute now we'll find out the winner and I need it to be me. Badly.

"Thank you to everyone who participated this year. You are a stellar class, but someone has to win, yes?" He grins and shrugs. "Please join us down front in no particular order: Andre Cornelius, William Green, and Ryan Landry."

My ears ring from the roar of applause. Tears sting my eyes, but I blink them back. This is not the time for crying. I'm a badass restaurant executive.

I give Weston a quick squeeze before walking up to join Andre and William in front of the table. We face the audience after shaking each other's hands. I gave William's an extra squeeze, then spare a moment's thought on why they brought two of us up here to put the non-winners' suffering on display. This wasn't mentioned when we were prepped. I vow if I don't win, I will not give them the satisfaction of showing how devastated I will be.

"Without further ado, the two runners-up are Andre Cornelius and…"

Time slows down, the room fills with an oppressive air, and my ears pressurize so much I can barely hear.

"Ryan Landry. William Green is this year's National Restaurant Executive of the Year."

I blink. Then smile and turn to William because congratulations are in order. It's a big deal that he won, and I'm happy for him. I'll worry about my plight later. That's the only way I'll get through this night.

I wait my turn because Andre is pumping William's hand.

"I'm so excited for you. Well done."

I reach out my hand, but he pulls me in for a quick embrace and says, "You deserved this just as much. I hope you know that."

He makes it difficult to keep my promise to myself of not crying. "Thank you." I smile and turn in time for the chefs to hand us our awards.

Weston is next in line with a huge smile on his face. He lifts me up in a familiar hug, warm and soft, scented with vanilla and sugar. "I'm so proud of you, Ryan. How you've broken through barriers here tonight." He pulls me even closer, and my feet nearly leave the floor.

"I know, and I am happy about it. Thanks, West."

With the ceremony over, we ride the elevator back up to our room. We have an early flight and both need to be in the restaurant by lunchtime tomorrow. The world goes on.

WESTON STUDIES ME as I pull out my journal from the bedside table, his long legs stretched across the bed, balancing his laptop. We had a grown-up talk with my sisters earlier because I was tired of hiding all of my entire relationship with Weston. I've never shied away from talking with the twins about sex, but I've never had someone spend the night, either. I've also never had a serious connection with anyone on this level before, so it was time for them to understand where Weston and I are in our relationship. I definitely didn't want to keep sneaking over to his house at every turn until they go off to college.

My hand trembles ever so slightly as I open the book and Weston closes his laptop. "What's that?"

"Remember a couple of months ago you pulled that grief card for me?"

He nods. "The Five of Cups. I remember."

I take a deep breath and run my hand over the open blank page. Then I flip to the beginning. "You challenged me to journal my good fortunes and not only focus on the hard parts of life that have been doled out to me." I release a small laugh. "Or, in some cases, of my own making."

He turns on his side, angling his whole body my way, patiently waiting.

"It was so hard at first, West. I mean damn hard. I could only wallow in my thoughts about my parents. Not good thoughts most of the time. I love my sisters so much, but I didn't appreciate how hard it would be to care for teenagers when I moved them out of Mimi and Papa's. I don't regret it because although I may not blame myself for what happened to Mama and Daddy anymore, I also have a sense of accomplishment. That I made something out of the terrible hand we were dealt."

Weston's thumb wipes away the tear that snuck out of my eye.

"So anyway, after that first session with my therapist, when I was finally able to start the process of forgiving myself, I wrote down how grateful I was for my sisters and our relationship. Our closeness." I shrug and turn the page.

"Then I wrote how grateful I was for your friendship." I angle his way and cup his cheek, and he turns his head and kisses my palm. "I'm still so grateful."

He offers me a toothless smile and misty eyes. "Thank you. I love you so much, Ryan. And your friendship is just as valuable to me. I hope you know that."

"I do, West. I promise I do."

We read through the remaining pages together, and when I turn to the contest passages, where I've written several pages on how I wasn't really ready for it but through Flynn's wisdom, and prodding I got ready for it, I release a heavy exhale. "I'm still grateful for all of this. I didn't win the grand prize, but I learned a lot about myself in the process of getting ready for it. Plus, I did get some money, and it'll be enough to cover the gap in Meagan's room and board plus pay for Saron's room and board, too. If she weren't going off to Howard, we'd be set I think." I bite the side of my lip and think about the loans Saron will have to take out to get her off to DC. Asking her not to go isn't an option. But I will ensure she only borrows what she needs instead of the full amount. I learned that the hard way.

"You could always—"

"I'm gonna go ahead and stop you right there. We will not put money in the middle of our relationship."

He executes a very unconvincing shrug, which makes me think I need to speak with the girls about not accepting money from Weston.

"So anyhoo, we're in a better position than we were three months ago. We'll figure it out, and I'm not going to stress about it."

Weston places an arm across my stomach and snuggles closer. "I agree that it'll work out. I hope you mean it when you say you won't stress. And I also hope that if you don't figure something else out, you'll let me help. I have a bunch of money sitting around I'll never use. My brother made sure of it with a lot of other stuff I don't pretend to understand."

From anyone else, that would almost sound pretentious, but Weston has never cared about money since I've known him. Then again, when you have it, you don't really need to care about it. His house is bigger than he needs for one person but the smallest in his neighborhood. He barely moves his vehicle out of the garage, preferring to walk or longboard if possible. And everything he enjoys—disc golfing, paddleboarding, kayaking, and camping—can be done with minimal spending. Even if Declan didn't have all his money invested, Weston would probably be well-off on his own from his salary from the restaurant.

I wrap my legs around his and push myself flat against him. "I'll consider it if I get absolutely desperate." I probably won't.

CHAPTER TWENTY-FIVE

You promised. Sigh.

FLYNN LEANS AGAINST the doorframe of my office, casual in trousers and a button-down shirt. It's not actual casual, but casual for Flynn. His arms are crossed but still conveys a relaxed posture. "I hear you were a runner-up."

"You hear correctly, Chef."

"That's quite an accomplishment." He taps his chin with a finger, then pushes off the doorway. "You have to wonder if Buccola wasn't one of the judges, if you would have won it all."

I allow my head to drop to my chest and take a couple of breaths before looking up. "Do you really believe that?"

He grumbles and sticks a hand into his pocket and jangles the change within. Lord, that's the most annoying habit in the history of habits. "I wouldn't put it past him."

"Do you think Knox would work for someone like that?"

He sighs and turns his head, glances around at the empty desks in the office. "Where is everyone?"

"Ace is handling a minor emergency in the kitchen with one of the automatic dishwashers. Kerry is supervising the transfer of an order that just arrived out back. And Nancy is in the small conference room interviewing a new host."

"You always interview the host. They're the first ones the customer sees when they enter."

"I'm delegating, Chef. What can I do for you?"

"Is Weston here?"

I swallow my own spit wrong and have to hit myself on the chest and cough a couple times to clear it. I stare at Flynn, trying desperately to read his mind. Does he suspect? Weston and I have been so careful to avoid any contact while at the restaurant. "Why would you ask me?"

He cocks his head to the side, and it reminds me of every one of his sons. Then he narrows his eyes. "Are you not in charge of the schedule anymore?"

"Yes, of course. I mean, Ace makes the schedule now and I approve it." I click the keys on my laptop and open the document, but of course I already know Weston is indeed working. "Yes, he should be in the kitchen." I stare at him, not able to help myself, barely containing the *why* in my mouth.

"Good. I'd like to meet with you both at..." He looks at the expensive watch of his. "Four. That should be enough time before the rush."

I blink a couple of times and regulate my breathing. "May I ask what this is concerning?"

He huffs. "Your future with this restaurant." With that verbal bomb, he turns on his heels and heads out the door.

I check the time on my laptop and pick up my phone to text Weston. *Meet me in the storage room. 911.* It doesn't matter if Flynn catches us there anyway. It's all falling apart.

I rush to the room, but Weston is already in our spot. "What's going on? What's the emergency?" He looks me up and down as if checking for an injury.

He won't see it because it's buried deep inside me. My hands are steady as I reach for him. There's no reason to panic now because what's done is done. "You father wants to meet with us at four."

"That's weird. Everyone, or just the chefs and you?"

I shake my head. "No. You don't understand. With only you and me. Just the two of us, and we only have a few hours to figure out what we're going to say."

He raises his arms in question. "Say about what, Ryan? Did he tell you what he wants?"

"He said it's about our future with the restaurant." All this time I never thought in a million years Flynn would fire his own son, but it appears I don't know Flynn Everheart as well as I thought I did.

"Oh."

"Oh? That's it?"

"I'm not sure what else to say, Ryan. That could mean anything. You don't still believe he would let you go, right?"

I raise my fists in the air and swing my arms around wildly. I need to scream, but that's impossible, so this is second best. My blood is pumping so hard, my ears are filled with the rushing sound of a river. No, check that—Niagara freaking Falls.

Weston reaches toward me ever so slowly and places his hands on my shoulders. "Breathe, Ryan. We don't know what he wants, and until we find out, what good will it do to speculate? I know Dad. He's not the best person in the world, but he's smart. This place would fall to pieces without you. Especially since he's barely been here these past few months."

I didn't realize Weston noticed Flynn's absence. When we're together, his dad is the last thing on either of our minds. We certainly don't discuss him. I lay my head on his chest. "I wish I had your faith."

He wraps his arms around me and kisses the top of my head. "We'll be okay, Ryan. I promise."

I sink farther into Weston, enveloped by his warmth, his sweet smell, our hearts beating in sync against the other, and his reassuring words. I somehow believe him. "Yes, we absolutely will because we have each other." I look up and touch his waiting lips with my own. Then my phones vibrates in my pocket. By itself, that wouldn't be abnormal, but Weston's phone vibrates against my stomach at the same time.

We stand back, each reaching for our devices.

"Weird, it's a text from Naomi. She wants to know if I'm free."

"Me, too." I shake my head at myself. It's a group text, so of course we have the same message. "That is weird." I text her back that we can call her.

We both look at our phones again. *Meet me out back.*

A pain reaches into my head from how hard I'm pulling my eyebrows together when I look at Weston.

He's clearly confused, too, but, in true Weston style, shrugs. "Come on. Let's see what she wants."

I grumble something to the effect of "You're not the boss of me" but follow him into the hallway leading to the back door. We're not even trying to be stealthy about it. What's the point?

Naomi stands next to her Audi, all fixed up like brand new after our accident. She's on her phone and has a tablet in her hands. When she spots us, she ends the call. "Hey, guys."

"Um, hey. What in the world is going on?" I flail my arms about like the wild woman I've become.

Weston leans in and they hug. "Hi, Naomi." His voice is cheerful and welcoming. Does nothing ever bother him truly?

"I'm sure you're wondering why I needed you out here, but I'm on my way to the airport to New York for a week and wanted to talk with both of you in person."

I scrub my face with both hands. "There's sure a lot of that going on today."

She scrunches her face up but waves me off. "I don't have time to unpack whatever that is, but I wanted you to be together when I gave you the news."

Weston is confused then, his eyebrows drawn together. "What's going on?"

"Your story, Weston. We want to offer you a contract for it. That and four more in the series." She grins with the toothiest smile I've ever seen from my all-business cousin.

My heart drops and I tense.

Weston's confusion deepens. "I don't understand. What story?"

"*Titanium Paradise*. We'll probably need to change that title, though. You're okay if we need to, right?"

His gaze hits the side of my face because I can't look at him. Weston, who's so good and loving. Who trusts so easily, and I've done the one thing he asked me not to do. I had one job.

I turn to him and reach out, but he backs up. "I'm sorry, West. I only showed it to Naomi because I knew it was so good and you were having confidence problems. I only wanted Naomi to give you some feedback."

She clears her throat. "I see you two need to work through some things and I can't be late for my flight, so, Weston, please give me a call later."

He doesn't say anything, but he doesn't even nod at Naomi. He's never rude.

Naomi drives away, and I want to be mad at her because I told her I was giving the manuscript to her without Weston's knowledge, that he didn't want me to share it with anyone. But that's on me, not Naomi.

"West?"

"I asked you not to show it to anyone." His shoulders are stiff, and he looks away at the street and the passing cars as he speaks.

"Yes, I know. I shouldn't have done that. I realize that now. That I had to control everything and make decisions for everyone because I thought I knew what was best. I was wrong, West."

He nods. "Yeah, you were definitely wrong. How come you can't understand I'm happy with my life? I don't need a big book deal or my own restaurant or chain of pastry shops. It doesn't seem like that's good enough for you, though."

I reach for him, but he backs up. "Weston. You can't believe that. You're so talented. I just wanted you to see it as much as I do. To point you in a direction, give you a purpose. Your dad has beaten you up so much you lost your confidence. I was only trying to help you get it back."

"My conf—Okay. I need to go back inside and get ready for lunch." He walks a couple of steps, then turns back to me. "I do need to go back inside, but I really just want to be away from you right now. I need you to understand how much of a betrayal this is and how hurt I am by what you did."

Tears stream down my face even though I tried to breathe through them. This is the whole reason Flynn didn't want fraternization. Times like this where I'm making a scene in his parking lot. My knees buckle, and I reach for the nearest car to hold myself up. "Are we done?" Everything I was afraid of before we got together—losing my job, losing Weston—is rushing at me, threatening to knock me over.

Weston closes his eyes, then steps my way and wraps his arms around me. "Of course not, Ryan. I meant it when I said you're it for me. I'm so angry with you right now, but I still love you. I'll always love you. I just can't be near you right this minute. Can you understand that?"

I cling to him but finally will myself to let go. "Yes, of course. I love you, too. So much."

He walks back into the building, and although I'm re-lieved he didn't break up with me, I'm torn up inside because I realize how badly I messed up. Everyone doesn't need to have some grand purpose in life. People are different, and just because I don't understand how someone can be happy living like that, it shouldn't matter. I never should have forced that on him.

I sag against the car and thank the universe I found such an amazing man.

WHEN FOUR COMES around, I trudge down to Flynn's office. May as well get this over with. I've already made a list of restaurants I would try to get in with. I wouldn't be able to start at this level, but that would be okay because the salary for an assistant somewhere would still keep me in range to get financial aid for the twins.

I look around for Weston, but he's nowhere to be found. I don't believe he ever left the kitchen after our fight.

Flynn sits behind his desk, hands steepled. He's not as relaxed as he was the last time I saw him. His shoulders are stiff, and his face is creased with something I don't recognize. I'd say hurt, but I've never witnessed that from Flynn and have no idea how he wears it.

I knock on the open door. "I'm here."

His head pops up as though he didn't realize I was standing there. He clears his throat. "Yes, Ryan. Come on in and have a seat."

I hold my head up high and walk the length of the floor, stepping around his golf grass, then sitting with a straight back across from him.

He raises an eyebrow.

I stare.

"Are you going to quit, too?"

"Am I not here for you to fire me?"

He narrows his eyes and frowns, deep lines crease the sides of his mouth. "What have you done?"

His first question hits me then. Something I missed when he initially said it. "What do you mean 'too'?"

He grumbles, then clears his throat. "Weston has decided to part ways with Everheart Bar and Fine Dining, his legacy."

I jump from my seat, looking around widely as if I can materialize Weston out of thin air. "Where is he? What do you mean 'part ways'?" Oh my G-d, what is happening?

"You mean to tell me you didn't know? I don't believe you. You've been sneaking around with my son for months."

"Oh, he's your son now. Wow."

He stands then, too, and places his hands on his hips. "What are you trying to say?"

"I've never once seen you speak to Weston directly. Not once."

"That's ridiculous. Even if he weren't my flesh and blood, he was the head pastry chef for the restaurant. Of course I talk to him."

"Ha—that's not true at all. You filter everything through me."

"Did Weston tell you that? He's always had a chip on his shoulder, that boy."

I clench my hands into fists by my sides because although I may talk about jumping on someone, I've never been in a fight in my life. I'd hate to start with my boyfriend's father who is also my employer. At least for now. "How dare you? You only had enough attention for Knox because you admired his talent and intellect. Declan got whatever was left over because of his business acumen. He was so far up your butt all the time, you couldn't help but notice him."

"Now you wait just a minute. You will not talk to me

this way in my own office."

I walk over to the bar hidden behind a credenza and slide the cabinet open, then reach in for a glass and fill it with water from the filtered sink. I eye the bottle of top-shelf scotch but think better of it. I need a clear head today. After I drain the glass, I fill up another in case the flames in my soul don't stop burning.

Marching back to Flynn's desk, I edge right up to the structure and point my finger. The digit is far from him with the desk between us but probably feels like it's right in his face judging from the way he flinches. "Poor Weston didn't even try to gain your approval or attention. He went out and found himself another family and was happy with them. Which is an even bigger shame."

A red vein throbs on the side of Flynn's neck, and I suddenly worry he might have a coronary right here in his office. "You don't know what you're talking about. Weston worked here with me and his brothers, his family. He'd still be here if it weren't for you."

"Weston worked here to honor his mother. He's a pastry chef, for goodness' sake. Can you really not see that? Do you really not see how deeply you've injured him? And what do you mean he quit because of me?"

Flynn wears his own path to his bar, but he doesn't pour water. He throws a few cubes into a glass and fills it with the whisky.

I've never been more envious of him, but I hold my resolve. "What's going on, Chef?"

He takes a long pull, then clinks the ice around in his glass. His shoulders rise and fall from his deep inhale and exhale, then he rotates my way. "For some reason, Weston was under the impression I was about to fire you both."

"Weren't you?"

"Of course not. Where'd either of you get that impression?"

I throw my arms in the air in frustration. "You said you needed to discuss my future with the restaurant. And you needed Weston there, too, so if not to fire us, why?"

He shakes his head. "How either of you could ever think I'd fire my own son, I'll never know." He makes it back to his desk and sits down hard.

I follow suit on my side of the barrier.

He takes another sip, but there's mostly only melted ice now. "Weston thought that if he preemptively left, there'd be no reason to fire you for fraternization." He snorts. "That kid is so much like his mother, it's almost impossible to bear."

I blink. And swallow hard. "What? I can't let him do that."

"Good luck convincing him otherwise. I made him understand I was not letting you go, but he quit anyway."

"I don't understand any of this."

He sets the glass on the table and sits back in his chair, staring at the ceiling. "A few months ago, I shared something personal with you—that I've been seeing a therapist. I never dealt with Lia's untimely death, and I recognized that in you."

I only nod.

"It's a long journey, but during the process, I've reevaluated what's important to me, especially once Knox and

Declan struck out on their own. That left the one son I could hardly be around because he's his mother's child through and through. It was too much, so I didn't deal with it. I ignored it, but I never meant to ignore Weston."

My mouth forms into an O, but I can't coax a sound from my throat.

"I've reconnected with my brothers and parents. I believe you met them a couple months ago. They were in for dinner."

I scrunch my face in thought. There's way too many customers coming through this restaurant for me to have a clue as to who it was, but there is a niggling at the back of my head that I'm supposed to remember.

"Well, anyway, I've been missing out on the important things in life by trying to out-success my perceived family disappointment. I've decided to step back and semi retire. I'd planned to turn it over to Weston and increase your duties." He raises his hand when I open my mouth to finally speak. "And increase your salary to go along with it. I challenged you to take your management to the next level, and you met that challenge, more than meeting my expectations. I have no doubt you can successfully run Everheart's with my part-time assistance. Looks like you'll need to find a new pastry chef, though, and I'll have to put off my semi-retirement status for a while." His face clouds over, and I've never seen him look so sad.

"So…you're not firing me? You're promoting me?"

"I bet you feel bad about your little tirade now, don't you?"

I shake my head and bark out a laugh. "Not even a little

bit."

He looks up to the ceiling, then back down to me. "We'll go over the paperwork tomorrow. I've had enough for today." He rises and picks up his phone and keys from the desk.

I follow him out of the office and back to my own without another word. I've got to somehow get through this dinner service and close up this restaurant before I can talk to Weston, but Lord only knows how I'll make it.

CHAPTER TWENTY-SIX

Tourist for a day. Okay.

WESTON KNOCKS ON the front door, a baker's box in hand when I open it. "Hi."

I nearly cry but hold on just enough to press my body against his. It's been a long, emotional night, and when I couldn't reach him, I nearly called the police and hospitals because Weston is never cruel no matter how upset he might be. Thankfully the text came through from him before I could figure out the phone number to call that's not 911.

"I missed you, too. I'm sorry we fought. And that I worried you when I didn't charge my phone. I should have known you'd call, but my mind was shattered into a thousand pieces, and it took nearly all night with Jerome to put myself back together."

I pull back and look up at him. "It's all my fault, West. I'm the one who's sorry. So, so sorry. Come on in. The girls will be up soon."

He walks through the living room and places the box on the kitchen table. "I also baked at Jerome's." He smiles and opens the box. There's every kind of pastry and breakfast roll anyone could want.

"Wow, you really worked out some stuff, huh?"

He grins and wraps me up in his arms, resting his cheek on top of my head. "I guess you heard I quit, right?"

"Yeah." I squeeze him a little tighter where my arms are joined around him. "Your dad told me."

He leans back. "I guess congratulations are in order. I have to say, you could have knocked me over with a feather when Dad said he was promoting you, not firing you." He kisses me, then breathes me in. "I'm so happy for you. This will help, right?"

I snort because I can't help myself. My emotions have been all over the place. "I'll say. The raise in pay will probably put me in a higher range for financial aid, but I'll cross that bridge next year. For now, I should have enough to cover Saron's tuition on a payment plan." I lay my head back on his chest because I need to be connected to him completely. "Tell me why you quit even after you found out I wasn't losing my job because of us."

He strokes my back, his breathing even. "It was time. I've never loved working there. It was nice with my brothers and, of course, with you, but I couldn't keep doing something that didn't bring me joy. We weren't able to spend time together there anyway, so I figured what's the point." He shrugs under my touch. "I took the book deal, so that'll give me purpose."

I step back from him so I can see his face. "Oh, West. I shouldn't have ever said anything close to that."

"I'm not doing it because of what you said."

"Then why? You were so upset with me giving Naomi your manuscript." I hurry and add to the statement. "Rightfully so, of course."

He takes a deep breath, then releases it slowly. "I didn't believe it was ready yet. After talking with Naomi, I realized that I could probably tinker with that story until the end of time and still think I had more to revise."

I hide a grin because those were exactly my thoughts.

"Why are you smiling?"

Busted. "I still understand how I was wrong and that I was basically mothering you and making your decisions instead of talking it out, but I guess that's basically why I handed it over to my cousin in the first place." I shrug. "I didn't believe you'd ever do it. Are you certain now?"

"I truly love writing, and this gives me a chance to get my words out in the world. I get to share them with others, and hopefully they'll love them as much as I love writing them. I still can't believe that *Titanium Paradise* will be the start of a series. I have so many ideas for the other four books." He smiles at me, and it's true and genuine, and Weston wouldn't tell me something just to appease me.

"This is huge, West. You seem really excited?" He does, but I can't help just making sure.

"I'm so happy, Ryan."

Tears threaten again, but before I can let go, Saron stumbles into the kitchen. "What's wrong?"

"Chill, Ryan. I'm just tired. I was up way too late listening to you spaz out last night."

Embarrassment heats my face. "I—"

"Whatever. Anyway, I have news."

I don't think I can take anything else at this point. "Is it good news or bad news?"

Weston slings an arm over my shoulder, pulling me into

his warm and comforting body.

"Hold on. I'm waiting for Meagan so I can tell you at the same time."

I turn my face into Weston's chest because I need to smother all my senses before I pass out.

Meagan comes in blasting music from her earbuds. "Hey, y'all." She hits a button on her phone to silence the noise. "Who died?"

We all face a serious Saron.

"So I got a full-ride cross-country scholarship to How-ard. I got the letter yesterday from my coach."

The kitchen explodes into a thousand questions at once, but Saron only stares at us like we've grown extra heads, then reaches into the pastry box and pulls out a cherry-filled butter horn.

"Saron Alexis Landry, put that down and tell us what's going on right this minute."

"What? I already told you. Oh, it's for four years as long as I stay eligible."

I fall to the floor in a wet puddle, but Weston's there to wrap me in his comfort. He's always there, and I couldn't be more grateful. I promise myself to be there for him, too. For whatever he needs, not just what I think he should need.

WHEN THE SILVERY light parts the vertical blinds in Wes-ton's bedroom, I begrudgingly open my eyes.

Weston stirs next to me, then stretches his long body, his feet extending off the bottom of the mattress.

I throw the covers back, then heave a leg over Weston's outstretched thighs. "Good morning. We really need to get you some curtains." I snuggle against his side, making myself comfortable for a few more winks.

"Hey, are you trying to go back to sleep? We have a busy day."

Why did I agree to an Austin-tourist day on the one day the restaurant is closed? With Flynn cutting back his hours and putting more responsibility on me, I'm not sure when I'll come up for air again. And on top of that, I still need to hire a new pastry chef. Thank goodness Knox can help me out in the open now, especially with Rowan's grand opening next week which will free up some of his time until his next assignment.

"We're not on a schedule, are we?" I rub myself against him, causing a little friction we might both enjoy.

He looks at the ceiling, then slowly closes his eyes. "You don't play fair." Without even opening his eyes, he reaches under me and pulls me on top of him in one swoop, then sits up to kiss me. His erection springs to life beneath me, making itself known. Weston is always ready.

My pelvis contracts and my blood sings in my veins, calling for him to be inside me. "Condom?" It's not really a question, but I had to explain why I broke our kiss. I reach for the nightstand and pull out the packet, tearing at it with my teeth.

Weston laughs and takes it from me. "Careful. Why are you in such a hurry?"

"I thought you were."

"Not for this." He sets the condom down on the headboard, still in its package, and reconnects our kiss. The humming in his throat travels through my lips onto my tongue and down into my belly, lighting my core on fire. He steadies my hips, with those big hands of his keeping me from upping the friction. "Let's take our time."

I grunt my reply and push him down onto his back and crawl up his long body until I'm positioned over his face.

He smiles against my mound but grips my butt and leans back, blowing a cool stream against my most sensitive spot.

"You are absolutely perfect."

He smiles and hums, "Thanks," and I'm heartened he takes my compliment without a self-deprecating reply. "Now come sit on my face."

He doesn't have to ask me twice. When I sink down on-to his waiting tongue, my eyes roll back in my head with the intense pleasure searing my pussy. He glides his tongue with lazy strokes, alternating between flattening and curling, and when I grab his hair because I can't take it anymore, he sucks on my clit, sending me all the way over the edge. His strong hands keep me from smothering him as I writhe through my release.

"Sorry. That was so intense." I roll off him and pull him in for a kiss. Just a quick peck as I catch my breath.

With his fingers, Weston swirls circles against my skin, traveling down my body, then trails kisses in the same path.

That orgasm took a lot out of me, but his touch perks my nerve endings right back up. I languidly stretch as he worships my nipples, slipping one in his mouth while tweaking the other. I put my hands in his hair again, this time pulling my fingers slowly through the wavy strands, then pulling him up for a deep kiss. Our tongues slow dance to our own, sweet rhythm until a sense of urgency has us writhing against each other.

Weston reaches for the condom. "Are you ready?"

I nod, my breath already coming faster, and take the condom from him.

He sits back on his haunches with his cock straining my way, and I roll the sheath down his shaft before positioning myself in his lap. He grins and nods, then pushes in. "I like."

Me, too, and I count on his strong legs to handle this position as long as he can because he is hitting that glorious place inside me just right. I hold on to his shoulders for the ride and meet his intense gaze. With the way he's looking at me, I want to cry.

"I love you so much."

"Me, too, West. I love you so, so much."

His lips meet mine as he pumps into me hard, digging his fingers into the flesh of my hips. I meet every stroke just as hard, rubbing against him at the perfect angle. Making love to Weston is a feeling like no other, and when my orgasm builds, I know deep in my heart he feels the same.

I bite down on his lip and pull it into my mouth when the tingling turns into pressure then throbbing as I come around his cock, pulsating and grabbing, dragging him in deeper. Somewhere in my gratified haze, he slams into me one last time and holds himself motionless deep inside.

CHAPTER TWENTY-SEVEN

Why are they all here? Oh.

THE AUSTIN WEATHER is cooling but still warm enough to dress in sleeveless shirts and shorts, but Weston opted for a nice pair of khaki pants and a button-down shirt, sleeves rolled up to the elbow, displaying gorgeously cut forearms, instead of his usual tank top and board shorts. To match his energy, I put on a nice sundress in my favorite color of green with comfortable sandals since we're doing a lot of walking on this little mini tour of Austin.

We arrive at our first destination—the Texas capitol building. Although the tour was Weston's idea, this one is my request. As long as I've lived here, I've never actually been inside the capitol. Which is doubly bad because I only work a few blocks away.

The building itself is lovely, up close as we are, shaded coral and stately. The grounds are spacious, and the first monument we come to is a huge African American History memorial to the state's stained past with slavery. This monument not only covers slavery but Juneteenth and Black revolutionary fighters. We moved along the back and check out the rest. I get a little teary-eyed reading about it, and Weston reaches out and puts and arm around my shoulders, his warmth a comfort.

We continue across the grass, then onto the sidewalk and cover the last few feet up to the steps of the capitol. There are two police offers standing at the top, holding intimidating automatic rifles. Inside, the air is cold, a welcome relief from the heat outside. I sag against Weston in relief. "We should have brought some water with us. Let's go downstairs and get some from the gift shop."

He leads me through the metal detectors, then over to the elevators and downstairs. The water is cold and sweet, an elixir to my soul. Nobody could ever say this Texas heat isn't lethal. But the air is cool, enabling us to walk wrapped up in each other.

"So where to next, West?"

"How about up?" He smiles, then kisses me long and slow until someone clears their throat nearby. "I guess we better go upstairs."

I'm tingling and warm again, so I take another sip of water. "I guess we better. Or..." I waggle my eyebrows at him.

His wide smile causes his eyes to crinkle, and it's the cutest thing, reminding me all the wonderful things I love about this man. His kindness and easy way, plus how amazing and freaky he is in the bedroom. I love that anyone looking from the outside in would never suspect that about him. It's for me alone.

We catch up with a tour guide on the main floor and explore along with other visitors. As a group, we marvel at the ground floor rotunda with its many iterations of Texas. I stand in the middle of the mosaic, right on the star, and look up. The breath nearly leaves my lungs with the view. The impossible layers that lead up to a matching star at the top will be an amazing shot, and I take my phone out of my purse to capture the image because it's impossible not to. I'm dizzy with the effect.

Next up is the second floor, where the house and senate chambers are located since neither are in session. The rooms are ancient and filled with history, and the smell reminds me of my visits to the San Jacinto monument in high school. Old and musty but at the same time salient. Everyone is quiet and respectful in this space. There's a huge painting covering one of the back walls, and Weston and I are compelled to walk over and study it. The painting is named *Dawn at the Alamo*. I scan it closely, but there's so much depicted. Our guide is knowledgeable and fills in the gaps.

When we exit the capitol, I check the time. "Wow, lunchtime already." My stomach growls to put a fine point on it.

Weston pulls me in for a hug and nuzzles into my neck. "Let's get you fed. I know a place not too far."

We walk the couple blocks down to the Roaring Fork restaurant, and my mouth waters thinking about their green-chili mac and cheese. "I hear they have an amazing brunch on Sundays." I'll probably never find out because Sundays are too busy for me to be out brunching around.

When we stop at the host stand, Weston smiles at the woman taking names. "Hi there. Landry for one p.m."

She scans the tablet in front of her. "Oh, yes, we have you, Mr. Landry. Please follow me."

I raise a thoroughly confused eyebrow at Weston and lower my voice as we follow the hostess. "Mr. Landry?"

He shrugs. "Imagine the questions if I used my last name."

That's a great point, but I wonder why we have a reservation at all. How did he know what time we'd be ready for lunch? And how did he know where we'd be?

When we're seated, Weston takes my hand and kisses the palm. "I love you."

"I love you, too?"

He chuckles. "That sure, are you?" Then he opens his menu like he hasn't got a care in the world.

Meanwhile, I'm freaking out. I pick up my menu with shaking hands and drop it back onto the table. The words are suddenly all blurred together.

"Hey, what's wrong? Why do you look like you're about to cry?"

"I, um…" I look around at the other people seated at nearby tables. Nobody's looking at us, but I get the feelings someone will jump out with a ring at any moment. "I, uh, what's happening right now?"

"We're about to eat? Did you not want to come here? Are you mad at me for picking without asking you?"

"What? No."

"Then why are you about to lose the lunch you haven't eaten yet?"

I take a couple breaths and think about it. Surely if Weston were about to propose, he wouldn't be so cool and relaxed right now. He nearly fainted just giving me the ruby necklace and earrings. "I'm too embarrassed to say."

He scoots nearer to me and puts a hand on my knee under the table. "Before we were together, we were best friends.

You know you can tell me anything, right?"

Yes, he's right, but it's still embarrassing. "Why did you have a reservation?"

"Are you averse to planning all of a sudden?"

"Well, no. But how did you know what time we'd have lunch?"

He smiles. "You wanted me to plan the day out since it was my idea." He shrugs and squeezes my knee. "So that's what I did. I've toured the capitol a thousand times. It wasn't that hard to figure out when we'd be here."

That makes a lot of sense, but I still feel uneasy. I pick up the napkins from underneath my water glass and tear at it.

"You don't have to tell me, but I'm worried about you."

I allow my head to flop back and look at the ceiling. "I thought maybe you were going to propose." Then I drop my head into my hands, shame flooding my cheeks.

Weston laughs uncontrollably in only the way Weston can. He wheezes and pulls me into his chest. "I'm happy I'm not because if this is how you'd react, I'd be worried about the answer." His chest vibrates under my head, but the tone of his words was tentative.

I sit back up and look into eyes, completely serious. "It's not you, West. We've already talked about it, and you're it for me, too. I think I freaked out a little because of the whole idea of not having my family near to share it. Sitting in a sterile restaurant with strangers. I'm so sorry."

He holds my head in his hands and leans his forehead against mine. "You scared me for a minute."

"I know. I could hear it in your voice." I kiss him and sit back. "Let's order. I'm famished."

AFTER A MEAL that did not disappoint, we walk back to my parked car, and I click my seat belt into place. "Where to next?"

"Straight down Congress over the river. Jo's Coffee Shop." His demeanor changes a little, and he wipes his palms down the front of his pants.

"Um, okay. You want coffee? Or is there something to see there?"

He grins at me. "There's definitely something to see there."

I shrug and drive us through downtown and across the Congress Street Bridge until Weston taps my thigh.

"Slow down and let's see if we can find a parking spot."

I'm doubtful because it's suddenly quite congested in this area. There's a crowd of people taking pictures next to a small building with a sign that reads *Jo's Coffee Shop*. "Oh, this is that mural, huh?"

He nods. "Turn right here and see if there's anywhere to park."

"Okay, but if we don't find a spot, I don't have to see it. I've passed that building a bunch of times."

"But I want to take a picture."

I snort a bark of a laugh but shrug. "If that'll make you happy, I'd love to take a picture with you."

He rubs my thigh distractedly, looking around presumably for a parking space.

We circle the block and, on the way back around, someone finally pulls out of a space on the street, and I maneuver into it before anyone else can swoop in and grab it. It's so crowded, it's unbelievable this little building has that big of an attraction.

Weston takes my hand as we walk down the block. His is a little clammy, and he snatches it back and wipes it on his pants before clasping mine again. "Do you know the story behind the mural?"

"Not really. I thought it was just graffiti like the Austin mural."

"It is, but the reason it's there is sort of interesting."

"Okay. Tell me about it."

"So there's a lesbian couple who owns the coffee shop. And one night they drank too much. Not coffee but spirits. And they got in this huge fight. And broke up."

When he stops speaking, I glance around and see a familiar face. "Knox? Hi."

"Hey, Ryan." He picks me up off the ground in a bear hug and spins me around.

I'm laughing when he sets me down and right myself against Weston's sturdy body. "What in the world? Hey, Rowan. What are you two doing over here?"

"Getting coffee. It's nice to see you, Ryan." She kisses me on the cheek, then rubs her hand up and down Weston's arm, somber. "Hey, Weston."

He nods at them. "We'll follow you. I was just telling Ryan about the mural."

They walk ahead of us, and I look over at Weston and lower my voice. "That's weird seeing them, right?"

He shrugs. "So the next morning, there were the words *I love you so much* written on the side of their little coffee shop.

That was, like, a few years ago, and they're still together."

We're standing right in front of the words as he finishes the story. "It's held up really well."

"Nah, they repaint it every so often. And people come here for all manners of romantic gestures or just to take pictures."

"Oh, neat. That's such a sweet story." I reach in my purse for my phone so I can take a few selfies. When I look up, my sisters, wide-eyed with grins on their near identical faces, are standing next to Papa and Mimi in her wheelchair. "Hi, baby." Papa takes a handkerchief from his pocket and swipes at his eyes.

Pushing Mimi's chair is a smiling Jerome, dimples popping all over the place, and his brothers behind him. All my Austin cousins—Naomi, Diedra, and Darryl—are next to them. Even Lisa pokes her head around from Jerome's side.

My heart takes off at a fast pace, and I frown when Declan comes from the other side where Knox and Rowan are standing and kisses my cheek. "What in the world are you doing here? Where's Kasi?"

"Kasi couldn't get away, but I would never miss this."

Tears prick my eyes and I gulp for air. "Miss what?"

When I turn back to Weston, he takes my hands in one of his and in his other hand holds out a small box with a beautiful emerald ring surrounded by diamonds. "Ryan, I need to ask you something. Here in front of our family."

I whimper as the tears flow, and nod.

"We Everhearts have a thing—a tradition, some might say, although involuntary. When we meet our true love, we know it right away."

I look over at Knox with Rowan tucked under his arm and a huge smile on his face. Then at Declan, true kindness in his eyes, holding up his phone with Kasi on the screen. She blows me a kiss and squeals.

Weston squeezes my hands, and I turn back to him. "The first day you came into the restaurant all those years ago and Dad introduced you to us, I knew it right away. But I couldn't say anything because we worked together. So I got to know you as a friend, and of course, we clicked like I knew we would. You are my best friend, Ryan. I'd love it if you'd be my wife, too." He lets go of my hands and takes the ring out of the box, eyes bright with unshed tears. "Because I love you so much. Will you—"

I'm nodding before he can finish the sentence. "So much yes."

He slips the ring onto my finger, then I wrap my arms around his waist and burrow into him as loud whoops and cheers fly up around us. He holds me so lovingly and gently but strong at the same time. So Weston.

I knew the Everhearts would be the death of me. I just didn't realize I'd die of happiness.

The End

Want more? Check out Kasi and Declan's story in
A Tasty Dish!

Join Tule Publishing's newsletter for more great reads and weekly deals!

Acknowledgements

In 2020, when outside closed, I wrote two books and started this one near the end of the year. It took me most of 2021 to finish. Meka doesn't know I was in a competition with her since we were both writing book threes and taking our time about it, but I'm a super-competitive person and thought this might help. She finished the night before I did but hung out the next night in a Zoom sprint and watched me finally cross the line. Thanks for running that race with me, Meka.

During that last couple weeks of finishing *Tastes So Sweet*, The Wordmakers were clutch. Thanks to Randi, Fortune, D. Ann, Mia, Lisa for running special sprints where the story finally caught fire and I wrote so much of this book.

Thanks, Book Besties, Jamie, Amanda, Bianca, and Cathie for your constant encouragement and telling me I'd finish the book and it would be wonderful. I hope you think I did right by Weston. Special thanks to Bianca for her grandmother's Zwetschgen-Blechkuchen recipe.

It's wonderful to talk with other authors who are in the same boat. Lots of love to my publishing siblings, Denise, Fortune, Mia, Stacey, Heather, Ieshia, and Lisa (I guess we're the Fierce Eight now, huh?). Knowing you're only a message away means everything.

Amy, you were the first to read *Tastes So Sweet*, and the

way you praised it made me teary. You've been in my corner on this Everheart journey, and I can't imagine taking it without you. You truly are a phenomenal agent.

Thank you to the wonderful folks at Tule for your immense patience and support, especially my editor, Sinclair.

Visit Kelly's website at kellycainauthor.com and connect with her on BookBub. Join Kelly's newsletter for inside info and exclusive content—Between The Sheets.

Are there recipes? Duh.

Zwetschgen Blechkuchen

(thanks to Bianca M. Schwarz for her grandmother's recipe)

3 cups fine white flour

½ teaspoon of salt

½ cup of sugar

5 tablespoons butter, divided

2½ tablespoons of yeast

1 cup whole milk, warm

2 eggs

The grated peel of one lemon

3 pounds of Italian purple plums, halved and de-stoned

Sugar for sprinkling over the fruit

½ teaspoon of cinnamon plus more to sprinkle over the fruit

Sieve flour into a glass or ceramic bowl and make an indent. Then sprinkle salt, sugar, and butter flakes around the rim so they don't interfere with the pre-dough. Combine crumbed yeast with one teaspoon of sugar and half the warm milk, then mix with the flour in the indent until it's a semiliquid dough. Sprinkle a little more flour over the mixture, cover with a towel and put the whole bowl into a warm place for

10 minutes or until the yeast has grown to double the size. You can also keep the pre-dough in a separate little bowl, but Grandma frowned on that. She said having all the ingredients warmed to the same temperature creates a better dough and therefore a better cake. Warm the yeast on a radiator, or in a very low open oven, or in a warm water bath.

Once the yeast has risen, add in the remaining milk, the eggs, and the lemon peel, and mix it all together with a strong spoon until the dough is smooth, shiny, and lifts easily from the side of the bowl. Form the dough into a globe and sprinkle flour into the bowl. Place the dough back into the bowl, cover, and put it back into the warm place to let the dough rise to double its size (30–45 minutes). This amount makes two sheets, so if you only want one, half the recipe or use the leftover half to make rolls or mix in nuts and raisins for fruit buns.

Grease a sheet pan with butter. Halve the risen dough, knead carefully back into a ball, then use a rolling pin or your hands to spread and cover the sheet pan. Brush the dough with melted butter and then slice and arrange the plums so they overlap like the scales of a fish with the flesh facing up. Bake in a medium-low oven (350 degrees F) for 35–45 minutes.

Once ready, slide onto a cooling rack and immediately sprinkle with sugar and cinnamon.

Serve with slightly sweetened, freshly whipped cream.

Weston's Linguine with Clam Sauce

For the pasta

2½ cups 00 flour

5 large egg yolks

1 whole large egg

1–2 tablespoons milk

5 teaspoons extra-virgin olive oil

1 tsp salt

For the clam sauce

¼ cup extra-virgin olive oil

2 shallots, finely chopped

5 garlic cloves, thinly sliced

1 teaspoon red-pepper flakes

½ teaspoon dried oregano

½ cup dry vermouth (or 1 cup dry white wine)

2 pounds littleneck clams (40 to 45), scrubbed

Salt to taste

Black pepper to taste

½ cup chopped Italian parsley, divided

3 tablespoons unsalted butter

1 teaspoon lemon zest (from 1–2 lemons)

1 tablespoon lemon juice

For the pasta

Use a pasta board (or large cutting board) and mound the flour. Scrape off to the side about 1/8 of the flour. Make a large well in the center of the flour mound and pour in the yolks, the whole egg, milk, olive oil, and salt. Swirl the ingredients together in the mound using fingers, and gradually add flour a little at a time. Scrape in flour from the reserve until the right tightness has been achieved. Knead until the dough resembles a smooth ball (about 10 minutes). Add flour as needed if too wet. Place dough in a sealable storage bag and let rest at room temperature for at least 30 minutes (can stay in the refrigerator up to a day).

Divide the dough into sections (roughly about 4x2x2 inches). Place pieces of dough not being used back into storage bag to prevent drying out. Flatten the piece of dough you are using into a rectangular piece (approximately ½ inch). Set the pasta machine on its widest setting, and run the dough through. Fold the dough in half, and run through the machine once again starting on the folded end. Repeat three to four times. Decrease the pasta machine width by one setting, and roll through twice more. Repeat by decreasing the pasta machine width by one setting until the dough is translucent. Cut the pasta sheet to length of noodles and hang on a pasta rack until no longer tacky. Lightly flour a pasta board (or large cutting board) and place pasta sheet on it, then lightly dust with flour. Roll lightly to flatten the pasta sheet and slice into 1/8-inch noodles.

Cook the linguine in a large pot of salted boiling water until al dente (about 1–2 minutes). Drain but reserve ½ cup of pasta water.

For the clam sauce
Using a very large, high-sided sauté pan, heat oil over

medium and add the shallots, garlic, and red-pepper flakes. Cook until almost golden (about 1 minute), and add oregano. Cook another 30 seconds, and add vermouth, clams, salt, black pepper, and ¼ cup of parsley. Bring to a simmer and cover, cooking until the clams open (5–8 min). Throw out any unopened clams.

Add the cooked pasta, butter, lemon zest, and lemon juice to the clam sauce, and toss until the butter has melted. If the sauce is too thick, add reserved pasta water as needed. Stir in the remaining parsley.

Ryan's Lasagna

1 pound ground meat (hamburger or turkey) (you can exclude meat to make it vegetarian)

Approximately 10 cups spaghetti sauce (use your favorite premade sauce)

2 large zucchini, sliced lengthwise (or alternatively 1 box lasagna noodles, al dente)

4 cups mozzarella plus 1 cup separated

3 eggs

24 ounces small curd cottage cheese

3 tablespoon fresh Italian flat leaf parsley, roughly chopped

Salt & pepper

5 ounces Parmesan cheese, grated

Preheat the oven to 400 degrees. Brown ground meat in a large skillet, add sauce, and simmer covered. Mix the 4 cups mozzarella with the eggs, cottage cheese, and parsley until well blended. Salt and pepper to taste.

Assemble the lasagna by using a 13x9x2-inch lasagna pan and adding layers. Start with a layer of the sauce, then a layer of zucchini or noodles, then a layer of the cheese mixture. Repeat this until near the top where the last two layers will be the zucchini, then sauce on top. Sprinkle with the Parmesan cheese and cover with foil. Place in the oven and cook for 45 minutes. Remove the foil and sprinkle the remaining cup of mozzarella cheese on top. Place back in the oven for about 10 minutes or until cheese is melted. Remove from oven and let cool at least 20–30 minutes. Cut into squares.

Portuguese Sweet Bread

2 packages of yeast
¼ cup warm water (105 to 115 degrees)
1 cup lukewarm milk—scalded, then cooled
¾ cup sugar
l teaspoon salt
4 eggs, separated
½ cup butter
5½–6 cups flour
Sugar for dusting top

Dissolve yeast in warm water in mixing bowl.

Stir in milk, sugar, salt, 3 eggs, butter, and 3 cups flour. Beat until smooth; stir in enough remaining flour to make dough easy to handle.

Knead until smooth and elastic, about 5 minutes. Place in greased bowl, and turn greased side up. Cover and let rise till double—about 1½–2 hours.

Punch down, and divide in half. Place each loaf in greased round 9-inch cake pan.

Cover and let rise to double, about 1 hour. Beat 1 egg, and brush on loaves, then dust with sugar.

Bake at 350 degrees for 35–45 minutes.

Yield: 2 loaves

Weston's Special Chocolate Cake for Ryan

For the cake:
8 eggs
1 cup plus 2 tablespoons sugar
⅓ cup unsweetened cocoa powder
1 cup bleached flour
1 teaspoon baking powder
2 tablespoon butter

For the frosting:
1 pound confectioners' sugar
½ cup unsweetened cocoa powder

1 stick butter, room temperature

1 teaspoon pure vanilla extract

⅓ cup boiling water

For the mousse:

2 cups heavy cream

8 ounces semisweet chocolate, melted

3 cups raspberries, plus more for garnish

¾ cup simple syrup (equal amounts sugar and water, simmered until sugar dissolves)

3 ounces semisweet chocolate, shaved into curls

Preheat the oven to 350 degrees.

For the cake:

Put the eggs and 1 cup of the sugar in a large mixing bowl, and with an electric mixer fitted with a wire whisk, beat on medium-high speed until the mixture is a pale yellow, thick, and has tripled in volume, about 8 minutes. Sift the cocoa, flour, and baking powder together in another large mixing bowl. Add the egg mixture and fold to mix thoroughly.

Grease two (9x2-inch) round cake pans with the butter. Sprinkle each with a tablespoon of the remaining sugar. Pour the cake batter evenly into the pans, and bake until the cake springs back when touched, about 25 minutes. Let cool for about 2 minutes. Using a thin knife, loosen the edges of the cakes and lip onto a wire rack. Let cool completely.

For the frosting:

Sift together the confectioners' sugar and cocoa powder into a medium-sized bowl. Add the butter, and mix with an electric mixer until incorporated. Add the vanilla and boiling water, and mix until smooth. Let cool.

For the mousse:
In the bowl of an electric mixer, combine the cream and the chocolate on medium speed. Whip until stiff peaks form, add raspberries, and set aside.

Assemble:
Line a baking sheet with parchment paper, and place a wire rack over it. Using a serrated knife, cut each cake in half horizontally. Brush the tops of three of the layers with ¼ cup of the simple syrup. Place the bottom layer on a 9-inch round of cardboard and set it on the wire rack.

Spread ¾ cups of the mousse evenly on top of the cake. Top with a second layer of cake. Spread another ¾ cup of the mousse over the top of the cake. Repeat the same process with the third layer. Top with the fourth layer.

If necessary, shave off any uneven pieces of the cake with a serrated knife so that it is smooth and even on all sides. Chill for 2 hours. Spread the frosting evenly over the sides and top of the cake. Refrigerate until the frosting sets. Place the chocolate curls and raspberries on top of the cake.

If you enjoyed *Tastes So Sweet*,
you'll love the other books in…

The Everheart Brothers of Texas series

Book 1: *An Acquired Taste*

Book 2: *A Tasty Dish*

Book 3: *Tastes So Sweet*

Available now at your favorite online retailer!

About the Author

Kelly Cain is a native Californian but has spent the last couple of decades in Texas, currently residing in the live music capital of the world, Austin. Consequently, most of her books are set somewhere between those two locations.

Kelly writes multicultural romance with determined women directing their own fates, and the swoon-worthy men who adore them. She loves reading most genres but please don't ask her to pick just one. However, she can pick her favorite book boyfriend – Will Herondale.

When she isn't reading or writing, Kelly is most likely using a genealogy site to research her extended family, both old and new. Or cooking/baking something delightful.

She has two adult daughters, and a new granddaughter. Visit her website kellycainauthor.com for more info.

Thank you for reading

Tastes So Sweet

If you enjoyed this book, you can find more from all our great authors at TulePublishing.com, or from your favorite online retailer.

TULE
PUBLISHING

CPSIA information can be obtained
at www.ICGtesting.com
Printed in the USA
LVHW112231130522
718552LV00001B/24